Hope Landing

MARTY AFTEWICZ

To my dad, Axel: thank you for teaching me to never give up.

CHAPTER ONE

Homecoming

Morning frost dampened Nolan's jeans as he knelt on the cemetery lawn. Dim light revealed lavish mausoleums and towering monuments with a silence disturbed by an occasional closing of a car door. Some people couldn't start their day without a brief sunrise visit to the resting place of a beloved spouse or family member. Many who came felt closer to their family and friends on the other side than most would understand. Dense cloud cover blocked brightness from entering, as the weather ignored the calendar's claim that it had slipped into spring.

Nolan David scooped the slush off the concrete marker. Dirt and mold had accumulated over the past forty years to fill the gaps between the letters, but "Kaminski" was still evident. He wondered if any of the priests or nuns from the orphanage were still in town and if the headmaster would still be angry with him.

The sixteen-hour drive to the shores of Lake Erie had drained his energy, but he was afraid to stop for a night's rest along the way. He'd mustered the courage to make this visit but feared any delay might persuade him to turn around.

"Hey, Mom and Dad. It's Nolan. I know it's been a long time." He paused and ran his fingers over the rough surface of the concrete tombstone. "I'm here to tell you I'm sorry. I should have come to the funeral, but worse than that, I should have been here many times since. All my life, I blamed you for everything that happened to me that I didn't like. This is overdue, but I'll do my best to honor your memory for the rest of my life. You both gave me life, and I repaid you with anger and hatred."

Nolan's fingers pulled the grime from the insets of his surname while he continued.

"First thing, I'm going to respect you properly, clean up your area here and get a headstone you both deserve. I always said my time in the orphanage was your fault, and I sure was a rotten kid after you left. I need to get over my anger and this visit is my initial step. I'm gonna make you proud."

He rose and pulled a cemetery plat map from his rear pocket, gazed at it and then his surroundings. The grid directed that his next stop was only a few hundred feet from his parents' graves.

Most of the snow had melted, but a thin coating of ice caused each footstep to crunch as his shoes sank into the soft grass. White patches still dotted the landscape, and Nolan felt that cemeteries were cold no matter the season.

And here he was, trying to solve all the problems in his life with one trip. Mary's eight-foot pink marble monument was imposing compared to others nearby. Its surface shined in contrast to the drab surroundings. The monolith was topped with a cast glass heart that reflected the minimal light and glowed like a beacon that attracted all who passed nearby. The entire site's care was meticulous, with a silk arrangement of white lilies placed with love in a bronze vase. He rested a few red carnations against the headstone.

"Mary, I often felt you were the only one who knew I was not responsible for your death. Funny how everyone turned against me with the speed of a shooting star. I came back to set things right. You know, I married a terrific woman and loved her deeply. But she's there with you now, and if you run into her, I'd appreciate you showing her the ropes to help get her acclimated. Odds are I won't see your sister when I'm in town, but you should know that as happy as I was in my marriage, part of me never stopped loving Ellie. I hope she's doing well."

Nolan hung his head, and a tear dribbled down his cheek. As he turned to leave, a stooped woman wobbled toward him, and even after all these years, Nolan recognized Mary's mother.

She selected each step with uncertainty, using a gold-stemmed cane to assist her balance. The old woman trudged right up to Nolan, lifted her walking stick above her shoulders and poked him in the chest.

Nolan stumbled back but held his footing.

"Humph," she said. "I was hoping you were a ghost. I'm disappointed you're still alive."

A severe line between her brows and a permanent frown marked the cantankerous woman's face.

"I'm sorry, Mrs. Thompson."

"Sorry you're alive? Sorry you were responsible for Mary's death? Or sorry that you're standing here in front of me?"

"Sorry for you feeling this way, ma'am. Many times in my life I thought I would trade places with Mary if it was possible."

The old woman's hand fidgeted in her large handbag.

"Does my daughter know you're in town?" she asked.

"Ellie?"

"Of course, you idiot," she said. "When you killed Mary, that left me with Ellie, and you're still not welcome near any part of my family and that includes Mary's grave."

"Ma'am, I didn't kill Mary. I had nothing to do with it, and the police cleared me before I left town. You know that."

She stared into Nolan's eyes with the ferocity of a branding iron and pointed a tiny revolver at his chest.

"I swore I would shoot you if I saw you again, but I'm giving you a warning instead. If I hear you've come around Mary's grave again or discover you bothered Ellie, I'll use my last ounce of strength to pull this trigger." Her breathing was shallow and her voice raspy. She remained quiet for several seconds while she rested her lungs. "And don't you think I won't use this gun. I put ole Tippy down a few years ago and I valued his life a lot more than yours."

Nolan froze in place, absorbing the words while peering at the gun that couldn't miss.

"And just because the police couldn't prove you were with Mary that night doesn't mean you're innocent either. So, if I were you, I would leave real fast. I may ask the police to reopen the case and use that new D and A testing to prove you're guilty."

Her hand wobbled, so she lifted her caned hand to aid the support. She teetered forward, and when Nolan grasped her shoulder, she recoiled, and the weapon slipped off her fingers and settled in the thick grass.

He stepped closer to stabilize her, then bent to retrieve the small revolver. He held it in his palm for a moment, noticing the pink-and-stainless steel weapon was designed with an enclosed hammer. Sorrow but not fear was in her eyes as he placed the gun in her palm. She hooked the cane about her arm and again gripped the gun with two hands and pointed it at Nolan's chest.

"Now get out of my sight before I shoot you just because I can't hold this gun out any longer. And you need to remember, at my age, I may forget that I gave you a second chance." She lowered the weapon to her side. Nolan backed up several steps before trotting away.

When he reached his vehicle, he discovered a man in a dark overcoat and black fedora leaning against the hood of his SUV. Their eyes met and Nolan halted in his steps, then eased forward.

The figure stood erect, and a slight smile cracked between his pocked cheeks. "I was getting ready to be a witness for the defense. Why didn't she shoot you?"

Nolan proceeded to his door.

"Just like all those years ago, Sly. Mistaken identity. She thought I was the one responsible for her daughter's death, then realized her mistake. Sound familiar?"

Cermak's grin widened. "Still a smart ass," he said. "What brings you to town, Kaminski? How fortunate for me to be visiting an old friend and stumble upon you. It's been a while but when I saw your tough guy walk, my stomach soured just like the old days."

"I don't use that name anymore. And I don't care if you're the chief of police now, my business is none of yours."

"Well, I suppose you're right. I'm not even on active duty, sort of on special assignment. If you don't start a crime wave, we should be just fine for the time of your visit," he said. "This is a visit? Just paying your overdue respects?"

Nolan opened the car door and slid behind the steering wheel, then lowered his window.

"I don't scare as easy as I did when I was a teenager, old man."

Sly took two brief steps toward the opening and whispered, "Since I'm officially retired, I don't need to bother with all those ridiculous rules. Gives me a lot more freedom to eliminate problems."

He edged back from the car as Nolan stomped the accelerator and sped through the cemetery gates.

CHAPTER TWO

Help Wanted

The chatter of the gulls at the pier was a welcome contrast to the silence of the cemetery. Alive and vibrant, they presented no threat of violence or imprisonment. As Nolan took in his surroundings, he noticed a solitary pickup truck parked near the end of the pier. Once outside his SUV, icy gusts of wind from the bay greeted him. Such was the start of spring in the Great Lakes region. The winds refreshed him after his all-night drive, while his graveside encounters cast some doubt about the wisdom of his visit.

"Looks like you're ready for the season opener." The vigorous voice jolted Nolan, who turned his gaze toward a grizzled angler preparing his lines. "How do you think Cleveland will do this year?" the fisherman asked.

Nolan rubbed his hand over the embroidered city name across the chest of his windbreaker. "Oh, yeah. I don't know. I'm ready for it to warm up so it will feel like baseball weather." He was shivering and rocked himself onto his toes.

"Well, I think it's too late. Opening day's this afternoon, you know."

Nolan shook his head. He had immersed himself so much in his personal life in recent months that he had lost touch with current events. He wasn't even aware of the start of the baseball season. The sport had been his emotional escape from the orphanage. Now he was back in Erie, standing on a frigid pier, listening to a stranger educate him about the game he still loved.

"They may get snowed out," Nolan said. The rhythmic clanging of a nylon rope against an aluminum flagpole added to the clatter, so he raised his voice a few decibels. "I think Cleveland leads the league every year in games canceled by snow."

"Keeps us from falling below five hundred," the angler said.

He set up his gear with stone-faced efficiency and displayed a metal prosthesis with hooked shiny fingers in place of a left hand. He maneuvered the artificial hand with a natural motion. He placed two fishing rods, a tackle box, a couple of buckets, and a propane heater all within easy reach.

"You've done this before," Nolan commented.

The angler smiled and nodded. Setting himself in a folding chair, he braced against a sculpture of a gigantic marble walleye. This gasp of winter didn't seem to bother him at all as he sipped from a steaming thermos that he gripped with his prosthesis. The man's parka, woolen cap, and insulated boots made Nolan appear dim-witted in his light windbreaker and athletic shoes.

Nolan nodded toward a small octagonal building in the center of the dock and pointed at the sign over the closed customer service window: Luigi's Bait & Burgers.

"I could use some coffee. When I was a kid, this food joint never closed. What time does it open nowadays?"

"Not 'til Memorial Day, if at all," the fisherman snickered. "Where you from, anyhow?"

Nolan continued to survey the surrounding area. "What about the restaurants over there? Do they serve breakfast?"

"Bayview closed about a year ago, and The Landing only serves dinner. They're hoping to keep afloat 'til the tourist season. So right now, you're out of luck."

Nolan stared at the dark buildings, then glanced up the hill toward the center of town and the interstate beyond that.

"I don't think there's anything open downtown either. The closest place is the diner up near the top of State Street by the stadium." The man pointed a silver index finger at the horizon above the city.

Nolan shifted and gazed over the skyline. The pier rested at the dead end of the city's main street. As he stood with his back to the bay, the many steeples appearing to be the tallest structures in town. Dawn started slowly this time of year, and the roads reflected little movement.

"I'm Clifton, by the way," the angler extended his gloved right hand while he gripped his pole with the crook of his arm.

"Nolan," he replied and accepted the greeting. "I just pulled into town. I spent many hours on this dock as a kid, drinking coffee or pop from that concession stand. Always worked out my big problems right here." He drifted off in thought, as he gazed at the whitecaps of the icy waters of the bay.

"I know what you mean. I do my fair share of thinking while I'm waiting for a nibble on my line. With the economy the way it is, my wife tells me not to come home unless I'm bringing Lake Erie perch or walleye. Some days I think she just as soon go hungry than eat any more fish."

"Well at least y'all have that. This recession's cost lots of jobs and money lost in the stock market."

"We got ourselves a new president now," said Clifton. "I didn't think McCain had much of a chance, so we need this new guy to jump start manufacturing."

Nolan shook his head. "Don't count on that too much. With new home-construction down and manufacturers leaving the country working class America in 2009 might be in for a tough climb."

"I'm here most mornings, so if you get back here, bring some coffee. Gets lonely here sometimes—especially on days like today."

"Thanks for the invite. I find myself with an unusual amount of free time," Nolan said. "I'll try to stop again in the next few days, and you can fill me in on what's new in town." His fingertip slid across the brim of his ball cap as he turned away.

The short drive revealed more of a city that had passed its prime. The few blocks of downtown exhibited a small number of moving cars, but a stoplight at every intersection hinted at a need for traffic control in the not-too-distant past. Potholes dotted the road while loose asphalt implied the aftermath of a mortar attack. Rock salt corrosion, plow blades that scraped the ice, and the expansion and contraction of the asphalt created a unique road surface.

Display windows of a former department store were painted white, while a green neon sign proclaimed Rest for the Weary: Full-Service Senior Living. Nolan passed city hall, a library, and a few banks. Most of the buildings were constructed of dark brick with elongated casement windows, representative of the construction boom after World War II. A banner above a furniture retailer displayed Reconditioned Loungers from $100. Nolan chuckled to himself as he envisioned a vinyl recliner with oiled springs and duct tape over the arms.

As he did his best to dodge the potholes, Nolan's mind recapped the events from the cemetery. Sly Cermak, still alive, now a sharp pebble that he couldn't shake loose from his shoe. What was he doing at the graveyard that early? Nolan never viewed the former detective as a man with an empathetic heart, so seeing him at a cemetery seemed out of character.

Now Mrs. Thompson, well, it was nice to see she had not

changed, although he was saddened that she still believed him to be responsible for her daughter's death. How he had loved Ellie. He recalled the young and sexy teenage girl who tugged at his heart with every move she made. That was thirty years ago, he thought, and if he hadn't left, he would have never fallen in love with Diane, the only woman he had called his wife. He missed her so much since she passed, and often felt she was riding in the front seat next to him, talking and keeping him awake during his long drive.

There was a section on his drive through Tennessee where he struck his first wall of exhaustion. He forced himself to blink his eyes to stay awake, and Diane's voice jolted him to awareness.

"The next exit is for the birthplace of Davy Crockett. I remember we visited there on one of our day trips before we were married."

He looked at the empty passenger seat and then noticed the blue historical reference sign.

"I thought he was a fairytale until you told me all about him. He was an actual congressman and fought for the freedom of Texas at the Alamo."

Once he reached the bottom of the exit ramp, it seemed her presence dissipated as quickly as it had arrived. But he spent some time at the nostalgic building and cherished the memories that flooded his senses.

He then realized he sat through the green light as he watched the flash of amber change to a commanding red. No other car had approached him from the rear to honk a reminder for him to move forward. But he caught the next green signal and continued his path away from the lake and up the hill. He smiled as he recognized the archaic structure that was the former home of the local brewery, filling the neighborhood with the aroma of hops during his childhood. Its edifice, once stately, was now in disrepair, with shattered windows protected by bars, and ornate doors sprayed with graffiti.

The diner was easy to identify since it was the one location with evidence of movement. Cars lined the curbs on both sides of the street, and the gravel parking lot was almost full. All the vehicles were glazed with a crust of salt, a by-product of road maintenance in an area of lake-effect snow.

The glowing red sign atop the entrance represented the city that Nolan had seen so far: the *n* was unlit to generate the message, *Erie Di-er*. The white paint was peeling off the frame structure, a con-verted home with the second floor perhaps used as living quarters or storage. A sparse evergreen hedge bordered the uneven front sidewalk.

The warmth fogged Nolan's eyeglasses as soon as he entered, but he hoisted himself upon the remaining stool at the counter. At first glance, lime-green walls covered with yellow triangles and red circles at precise intervals shocked his senses. He wondered if the painter created an intentional art deco design.

The drop ceiling tiles appeared new, but several were missing with an ice tub positioned beneath the opening. Cracks and bub-bles were abundant on the linoleum floor, perhaps from the snow melting off boots or a roof leak, he thought.

"Regular?"

He peered up at the bulk of scarlet hair that framed a pint-sized server. She chewed with aggression on something he hoped was gum and not the breakfast special.

Before he could respond, she slid a sloshing cup of brew between his hands.

"I read you as high octane when I saw you come in. I'm right almost all the time."

11

Her pink-and-white striped uniform reminded him of candy stripers, hospital volunteers who were predominantly high school students. She still possessed the figure of a teenager with all the proper curves. The freckles on her cheeks had faded, but she still had an abundance that made judging her age difficult.

"What'll it be, hon?"

"Uh, can I see a menu, or do you have any specials?" He wasn't on the fast-food track and looked forward to a relaxing breakfast. She stared at him like he had asked her to disrobe on a first date, then lifted her eyes upward to a whiteboard.

"Menu's up there, so read it all you want, but don't order nothin' fancy. Rose is back there cooking, and she can't figure out why hash browns don't come in a can. You just wink when you want me." She squeezed one eye shut and popped it open, then smiled while she continued to chew. A patron at the other end of the counter raised his hand, and she strolled toward him.

Nolan gazed out the window, but without focus. "Perhaps I'm not ready to mix with people just yet," he said aloud. He slid his keys into his jacket pocket and sat in place.

He picked up a section of the *Erie Gazette* that lay unclaimed and read the headlines:

MAYOR PROPOSES BANKRUPTCY —CUTS NON-ESSENTIAL SERVICES

At an emergency session of the city council yesterday, Mayor Lindsay Bennett proposed Erie pursue bankruptcy to ease its financial woes. Bennett further indicated that the city would stop all non-essential services effective today. This announcement came on the eve of yet another significant snowfall predicted in our area.

The mayor explained the reason for this drastic action at a press conference held after the council meeting.

"Our tax base continues to erode each year with the departure of industry and residents. Erie can no longer support all existing public services."

The mayor went on to say this decision will affect snow removal and road maintenance throughout the municipality, as well as a reduction in bus service and the elimination of all routes on Sundays. Trash collection for now will remain unchanged.

Councilwoman Ashley Pershing opposed the action, citing the future opening of the Lake Erie Racetrack that would soon contribute to tax revenues. "There is no logical reason to take these severe steps. The state government has emergency funds available for such cases. These monies would sustain all city of Erie services until the horse racetrack makes their significant contributions."

Two enormous young men with knee-high green boots and bulky parkas distracted Nolan as they entered and stomped on the linoleum. Snow! Nolan pivoted his head to capture the image of his already blanketed SUV. Flurries zipped across the landscape parallel to the ground, but the town residents seemed neither bothered nor surprised by what appeared to be an incoming blizzard.

The coffee refills were on a "grab your own" basis, so Nolan followed suit.

"You ready to order yet, hon?" She rested her pink uniform against the countertop so her nametag, with "Marge" printed on it and formidable chest projected toward Nolan. "Rose is caught up on her orders, so what'll it be?" Nolan almost pointed out her top button needed reinforcement, but then figured she already knew that.

The pale, flushed hue of her skin posed little contrast to her attire. "Marge, surprise me. Pass your recommendation onto the chef and I'll eat it."

A few minutes later, Marge delivered his breakfast. "Just so you know, when Rose is cooking, we have a no return policy."

Nolan looked at his plate of charred scrambled eggs, under-cooked bacon and cold hash browns that could have indeed come from a can. Undaunted, Nolan downed the breakfast in huge bites. He held the philosophy that he should nibble exceptional food but gulp the nasty stuff before his taste buds revolted.

Marge stuffed a dark, thin stick of something in her mouth, and the labor of her chomping began anew. *Was that chewing tobacco?*

"You're either real polite or awful hungry," said Marge as she glanced at the empty plate. Nolan didn't respond, staring at the snow, which continued to accumulate.

As the squall intensified, the diner's clients thinned out. Nolan's destination would wait, so he allowed his digestion the ample time required to challenge the mess he delivered to his intestines.

Marge once again leaned her torso to the Formica counter and clasped her hands in front of her. "I'm guessing a funeral. Rose is betting you're on the run from the law. Of course, she always guesses that, but no one is ever going to tell her she got it right. So, which is it with you?"

A frail woman slid around the corner from the kitchen and leaned against the wall, gripping a steaming mug. The food-stained apron snug about her waist identified her as the cook that Marge had been criticizing. Her thin black hair curled up at her shoulders, and Nolan recalled this style from 1950s black-and-white sitcoms.

"I'm here for no particular reason," Nolan said, "got off the interstate and wanted some breakfast."

Rose whooped like a teenage girl after a prom invitation, rushed to Nolan's side and plopped on a vacant stool. "So, tell us why you're runnin'. We promise we won't breathe a word." Her eyes widened in anticipation.

"I hate to disappoint you ladies, but I don't have a special story. I got tired of driving and thought I would take a break from all those chain restaurants by the highway and enjoy some local cooking. That's it."

Rose's immediate look of dejection caught Nolan's attention, and he almost retracted his comments. Marge, however, sighed and rolled her moss-green eyes. She evidently didn't buy in quite as quickly, but neither did she challenge her customer. Nolan kept his silence.

Rose rested her chin atop her hands clasped on the countertop. "I can do lunch today, but I can't pull the dinner shift. Karl's bowling banquet is tonight, and I promised to go. Sorry."

Marge huffed. "I should have known I could never rely on my sister. After everything I've done for you, here I am up the creek again. Why didn't you tell me this before? They didn't schedule this dinner this morning."

Rose sat erect. "Listen, Marge. Karl's been pressuring me to quit. I had to give in a little. We agreed I would help out for a few days. Well, it's over a month now, and you haven't got one person who's even applied for the job. Can't you let Jake work tonight?"

"He can't handle it; you know that. He gets the orders all mixed up." Marge raised her hands to her hips and squinted as she leaned toward Rose. "It's just as well you quit. Hell, thanks to your cooking, I've lost half my regulars anyhow. I thought if you got some experience, you'd improve. Why the one customer who's cleaned his plate since you've been working is this gentleman right here, and I think he was only being courteous."

Nolan held his hands up in a gesture of surrender. "Don't involve me in this. I was hungry."

"I'm not sure the Donner family was that hungry," said Marge.

"Karl thinks I cook just fine, so I don't need to im-prove. Besides, he didn't marry me for my cooking, if you know what I mean." Rose's index finger notched an imaginary mark in the air to show one point for her on the abstract scorecard. And she wasn't finished, "And did you ever think that you might be chasing off your own customers? You look like a damn cow chewing that stuff and your breath smells like garlic!"

"Thanks for the support, Sis." Marge pivoted away and grabbed a steaming carafe of coffee from the warmers, sloshing some onto the floor as she headed for the table.

"Go ahead. Put me on a guilt trip." Rose raised her voice. "You can't force me to work for what you're paying me." She looked at Nolan and spoke in a soft mumble. "Least she could do is share the tips," and she mumbled something about family as she strode toward the kitchen.

Nolan remained the casual observer. Marge finished topping coffee cups of the few remaining diners, then returned and filled Nolan's cup to the brim then over and onto the saucer. Nolan saw no upside in complaining, so he picked a few napkins from the dispenser and placed them under the cup.

The snowfall's pace appeared to accelerate, so he made a tactical decision to stay nearby. He still had over $700 remaining in his wallet, plus the cash he set aside for his parents' monument.

Marge, having composed herself, slid Nolan's check onto the

counter and ambled out of sight and in Rose's direction. A renewal of the fireworks seemed certain, but the conversation remained peaceful. Nolan anchored his payment and tip beneath his mug and zipped his jacket to prepare for the weather.

"Hey, hon. Rose and I are sorry we acted that way. I hope that won't keep you away while you're in town."

"No need to apologize; I'll be back. In fact, I'll be glad to pitch in tonight, if you want."

"You must have something better to do on a Friday night. Jake and I will be okay. Most everybody will order the fish fry anyway, so he shouldn't get too many orders messed up."

"I have no plans, and I'm not looking forward to driving in this snow. How about I come back later and if you need me, great; if not, then I'll enjoy the gourmet food."

She wiped her hand on a towel and reached to introduce herself. "That's a generous offer, but not necessary. I'm Marge Kelly, and this is my place. I'll have Jake help out, but if you're still in town, the fish fry is all-you-can-eat, and I'll be the one cooking."

Her skin felt rough, her grip firm. He introduced himself again with only his first name.

"What time do you expect Rose to leave?"

"Around four, but sooner if it's quiet. If you want to beat the crowd, I suggest coming before five."

Back on the road, Nolan discovered his skills of driving on ice and snow had diminished. The squall had already dropped several inches of snow, and the roads were slick as he maneuvered toward a stone mason across from the cemetery.

CHAPTER THREE

Fresh Lake Erie Perch

"I wasn't certain you would still be open." Nolan caught Marge's curious eyes as he slapped the melting snow off his windbreaker.

"What are you talking about? You mean the snow? This ain't a big deal." She scowled at him, scanning his clothing from head to toe. "Tennis shoes? And that jacket you've got wouldn't keep you warm during a cool summer's night."

A blond teenager with broad shoulders stepped into the conversation. "Mom, is this the hot new guy in town you and Aunt Rose were talking about?"

She ruffled his hair, and he stepped away. "Don't Mom. It takes me a long time to get all those hairs in their place."

"This is my son, Jake. He can help you serve if we get real busy. You never told me your full name."

"Sorry, I'm Nolan David." His spoken name didn't cause a reaction. Marge was looking right at him and didn't appear alarmed. He scanned the diner and saw the lone customer was an elderly gentleman on a stool at the end of the counter. No one was calling 911. He continued to remind himself he was cleared of all criminal charges before he left town so long ago. The only person he was running from was himself.

Jake shook Nolan's hand with extended enthusiasm, causing him to wrench his arm free of the young man's grip.

"But Marge, I'm a bit confused. You said Jake would help me serve. I . . . uh . . .thought I was going take Rose's place . . . to cook."

Rose released a raucous cheer, ran from the kitchen, then her bony arms enveloped Nolan. "I knew you were an angel when I laid eyes on you. You hear that, Marge? He can cook!"

"You know this is quite a bit different from flipping burgers on a backyard barbecue." Marge's eyebrows raised. "You ever actually cooked, like as a job?"

"I've owned some restaurants. Just give me a few minutes to set up, and your regulars will spread the word in town tomorrow."

"Well, I'm leaving with a dream to sleep on tonight," Rose said.

She was wrapped in blazing red, including her parka, boots, mittens and knit cap tugged over her ears—easier to locate if she fell into a snowdrift.

"Sis, offer him anything to get him to stay and don't stop at money," Rose added as she slid out the door.

"Don't pay any attention to my sister. She uses sex as a motivational tool."

She pivoted and pointed at the open doorway behind the counter. "I'm reluctant to allow this, but hell, there's no way you'll cook worse than my sister. Follow me and I'll give you the grand tour of the kitchen."

As Marge showed him the supplies and equipment, Nolan observed her. She chomped continuously while her hands seemed to move without purpose. There was a constant motion of hands to her face. Sometimes she scratched her cheek, rubbed her lips, pinched her brows, or arranged a few wayward strands of her red hair. Cinnamon, Nolan thought that was the best match for the color of her locks.

"Fish fry starts at five and we always have some early birds. I'll let you get comfortable. Holler if you need me for any reason." She hesitated. "As long as you don't think Rose's implied offering of my body was legit."

Cooking at the diner seemed like the perfect therapy. Nolan could rest his worries and adjust to his lifestyle change. He was starting life anew, trying to suppress the sorrowful times.

He added a bit of creativity to the customary fish fry, and per Jake, all the customers were pleased. Jake became Nolan's companion and spent more time chatting than he did bussing tables and serving food.

"You sure know how to put food on a plate, mister. I usually have to move Aunt Rose's all around to get everything in place. You had a few too many fries on some orders, but I ate some to get them all to twenty."

Clifton, the angler from the pier, entered the diner. His shiny fingers clenched a woman's upper arm as he guided his companion to a rear table. Nolan wanted to at least say hello to his new acquaintance, but he was caught up in the evening's peak of orders. By the time he glanced back to Clifton's table, only crumbs and crumpled napkins remained.

At nine, the all-you-can-eat fish fry ended, the crowd thinned, and Nolan got a chance to take an overdue breather. He poured some coffee and sat at the end stool at the counter where Jake joined him a moment later.

Marge wrapped her arms around her son, leaned in and whispered in his ear.

"Aw, Mom, I've been working real hard." He stopped his protest when he saw her stern look, then he trudged to the kitchen and began washing dishes.

Marge grabbed a cup of coffee and sat next to her new cook. She was still munching on something, and her breath projected a mild spice scent. As she renewed her hands to her face motion, Nolan remembered his days after he quit smoking many years before. He bit his fingernails for a short time and thought this might be the explanation for Marge's chewing as well. Must be a nicotine substitute, he thought.

"I appreciate you being kind to my son. Most people aren't that considerate. And I especially thank you for getting me out of a jam. I love my sister, but she caters to her husband's every whim. I often tell her she needs to grow a set, but her Karl can do no wrong. The bowling banquet is at the Elks Club, and I happen to know almost none of the wives show up. It's not exactly the social event of the year."

"Well, it was good therapy for me—gave me a break from too much thinking."

Marge grinned. "I know that feeling. We were swamped tonight, and I would have lost more customers if you hadn't helped. Rose's cooking isn't only bad, but slow too. Sometimes this weather is an advantage for my diner. The lazy and hungry don't want to drive the extra few miles toward the chains, so I get lucky."

"Jake's a good kid. He didn't bother me at all."

Up close, Nolan noticed Marge showed her years, though her smooth skin and fine lines suggested genuine beauty was not far behind. Her ring finger revealed a slight indentation from recent wear. Perhaps her job provided too many hazards for losing a ring, but based on Rose's comments, Nolan guessed that wasn't the case.

"Pan-fried fish; nobody does that around here for a fish fry. I thought you were going to be in trouble, but you kept pace. And the folks gobbled 'em and asked for more. I know you used some garlic in the breading. What else was in there?"

"Nothing fancy. I found some basil and added that. I ran out of cracker meal and switched to cornmeal about halfway through. But I didn't hear any complaints."

The pair sat sipping their coffee, resting from the previous hectic hours.

"Any recommendations on nearby motels?"

"About any place up near the interstate should have a room. We had a hotel downtown, but it closed last year."

"I'll leave soon; not that accustomed to driving on icy roads."

"Well, I thank you again. We never talked about how much you would get paid. Rose was free except for the food she took home, but she's my sister."

"How about I cook myself a pile of lake perch and fries and we call it even? I actually had a great time."

Marge rested on her stool and scrutinized her visitor. Then she rolled her head back, closed her eyes and expelled a long sigh. "I think I just had an orgasm." She burst out laughing so hard that the few remaining customers all stared. Nolan blushed but didn't comment.

"You're not going to tell me your story, are you?" Marge asked.

"I don't have a story. I wanted to help. That's it."

"Then I assume my sister was right. You're an escaped convict. But don't worry, your secret is safe with us." Her joking tone hung in the air as they relaxed and surrendered the day.

Nolan thought about his plans as he watched the swirls of white flakes. He estimated seven or eight inches so far. The stone mason said he could start the work but couldn't put anything in the ground until the thaw was here to stay. And this night's snowfall would take some time to melt, even if the temperature climbed above freezing.

"You fix your dinner and some extra for Jake if you don't mind. We'll be closing up soon and I can handle anyone else who comes in," She swiveled her stool and looked into her visitor's eyes. "Are you leaving in the morning?"

"No, I'll be in town for a week or so—maybe longer. Need to tend to some old business before I can move on." Nolan spoke to Marge, but his mind was already pondering his next steps. He never imagined the players in Mary's death would have appeared so soon after his arrival. But they were all here, Ellie's mother, her family, and that damn detective Sly Cermack. He felt a sudden urge to return to the cemetery and talk to his mom and dad.

"I'd like to help you if I could. There's gotta be a way I can repay you."

Marge was talking but Nolan seemed to be staring at the linoleum. She reached out and touched the top of his hand.

He jerked and looked up at her. "Oh sorry. I was thinking about my to-do list."

"Well, come back to the present. Is there anything this owner of a floundering diner can do to make your life better?"

"Not much anyone can do. Truth is, I'm in town for a funeral, but I'm about forty years too late."

CHAPTER FOUR

Don't Sleep in the Subway

Nolan fidgeted in the driver's seat. He was wrapped in a woolen blanket but couldn't recline to a more comfortable position. Everything he owned was crammed in his SUV. He had packed the key items of his vast baseball memorabilia collection, so little room remained for clothing or much else. Prior to his departure from Atlanta, he sold almost all his life's remaining objects. If he didn't foresee an urgent need for the item, he peddled it at his garage sale, donated it, or bagged it and placed it curbside. Only a small number of articles made it to a self-storage unit. Very few sentimental items survived the cut.

His first evening back in Erie was restless. Nolan was too afraid of the icy roads to search in the blinding storm for a motel, so he made do with his vehicle and saved some money as well. The parking area behind the diner was quiet, and he felt safe. The sub-freezing temperature required him to start his car and run his heater on occasion, and he was approaching another time for a warm-up.

His car wasn't visible from the street, and snow-covered windows blocked any view of the interior, even if someone walked past. The lone lamppost was unlit, and Nolan guessed the circuit was connected to the diner's neon sign. As had become his custom since a preteen, he entered some notes in his journal before he dozed off. The chance to write initial perceptions of the city and the people he had met remained fresh in his mind. The snow provided enough reflective light for him to complete his task.

While at the orphanage, a priest counseled him that writing his recollections of the night his parents died would make him feel better. As he crafted his journal, he soon learned the priest was reading his entries. Still, he continued this habit and had fun with the invader of his privacy for over a year. The priest would console him and offer him special privileges whenever Nolan would scribe a sorrowful tale. He exposed his trick when the priest counseled him about his passions for Sister Bernadine. The priest became frustrated when his kind words failed to provide comfort. After a few counseling sessions, Nolan released an outburst of laughter. From that day, Nolan shelved his writing until he left the institution on his eighteenth birthday.

He hadn't had a decent night's sleep since his wife passed, and his nightmares focused on all the unpleasant occurrences of the last few years. But he was in Erie to forget the recent past and discover the truth behind Mary's death.

His parents and cherished childhood recollections lured him home. There were few, but he was hopeful this visit would jog some better times he had forgotten.

A tapping at his window startled Nolan and disturbed the snow.

"Nolan, are you all right?" The rapping intensified as gloves swept wet snow off the side window. Nolan's eyes widened when he recognized Marge's voice. She tugged on the door handle to no avail.

"Hold on, hold on, Marge." Nolan started the ignition, lowering the window as wet clusters fell onto his lap. "I'm fine, Marge. Sorry to alarm you."

"What the hell are you doing back here?" Marge's fiery eyes were searching the inside of the vehicle. "You slept out here last night. Are you crazy? You could've died from carbon monoxide or froze to death. You get out here right now."

"Now Marge, don't get excited. I'm okay and would never go to sleep with the car running. Besides, this blanket kept me pretty warm."

Marge's cheeks flushed as she glared at him. "You either step out of that truck and come in the diner or drive out of here. I can't have you nesting in my parking lot. It's creepy!"

She turned and trudged into the rear entrance of the building. Nolan felt perhaps Marge overreacted a bit, but also admitted he should have asked her permission. He wiggled out of his wrapping then made his way to the diner. He stomped the snow off his feet on the floor mat in the tiny alcove while the aroma of brewing coffee welcomed him.

He pushed open the door to the kitchen and saw Marge at the butcher-block top. She mumbled to herself while she attacked a golden potato with a butcher knife. She lifted her head and pointed the blade at his chest. "You tell me who you are, and what you're doing here right now, or I'm calling the police. And don't start with that wild story about a forty-year-old funeral." She picked up the phone with her left hand then poised her thumb to back her threat.

Nolan spread his arms and remained in place. "Marge, I'm really sorry. I wasn't thinking. But when I left here last night, I was afraid of driving. Cars were sliding all over, so I came back to be safe. Honest."

Marge's knuckles were white from her grip on the long knife.

"All right, I should have known that any guy sleeping in your parking lot would alarm you."

"Keep talking. You still haven't answered any questions."

"There isn't much to tell. I grew up here as a kid and came back to visit the graves of my mom and dad. That's all there is to it."

"You were raised here." She shook her head. "You sure don't dress for the weather. You should have expected this if you're from around here."

"I haven't been back in over thirty years. When I left my home in Georgia, it was almost eighty degrees. I didn't plan for this dramatic change. I don't even own any winter clothes."

Marge slipped the phone into her hip pocket and returned to dicing the potato. She was pushing the blade down so hard Nolan was fearful she would slice off a fingertip. She glanced up. "Where did you live when you were here?"

"Off Raspberry and Thirty-Third." Nolan had referred to that location many times while he was in the orphanage. He was too embarrassed to reveal the truth, so he often used the address of a close friend.

"School . . . what high school did you go to?"

"I graduated from Highland, but I understand it closed a few years ago. I attended Haven College for three semesters before I moved out of town."

"One more question." The flare in her eyes had diminished, and she lowered the knife to her side. "Why is your truck so jammed with boxes? There's too much shit in there for any vacation."

Nolan hesitated, "Marge, I don't want to talk about that." She brushed her bangs aside as he continued, "I can only tell you I mean no harm and apologize if I frightened you."

She flung the knife onto the counter. "You can't be sleeping in the parking lot. If I find you dead back there some morning, my business is a goner. The *Gazette* would splash that on the front page and people would just find some other favorite place." She pivoted away. "I need to get ready for breakfast, but this conversation is not over."

She poured herself some coffee, and once again inserted a dark stick into her mouth. This time Nolan guessed it was a chocolate bar, but the labored chomping didn't match. He thought Marge's reaction to his stay in the parking lot was too extreme and wondered if there was a hidden reason.

After about fifteen minutes, Rose entered with an amused grin and broke the uncomfortable silence.

"I see two cars out there and one of them never left last night." A glaring look from Marge counted her comment. "Sis, is there trouble in the love nest already? Perhaps a little morning-after remorse?"

Marge pointed an authoritative finger at Nolan. "You keep quiet," then turned to her sister. "Nothing happened; nothing is going to happen. Idiot slept in his car last night and scared the hell out of me this morning. I thought he died from the exhaust fumes, but he was just asleep."

"Well, why didn't he stay and sleep upstairs since you both were already up there? You guys aren't teenagers anymore. There's no reason to . . ."

Marge interrupted, "Don't be making up rumors, Rose. I went home. He slept in the car. I didn't know he was borderline suicidal."

"My, my, we are touchy this morning, aren't we? Why don't you just have a cigarette and stop chewing that silly stuff?" She glanced at Nolan and lifted her hand to the side of her mouth, whispering, "She chews those spicy sausage sticks so she doesn't smoke."

Nolan chuckled, and Marge scowled at him. "You stay out of this."

"Marge, how about if I go back home?" Rose asked. "I stayed up dancing 'til the wee hours and could use some more sleep. Besides, I heard the fish fry was an enormous success. Your new cook wowed them."

"He's not my new cook. He just did me a favor is all."

"I can work today if you want," Nolan said. "Sort of owe you for upsetting you this morning," The pair looked at him with uncertainty. "I don't mind. Can't do what I came for until some of this snow melts anyhow."

"Well, that should be soon," Rose stated. "Got a warm front coming through. Winds are picking up already. It's supposed to hit fifty-five tomorrow, a beautiful Easter Sunday." She turned to leave and added in a saucy tone, "I'm going back to snuggle with my Karl. Don't call unless it's an emergency."

Nolan tied on an apron and warmed up the grill, looking forward to a busy day. The snow was quick to melt with bright sunshine and temperatures in the high forties. By midafternoon, over half of the thirteen inches accumulation had turned to a dirty slush. The climate in the diner was chillier than that outside as Marge avoided any conversation not related to serving customers. She took a break around three and told Nolan to call her cell phone if they got hectic. Nolan didn't see her drive away, so he guessed she was upstairs working on business. No matter, he told himself, her whereabouts were not his concern.

Her temperament had calmed when she returned. "The folks enjoyed your omelets this morning. I have to admit they were better than even I can make them, light, fluffy and tasty—perfect combination."

"Thanks," he muttered.

"I thawed some cube steak and I'm thinking about a Swiss steak special for tonight's dinner. You up for that?" Marge asked.

"It's your diner. I can make a not-too-exciting Swiss steak or use that same meat and jazz the menu up a little with country-fried steak."

Marge thought for a moment. "Not too spicy? Bland seems to be the common thread for most of the food my customers eat."

Nolan shook his head. "Not spicy. Flavorful. Traditional white gravy with mushrooms. I could add a side vegetable of sautéed seasoned tomatoes. Again, not spicy, but tender and with a slight burst of taste."

"I don't know. Sounds like I may lose money on that offering. People come here for cheap, with so many workers in town without jobs."

"Try it out at a dollar more than your Swiss steak. If you get wind of anyone unhappy about the food or the price, we can drop the buck, and I'll drop the tomatoes."

She agreed and swiveled away on her heel but turned back in slow motion. "Listen, I feel I came across too harsh this morning."

"I was wrong," Nolan said.

She held up her hand to stop him. "Let me finish. I know you must be short on cash if you slept in your truck last night. I should have picked up on that before. And I can't pay you for all you've done for me. Don't believe you would take my money anyhow. So, I fixed an area upstairs for you to stay here tonight and tomorrow night if you want. We're closed for Easter like most everyone in town, so you can cook something for yourself here. This key's for the back door."

Nolan accepted the envelope and thanked her. "I'll leave early next week, but not before I test Rose's cooking again."

*   *   *   *   *

It was past midnight when he trudged up the stairs to crash. An assortment of model airplanes and ships displayed in antique oak curios filled the room. Upon closer inspection, he noticed that the collection was assembled with remarkable craftsmanship. Perhaps Jake had a hidden talent, Nolan thought.

There were well over fifty models of all sizes, including several tall wooden ships displayed with pride. Most were under twelve inches in length, but that miniaturization seemed to make the accomplishment more impressive. The HMS *Bounty* was over three feet long with intricate rigging and detailed armaments. Closer inspection of the others showed these were the work of a talented artist, not a child. Perhaps Marge's husband was responsible.

He felt comfortable bringing in a few of his most precious collectibles and journals from his vehicle. They were in good company here and would be safe when he left for the cemetery in the morning. The weather was turning in his favor. Now all he needed was courage.

CHAPTER FIVE

A Wink, a Smile and a Tear

Nolan buried his head in the pillows, away from the morning light that streaked through the cracks in the window shades. Seven hours of uninterrupted sleep was a mark he had not achieved since his wife's passing. He rolled onto his back and stretched his arms across the mattress, hoping to find the warmth of her body next to him, to wake him from this horrific nightmare. A solitary tear streamed down his cheek. He allowed it to leave a chilling trail to his chin before he smothered it with a blanket. Damn, he really was in Erie.

An amazing and familiar fragrance filled his senses. He sat up and looked about the room. He recognized the bouquet as one which was always present in their bedroom when his wife prepared for a special evening out. The identical scent of perfume mixed with talc flooded him with memories. Her spirit found him, and her aroma was there to alert him. Nolan calmed himself and rested on the edge of the bed, then inhaled with awareness, enjoying the moment and wanting it never to end. This was a wonderful Easter gift and told him his wife somehow found a way to follow him to his hometown. He had experienced sensual visitations before, but their frequency had dropped off over the past two years. After several minutes, he could no longer recognize her scent and thought perhaps he had just become accustomed to it. He wandered into the hall, took a few deep breaths to renew his sense of smell, then re-entered the space. The redolence was gone.

Nolan was neither shocked nor surprised by this event. Instead, he had grown to appreciate these now-rare moments that caused him to feel as if his wife had never left. This Easter gift had passed, and he needed to step out into the brisk Erie air. He grabbed his journal to jot down this morning's experience while it was still vivid in his mind.

More snow had melted overnight, and the rising sun shimmered off the white ground. He drove toward the pier to enjoy the view while he drank his morning brew. He was pleased to find Clifton's familiar figure huddled against the polished walleye.

"I see you brought your coffee this time," Clifton shouted over the sounds of the bay as Nolan strode across the parking area. Nolan handed him an insulated cup filled with black java and rested on the pedestal of the fish.

They talked about baseball, fishing, and the weather with an occasional interruption from a Lake Erie perch that gobbled Clifton's bait. After almost an hour, Nolan went to his car to replenish his drink and returned with a green-checkered thermos.

A solemn grimace replaced Clifton's grin as he stared at the container while Nolan poured him a refill.

"That's Mike's thermos, ain't it?"

Nolan hesitated, and a wave of guilt overcame him, but he wasn't positive of the reason. "I borrowed this from the diner. I didn't think Marge would mind."

Clifton frowned and shook his head. "Shit, Marge would kill you if you lost or broke it. Mike had that thermos with him when he died."

"I'm sorry. I would have never taken it if I had known." Nolan turned and wiped his eyes with his arm, cursing at himself.

"I lost my wife not too long ago. I don't think I cried for most of my life, you know, all about men not showing weakness. But since she passed, I tear up at the sight of a puppy. Sorry about that."

"You didn't know. Just get it back in one piece before she finds out."

Nolan sat next to Clifton and cradled the thermos.

"Mike and I worked together at the old forge plant. When they shut down about five years ago, he took it harder than most. He couldn't find another job and then started drinking. Marge did everything she could to support him and lift his spirits. She even helped him get a job as a night watchman at the paper mill. Then, one night, he told her he was on his way to work, and she found him the next morning in his truck in the garage. The truck had run out of gas, but the carbon monoxide already killed him. He held that thermos in his hands. We learned later that he got fired the day before but was just too ashamed to tell Marge."

"No wonder she was so upset yesterday."

"Yeah, I heard about that. There's not much that happens around here people don't talk about, especially in the winter. Marge and my wife, Evelyn, are very close friends."

Nolan continued his protective grip around the thermos while he just stared at the cresting waves.

"Hey Nolan, how about you have Easter dinner at my house this afternoon? My kids are in town, but my wife would enjoy meeting you. Besides, I think she wants to hook you up with Marge, so don't be surprised. Evelyn's always trying to find Marge another husband."

Nolan rejected his offer at once and got up to leave, but Clifton snagged his windbreaker with his stainless-steel fingers. "I'd like you to come. You're in town all alone, and we can watch the ball game. My two daughters will hang around Evelyn in the kitchen, and I'll be stuck with my sons-in-law watching economic forecasts and stock reports. I could use you as my excuse to change the channel."

"I don't know, Clifton. I'll be at the cemetery today for quite a while."

"You'll be doing me a favor. Honest. Evelyn will be thrilled, but I won't tell her 'til the last moment. Otherwise, she'll con Marge into coming over too, and you'll be trapped. I've seen my wife work like this before. The game starts at four, and we should eat around the third or fourth inning."

"Truth is, I could use the company today, too. What can I bring?"

"Don't insult me. Come hungry, and I'll have cold beers."

Clifton jotted down his address, directions, and phone number.

"Well, I'm going to coddle this thermos in my lap until I get to the diner, then I'll place it with tender care right back where I found it."

On his way to the cemetery, Nolan was reminded that most retail stores closed on Easter Sunday. He couldn't locate an open hardware store, supermarket, or florist. He finally stumbled upon a convenience store housed in a brilliant red A-frame structure.

Of course, they had no gardening tools, so he had to settle for a snow shovel and an implement with an ice scraper on one end and a snowbrush on the other. He added window cleaner and paper towels to his order, then noticed a flower display at checkout. The white roses and red carnations were individually encased in clear plastic tubes, and he placed a handful of white roses and all the red carnations onto the counter, then was on his way.

His parents' marker was dull concrete, with just their names and years of life. Beyond this modest nameplate, Nolan remained as the only other evidence of his parents' existence. He worked with devotion, pulling weeds and overgrown grass to bare a few inches around the plate. Dirt and grime had filled the area within the raised letters, but his efforts did a credible job of returning some respect to their names. The surname Kaminski was almost as clear as the day it first greeted the sun.

He stood to assess his work and placed two small bouquets over their markers.

"Mom, this is a long time coming, but here are some white roses that I got for you after all these years. I'm sorry I've ignored you, and I will do my best to keep this area more presentable in the future.

"And Dad, I remember you always wore a red carnation in your lapel every time you and Mom went dancing, so here's a few of those to honor that memory. I'm sorry I disappointed you by not being a better son. I love you both very much, and I'm not embarrassed to tell myself that any longer."

Nolan stood and scanned the cemetery. A few dozen people were evident, with more cars entering in intermittent streams. As they exited their vehicles, most were dressed in their Easter finery and carried colorful bouquets or pots of silk flowers.

"Dad, I recall you taking me around these grounds once and pointing out the resting places of our relatives. I guess I should have paid more attention. I'll get locations from the office and tend to their spaces too—a spring cleaning of sorts."

Nolan then took a couple of quick steps toward his car, then glanced at the markers' names.

"Of course," he whispered, "Sly was probably here visiting family. Why else would he come to a cemetery?"

Nolan then began a patterned search from his parents' graves. After almost thirty minutes, he finished looking at the headstones in the square where his parents rested and located none with "Cermak" listed. He crossed a street to another block area when his line of sight stopped at a group of people near Mary's pink marble monument. He moved closer without attracting attention and noticed the same pistol-packing woman who had threatened him.

She was accompanied by two teenage boys and a woman who stabilized her gait. Nolan gasped at the sight of Ellie, who had been his first love. With the cloud of mystery surrounding her sister's death still remaining, Nolan's best choice was to leave town.

Though he was still thirty yards away, he could tell the years had been kind. Her wafer-thin teenage profile had matured into a shapeliness that was obvious even concealed by a knee-length beige coat. Although Nolan did not see her face, he knew it was Ellie when she brushed a wayward strand of hair behind her left ear. That fluid motion was a mannerism that confirmed her identity. Beyond that, Nolan sensed her presence. He stood immobile for several minutes while he remembered the essence that made him fall in love for the first time after ten hard years in the orphanage.

He would never trade one second of his life with his deceased wife, but those passionate years did not tarnish his admiration for Ellie as a teenager. The four of them wore soft pastels, and the two teenagers acted patient and respectful, not begging to leave for their personal activities. At least their behavior was well-mannered in the presence of their grandmother. Both boys were already taller than Ellie, and she appeared as tall as she was in college. She used to joke that her eyes were at the perfect height to gaze at his luscious lips, and Nolan smiled.

She then turned in his direction, and Nolan dropped to the ground behind a headstone. He lay there for several minutes and listened, then heard a sequential slamming of car doors and the fading sound of a motor. When he rose, the family was gone, and he was a muddy mess.

CHAPTER SIX

Accustomed to Loss

He had just enough time to clean up and arrive at Clifton's for Easter dinner. He withdrew his smartphone from his back pocket, touched the screen, and then spoke, "Check on Cermak names at the cemetery."

As he drove toward the Clifton's house, he made a slight detour and stopped in the parking lot of the building where the priest had dragged him so long ago. The expectation of his new lifestyle with a priest showed how little he knew as an eight-year-old. Nolan envisioned living in the rectory in his private bedroom with access to the gymnasium and playground. Instead, he spent the next ten years sharing a room with revolving strangers in the orphanage.

The solid brick structure was a converted elementary school, with the east side dedicated for the boys and the west for the girls. The nuns displayed no mercy for those who had directional problems. He looked at the remodeled building that was now the Serenity Nursing Home. Sand-blasted and new windows and doors with gloss-white framing projected a more inviting impression than the old orphanage. He chuckled at the thought that gender may still segregate the senior citizens.

He next headed along a route that he and his parents had taken on a Fourth of July holiday turned macabre. As he approached the railroad tracks where their car collided with a train, he noticed they had installed a signal with an arm to halt the traffic flow. But he made a U-turn a half-block from the site, still not possessing the courage to cross and see the house where he last lived with his folks.

Clifton's home was a modest one and one-half story frame dwelling amidst a group of similar cookie-cutter homes. His was well maintained, and the exterior porch appeared as a recent expansion. This addition would be a sunroom in the South, but partly cloudy and gray was a good day in Erie. The steel mailbox affixed to the frame outside the front door had a wrought iron plate displaying Bell swinging from hooks at the box's bottom. Nolan defied Clifton's instructions of not bringing anything, and he greeted Evelyn with a bouquet of red carnations. She followed up with a persistent badgering of Clifton for never giving her flowers. Clifton took it in stride.

The afternoon proceeded per Clifton's outline. His eldest daughter Tamekia was married to Jesse, while Brittany was engaged to Brent. With the introductions over, Clifton and Nolan moved into the family room and shared beers. While they watched the baseball game, Nolan learned that Brittany and Brent had been engaged much longer than pleased Clifton, who launched verbal barbs at Brent at every opportunity. Clifton practiced old- school ideas of morality, so he referenced Brent as his son-in-law.

"If I call him my son-in-law whenever I introduce him to some-one, then maybe he'll be ashamed enough someday to make a gen-uine commitment."

Evelyn announced dinner at the top of the fourth, and Brent sprung from the sofa and grabbed a seat at the table as far from Clifton as possible. It didn't appear that Clifton's plan was working well.

Nolan hadn't eaten, so he salivated at the home-cooked meal: roast turkey with all the accompaniments, cornbread dressing, sweet potato pie, collard greens, macaroni and cheese, rolls, and a tossed salad.

"Evelyn, thanks for sharing this special day with me. My wife and I would have the traditional ham on Easter when she would wear all her spring colors."

He wiped a renegade tear away from his cheek, and the motion caught Evelyn's attention.

"Nolan, you sit here next to me so I can find out more about you." Evelyn guided her hand to the chair to her right, and he had no choice. "The girls don't make it back for Thanksgiving anymore, so we just moved our traditional turkey dinner to Easter. We're glad you could join us."

Evelyn's questions were all broad in nature, and Nolan deflected them like a politician at a press conference. Her limited knowledge of Nolan meant her interrogation was not pointed enough to require lies. Family? Nolan had none. Occupation? Taking some time off right now to relax and attend to some long overdue personal business.

"How long has it been?" asked Evelyn.

"Well, I can't decide if it's been too long or too soon. See, when my wife passed, that grief, that fog enveloped me with more power than it did with most folks. Anyhow, I ended up going from being a successful owner of several restaurants to bankruptcy. I'm here in Erie as part of my healing process, and so far, partly because of people like you and Clifton, I'm glad I made the trip."

"How long will you be in town?"

Nolan was active with Evelyn's conversation, but his head tilted toward the exchange at the end of the table.

"Probably a few weeks. It depends on the progress with new headstones for my parents' graves and a few other items I'm working on."

Nolan leaned back in his chair and spoke away from Evelyn.

"Please excuse me, Evelyn, but I'm curious about what the guys are discussing down there." Nolan raised his voice to project to the other end of the table. "Clifton, so you're in favor of the mayor's idea to file bankruptcy?"

"I'm not sure if I have enough of the details to back Mayor Bennett on this. But I don't believe that this horse track is the answer to our problems either. I don't have the solution, but we have to do something soon, or Erie will be a ghost town."

Jesse's voice projected authority, "We had a similar financial crisis a few years ago in California. The governor pushed the legislature to create some attractive municipal bond programs and tax incentives to attract new companies into the state. We're not 100 percent solvent yet but have made significant improvement."

Clifton shook his head as a futile gesture. "Attract new companies? We can't even keep the ones we have. Winkelman's is shutting down and moving to New Mexico. That will put another three hundred plus workers out of a job. A few will transfer out there, some will move to wherever they can get a job, and the rest will be on welfare and union severance. There are just no jobs here."

Brent mumbled, "Not at union wages anyhow."

Clifton responded. "Now listen to me. The union protected me as long as they could at the forge. And they put in a good word for me at the IBEW so I could at least get enough work to help us pay our bills. They paid for the girls' college."

"Daddy, don't be silly. You paid for our college by working sixty hours a week at that smelly factory," Brittany said. "You act like the union gave us a scholarship."

"I'll sort of miss Winkie's," Evelyn said. "I pass by their plant all the time. They've got a big yellow smiley face painted on the side of their building, and he's got the cutest wink." Evelyn's comments drifted into silence, then Clifton restarted.

"The problem is the illegal immigrants we have in this country. What am I supposed to call them now?"

"Undocumented immigrants, Dad," said Brittany.

"Well," Clifton continued, "Winkelman's told everyone at the beginning of the year that the company may relocate to be closer to the bulk of their market to save on shipping costs. They manufacture foam products like life preservers, seat cushions, and other boat accessories. Then they announce they're going to New Mexico. I don't need a college education to know there are not a helluva lot of ports in New Mexico. They're moving for cheap labor." Clifton pointed at Nolan, who was slinking behind Brittany and away from Clifton's line of sight. "Nolan, where do you stand on this?"

He hesitated for a moment. "I agree the influx of undocumented workers is a major problem for our country. And on the surface, this Winkie's company is probably moving to take advantage of that situation." Clifton sat back in his chair, appearing proud that his new friend agreed. "But I also believe that the unions have outlived their usefulness as they are currently structured." Clifton eased forward in his seat with a frown. "I mean you no disrespect, Clifton. But the labor unions rose to power primarily to provide better working conditions and fair wages. That was over a century ago, and workplace conditions are no longer as important an issue. Now Clifton, perhaps the union came through big time when you had the accident which caused the loss of your hand, but overall, those types of injuries have almost disappeared."

Clifton raised his prosthesis to get attention, and Nolan nodded in his direction.

"I don't want you to get the wrong idea, bud. This here injury wasn't work-related," Clifton said. "We don't need to get into all the details right now, but I lost my hand in sort of a fishing accident."

"A fishing accident?" Evelyn asked.

"Evie, I don't see the need to get into that now." Clifton glanced at Nolan who continued.

"As I was saying, the union's goal is to not only provide you with a fair wage but to control you and your ability to work elsewhere."

The sound of a few forks clicking at plates was heard as Clifton mumbled to himself and then spoke. "Nolan, you know that Winkie's is going to pay next to nothing for their workforce when they move, with no benefits and no pension. That's not fair."

Nolan replied. "I'm sure they will have lower labor costs and probably no retirement plan. Benefits? I'm not positive about that one. Just like you with the mayor's decision, I don't have all the facts. I imagine the company is also moving to offer more competitive prices to increase their revenues. Allow me to pose a scenario."

Clifton glared at Nolan. "Go ahead," he muttered.

"Let's propose for a minute there is no union at Winkelman's. I'm Mr. Winkie, and you're the employee." Clifton nodded and crossed his arms over his chest. "I tell you, we are going out of business if we continue the way we are structured today. I have made some cash flow projections and arrived at a plan to keep the company in town if you agree."

"You with me so far?"

"I got you. You're the boss, and I'm getting screwed again." The sound of muffled laughter around the table made Clifton's expression turn into a slight snarl.

"All right, I propose a plan that will eliminate the company contribution to your retirement and replace that with a profit-sharing plan. We limit overtime pay to the normal hourly wage, reduce paid vacations to a maximum of ten days per year, and you pay half the cost of your benefits. It's that or the company closes or moves. Would you go for that?"

All eyes at the table were now on Clifton as he squirmed in his chair.

"I might. But you'd have to pay time and a half for sure. Anything over forty hours a week has to be time and a half," Clifton said.

"Then I'll tell you we will never work overtime, no matter what. Would you go for it then?" Nolan asked.

"Well, I wouldn't have much choice. That's why we would need a union to help us out and stop such nonsense."

"But I can't negotiate a better deal for you with the union, Clifton. My competition is selling their foam cushions at my cost with the structure I have in place now. And that's my point. The union won't work in partnership with management for the good of all concerned. Their need for control and lack of trust in ownership is just too overwhelming to allow such a negotiation. And owners cannot afford the demands of unions."

"Well, I don't think Winkie ever tried. The forge owners didn't try, nor did the people who took the paper mill out of town a few years ago. Maybe if someone tried, oh hell, I don't know." He lifted his coffee cup with his prosthesis toward Evelyn, perhaps half for coffee and half surrender. "So, you're saying unions are all bad and should be eliminated."

"No, not at all. Unions are a necessary cog in our checks and balances. The organizations have and will continue to strengthen America. But in some instances, the power of unions needs to be controlled."

"But we have to do something. I haven't had a job since we finished the wiring at the horse track last month, and I see no new projects coming open."

Evelyn rose, and she and her daughters started cleaning and serving more coffee. Nolan carried his dish into the kitchen, and Evelyn grabbed his elbow and whispered. "Clifton thinks highly of you, or he would never have let you go on. The union is all he has ever known, so please indulge him. He's not as harsh as he makes out to be."

Nolan smiled and nodded in understanding as she took the plate from his hands. "That was a splendid dinner. Thank you for allowing me to share Easter with you and your family."

"Marge told me you were a smooth talker." Evelyn grinned and waved Nolan back toward the dining room. "You come back in here and get ready for dessert. Coconut-cream pie or chocolate fudge cake?"

"Coconut's my favorite, but only if you have that left after everyone else has some. I love both choices. But I will take some coffee if I may."

Nolan returned to the dining room, and Clifton ignored him until Evelyn set an enormous slice of coconut-cream pie before her guest.

"Oh boy," Clifton said, "that slice is going to cost you plenty, believe me," he snickered.

Nolan then learned all about Marge and a tidbit of her deceased husband, Mike. She was a caring woman, dedicated to her husband, and kept her youthful figure. For a moment, Nolan imagined they would drag Marge in to model for him. She was only thirty-eight years old. That surprised Nolan since he misjudged by perhaps ten years and not in the favorable direction. His facial expression must have betrayed his surprise when Evelyn added, "She's had a very stressful life."

His attentiveness increased when he learned Jake was autistic. Evelyn presented this as yet another challenge for Marge and her husband but emphasized the progress Jake made toward caring for himself. Evelyn was earning extra credits for statesmanship as she bolstered Marge's abilities to care for someone like her son, yet also depicted Jake as a young man who would represent no inconvenience to anybody who wanted a relationship with his mother. Hers was a polished presentation.

Triumphant cheers from the family room distracted Nolan from signing an official letter of intent for Marge. Brent stuck his head into the kitchen to create the diversion Nolan needed. "Cleveland just hit a grand slam to tie it up!"

Nolan peered at Evelyn, then she patted his hand.

"You go ahead with the boys and watch your game. But remember what I said. Everyone is meant to have a companion, and your wife wouldn't want you grieving forever."

"Well, thanks again for dinner, Evelyn. Everything was truly spectacular."

He joined Clifton and the guys and sipped another beer. This couch-potato life was not all bad, he thought. Cleveland lost in the eleventh, but the men felt little dejection. None of them were alive when their team last won a World Series in 1948, so they were accustomed to losing.

As Nolan said his goodbyes and drove away, he recognized Erie residents faced disappointments of more importance than losing a baseball game. He wondered if that would ever change, and if there was any way he could help facilitate a recovery.

CHAPTER SEVEN

False Hope

Nolan drove about the city, in no rush to return to an empty room. He located another convenience store and bought some bitter coffee. But it was hot and filled with caffeine, so it satisfied his habit.

He steered toward the isle that projected into Lake Erie but encountered closed gates, with a sign: Park closes at dusk. Open at 9 AM. So much for a walk in the park, he thought. He next went to the pier and pulled his SUV into a parking spot near the octagonal building across from the concrete walleye. He had some good times there as a teenager and recalled he was pretty much a loner even at that age. Erie was a vastly different city then, bulging with 125,000 people and a healthy economy. This dock area was usually filled with the constant energy of car radios, street vendors, and restaurant patrons. This odd-shaped structure was a twenty-four-hour snack bar.

The Landing restaurant was fully lit with a few cars parked in front, so he ambled over. A man with skin the color of rich cappuccino and thick carbon-black hair noticed Nolan standing inside the entrance. Only the eyebrows displayed a mixture of gray.

"I'm sorry, sir, but the kitchen is closed." He spoke with a mild accent as he was untying his chef's apron. *European*? Nolan wondered.

Nolan lifted his foam cup, "Oh, that's fine. Is it possible to buy a cup of coffee?"

"Sure, sure, I will get one for you." He strode away and spoke over his shoulder, "Cream or sugar, sir?"

"Just some fake sugar, please."

The man returned a moment later and handed Nolan a paper cup filled with steaming coffee. He pointed to the nearby packets of artificial sweeteners.

"No charge, sir. Perhaps you will return with your family for dinner."

"Sorry, I'm a visitor alone in town. But your food smells very tempting; maybe I should extend my stay."

He smiled. "Our kitchen is cleaned, but do you have time for dessert? Some baklava? I made it myself and guarantee you will enjoy it."

"Yes, please. I'm certain it will be excellent." In the recent past, Nolan never would have allowed himself a moment to relax with such an offer. He had focused on caring for his ailing wife and then trying to recover his sinking business. Gradually, he was learning to take care of his own needs. His shrink would approve.

The two tables of dinner guests were preparing to leave when the chef delivered the baklava. With a confident grin, he said, "Please tell me what you think. My son makes the entrées, but I focus on desserts."

The chef attended to his last customers, then returned for Nolan's critique. "Magnificent," he raved. "Not too sweet and very flaky. Working with phyllo dough is an art, Mister . . ."

"Aaron. Call me Aaron. I am very pleased." He spoke with a definite accent, but his pronunciation was crisp and accurate. His toned skin gave him a youthful appearance, but he was old enough to have a son who worked with him.

"Well, Aaron, I'm trying to guess the nuts you used. They are not walnuts or pecans—much more tender and a distinct flavor. Pistachios?" he asked.

"You are correct; few of my customers are able to guess. Now, you have me at a disadvantage, Mister . . ."

"Nolan." The pair shook hands, then Aaron joined him with a cup of coffee.

"I should confess my guess at the pistachios had some experience behind it. I used to manage several restaurants in Atlanta."

Aaron, too, was born in Erie, but he returned to Turkey when he was a boy. As a young man, he worked in his father's establishment there, then married and returned to open The Landing. It excited him to learn Nolan had once owned restaurants and joked that Nolan cheated when he guessed at the type of nuts in the baklava. He settled in Erie because of his fond memories of the area and believed this would be a proper place to raise his family.

"But Erie, she is dying. Every year we make less than the year before. My son is not interested in taking my place. He makes me angry, but I cannot fault him. He wants me to move back to Turkey to open a restaurant in the city of my home when I was a boy. I do not know." He looked at Nolan with raised brows.

"I grew up here, Aaron. I am saddened by what has happened to the city."

"We have no new jobs, no new business. Taxes are higher each year, so more businesses leave. Then people give up. Now we have horses coming. Horses will do nothing for The Landing. Families do not come to this city to bet on horses. Men will come and go to the racetrack and bars, but few businesses will benefit. The hotels by the track will do well."

"I remember there was a horse track here when I was a young boy. I recall little about it other than it failed."

"Yes, yes. I read about that. Council says it closed because it was a different type of horse and was only open in the summer."

"I remember now. That track was for trotters—harness racing. You know, with a little buggy behind the horse. This new one must be a traditional horse racing track. I don't know much about horses either way but agree any horse track will not solve the problem. I don't see people moving back to Erie or businesses staying just because there's a horserace track."

Nolan stood from the table. "Well, Aaron, I appreciate your hospitality. I'm going to walk for a bit around the pier and will definitely stop for dinner before I leave town."

"If you do not mind, I will come and walk with you. My legs could use the exercise. Let me warm up your coffee."

Aaron flung on his coat as the pair entered the brisk air.

"I must admit you appear to have a great location here, Aaron. I guess the local economy is choking you."

"Yes, that is true. My friends at Bayview across the street," he pointed, "have already left, but I'm trying to hang on."

"The people who live here, from those I have met so far, they seem to have kind souls."

Aaron nodded as they stopped and leaned on an iron rail, then gazed out over the dark waters of the bay.

"I used to live in Erie, but oh so long ago. In fact, the last day of my life with my parents was right across the water here at the Fourth of July celebration back about forty years ago."

The splashing of the waves against the concrete pier was soothing therapy to one's anxieties.

After a few moments, Aaron said, "Those memories still trouble you."

"Yeah, it's why I came back. I was only eight years old when my folks and I were returning home from the fireworks. A train hit our car, and I was thrown free. My parents didn't make it. So, I spent ten years at a Catholic orphanage and blamed my parents for every-thing that ever went wrong in my life."

"I am sorry for you, my friend."

"Well, when my wife died recently, I got a fresh perspective on life. I'm here to get a proper headstone for my parents and try to right a wrong that happened when I was a teenager. Perhaps I'll tell you about it sometime. The most important thing for me now is to honor my parents. It's long overdue and I feel very guilty."

"You seem like a decent man. I am glad you stopped in for cof-fee. I look forward to serving you authentic Turkish cuisine on your next visit. But . . ." Aaron turned and looked at the bright neon sign above his restaurant, "I fear you must come soon."

They shook hands, then Nolan walked back to his SUV and headed to the diner. He planned more research for the following morning and hoped to find a way to help these people. After all, what else was he going to do? Perhaps it was time to attract atten-tion to himself. Someone knew what happened to Mary, and their curiosity may draw them out.

CHAPTER EIGHT

Catch and Release

The aroma of baking blueberry muffins and freshly brewed coffee greeted Marge as she strolled through the diner's back entrance. At a glance, Nolan noticed a Marge upgrade had been installed overnight.

Her gait displayed a spring in her step, accompanied by a smile that would tempt the heart of many a man. Nolan stuttered a weak greeting as he studied a redesigned Marge. She was wearing makeup, and a scent of sweet perfume permeated the room. The same striped uniform covered her torso, but the addition of nylons and low pumps gave her a more elegant image. Damn, Nolan thought. She had spoken with Evelyn last night and was now on the hunt.

"Nolan, are you still leaving this morning?" She combined her pleading expression with a provocative grin.

"Well, Marge, I wanted to speak with you about that. I'd like to stick around for a few days—more if necessary."

She fidgeted on the stool. "Have you more, uh, business here in town? Uh, perhaps another reason to stay?"

She projected that puppy-dog look with soft eyes open and ears perked with anticipation.

"I need to do some research for a new business idea. I'd like to design a plan where I can continue to cook here and still have some free time to work up some background details. Of course, I'd prefer to stay upstairs if possible."

"That's glorious news. I'm eager to hear more about your project. I don't mean to be rude, but are you planning to work the breakfast shift today? I can call Rose and tell her to stay home, if you're going to handle it." There was that smile again, and her hand patted his arm.

"Holy crap," Nolan mumbled. "Yes, I can work this morning." A twinkle of hope seemed to fill Marge's eyes. "Why don't you call Rose while I get the muffins out of the oven? Then we need to talk." Nolan gave her a most professional and solemn stare.

Nolan sat at the counter, and she perched next to him with not a seat between for comfort or elbow room. Then she swiveled her stool toward him, and her knee brushed his leg.

"Marge, I don't know your specific arrangement with Rose, but I'd prefer either the breakfast or dinner shift as a regular schedule. I can do lunch most days as well. But I need time to do this research, and most of it will be necessary during normal business hours."

She swiveled a bit, reminding Nolan of moving bait in the water. "I can get along for a while longer with you helping and Rose staying away. The hours are killing me, but I can hire a server soon with the money I'm saving. That will put me back in the kitchen for whatever shift you don't work. I would rather have you cook the dinner shift. You seem to have a creative touch, which may attract a few more people." She was staring into his eyes with a few flecks of gold sparkling on her eyelids.

"Dinner shift is perfect, and we can work out the details later." Nolan paused and turned away, then pivoted back.

"Marge, there's something you need to know about me," Nolan said.

"Oh no, here it comes. Please don't tell me you're married, but you have an open marriage."

Nolan laughed and shook his head. "No, I'm not married. But I am a recent widower. My wife passed away about two years ago. That's part of the reason I'm traveling. I needed to get away from the memories. We were wonderful together, but the only visions I can recall since her death are the futile months of pain and anguish. I hope soon I will remember only the reflections of the happy moments we shared."

Now her teal-blue eyes were tearing.

"I don't want your pity, Marge. People go through this all the time. Losing my wife hit me harder than most. From what I've been told, you will understand. I can't have feelings for another woman right now. I might never or I may change tomorrow. But for now, I feel like I'm still married. I can't even romantically think of you." She wiped the tears from her cheeks with a napkin. "I'm not ready yet, and I hope you understand."

"I'm sorry, Nolan. I didn't know. Evelyn told me you seemed interested last night, and I allowed a dim light to enter my heart. I knew it was silly putting on this makeup and perfume. It's not who I am."

"You shouldn't change from who you are to attract a man. Relationships built on lies are doomed to fail. I know little about you as a person. But I see you're attractive, sense you're kind, and Evelyn said you've experienced more than your share of life's disappointments. People today don't always need to find a mate to be happy. If it's what you want, then pursue it. I think someone will enter your life someday who will appreciate the real Marge, the hot tempered, sarcastic, lovely Irish lass with spicy breath."

She suppressed her laugh and raised her hand to cover her smile.

"Now, let's work out a schedule for this week so that I can plan a bit," he said. "Friends?" he extended his open right hand.

"Of course," she replied and grasped his hand, both of them smiling with ease.

"I'm going to call Bootsie. She was my server for over a year but got a better offer at the Waffle Palace. I heard she hates it and uses her pay increase on gas money. She lives down the street. And Jake will be out of school soon and can pitch in to help. Hell, things are looking up."

Her beam returned, and Nolan tapped the top of her forearm. "Marge, thank you for listening. I hope I didn't hurt your feelings."

"Me?" She pushed away from the counter and fanned her open hand in the air. "Hon, you misunderstood me. If I were serious, I'd have you wrapped up already. You wouldn't stand a chance. I was hoping you might stay on a few more days and give Rose a rest. I was teasing, that's all."

Nolan mumbled to himself. "God help the man . . ."

CHAPTER NINE

Payback

The statistical information Nolan gathered was data he felt the Erie Chamber of Commerce would prefer to keep secret. Erie's population was indeed shrinking at a dramatic rate, with several causes. The number of failed or relocated businesses appeared significant, as people left the city for more opportunities. However, the aging community was most alarming.

Thirty years earlier, five public and four private high schools bustled with teenagers. Today, there was one of each. That fact alone forebodes a depressed economy. The pattern was similar for elementary schools. When Nolan was new at the orphanage, Little League baseball was at the height of popularity. At least fifty teams competed across the city. Now, the league had dissolved and organized baseball no longer existed for boys or girls in the area.

A simple calculation of births versus deaths over the most recent five years revealed a negative balance of nearly nine-thousand people. If that trend continued, someone would turn out the lights in Erie in a few generations.

Nolan spent a considerable amount of time in the clerk of court's office. Mrs. Castillo was so intrigued by his perseverance that she assisted with his research while he was at the diner. She developed into a consistent patron at Marge's place, and her recommendation led several others there, particularly for lunch. After a week of daily appearances at the courthouse, she told Nolan he could call her Isabel but wanted to know his motives.

"Isabel, I assure you I have the best interests of Erie at heart. I realize this sounds like I'm a politician, but I am certainly not. I have a business idea which may help generate some revenue for the city and your dwindling population."

"Well, then tell me about it."

"Actually, you're telling me about it. Your statistics give me valuable information, which tells me if my whacky concept has a realistic chance. If I believe it does, then I'll have a meeting in a few days with some folks in town and invite you. If I don't think we have a shot, I'll at least share my thoughts so you can confirm your efforts were legitimate."

Meanwhile, life at the diner settled into a comfortable pattern and business picked up. Nolan learned the palate of the average Erieite did not accept a high level of spice in their diet. His attempt at chicken étouffée was a bust, so he aborted his plans for sautéed Cajun catfish.

Clifton helped Nolan unpack his SUV and sort the baseball memorabilia. The angler even cut back on his fishing so he could spend time appreciating the collection.

"Hey Nolan, how about we go to the Cleveland game tomorrow? We could stay over and make the Saturday night game too. You've gotta see a couple games before you leave town."

"That's awfully tempting, but Marge would have a cow if I told her I was taking off for two days."

"Gee, you gotta have some fun. Tell her you're going to Cleveland for research, and I'll tag along. She may buy that one."

"Clifton, don't you even think about stealin' my cook." Marge's hollow voice boomed through the vent next to the bed where the men sat. In an instant, she stood at the doorway with her hands gripping the apron at her hips.

"Clifton, before you make plans to go off on a baseball junket, I should warn you I saw your truck over at Ida Kensington's last week," Marge said.

"What? You know better than that, Marge. I'm a faithful husband to Evelyn."

"I can't testify to that. All I know is I'm finally getting some debtors off my ass, and you plot to take my cook away to a ball game for my two best nights. And I recall you and Ida were an item in high school and ever since her husband left her a few years ago, she's made it clear to everyone she would be happy to have you back in her life."

"Marge, where did you hear such nonsense? I haven't spoken with Ida Kensington since she was Ida Filipkowski, and that was a long time ago. So, don't you go starting rumors that aren't true."

Marge kept her hands on her hips and glared at Clifton. "You should know rumors are the worst kind of evidence. It's hard to prove you hadn't done anything when there's no one there to see you hadn't done it."

Clifton looked puzzled. "Marge, I don't even understand what you said. I think I better postpone our baseball trip. But it's just not fair blackmailing me with something I ain't even done."

Marge turned and sped down the stairs with Clifton on her heels.

Nolan's memory flashed back to the night of Mary Thompson's accident and his lack of an alibi. *How different would his life be today if he had proof of his whereabouts?*

He could hear his friend downstairs pleading his case with Marge, so he joined them and leaned against the counter.

"Listen, while I have you both here, I know you've been curious about my research, and I plan to gather some people and talk about my idea."

"Let's hear it. Evelyn doesn't believe you haven't shared this with me, so I'm ready." Clifton pulled up a seat at a nearby table and folded his hands. Marge slowed her pacing.

"Not here, Clifton," Nolan said. "It's more complicated than we have time for right now. I was hoping we could close an hour early on Monday and meet at The Landing."

Marge had that scowl on her face again, "Why can't we just meet here when we close? You both want to cost me money. First, you want to go to a ball game, and now you want me to close early. And why down there?"

"We don't have much late business on Monday anyhow. You know that. And I'd like Evelyn and Rose to come if they can make it. Rose can bring her husband too."

"I'm in. Ten o'clock on Monday?" Clifton asked as he looked up at Marge.

"Well, all right. I guess you've done me enough favors here that I can give you an hour back. But this better be good."

CHAPTER TEN

Twinkle Little Star

Aaron greeted most members of the assemblage of eight with a boisterous hug. The group overall was rather apathetic, like attendees at a Tupperware party. They came out of respect to Nolan's friendship, but they weren't about to buy anything. Only Aaron was gregarious as he produced a tray of baklava and tartlets which he announced held another mystery ingredient to challenge Nolan.

Marge brought her son, Jake, but Nolan's expression displayed his disappointment Rose's husband, Karl, would not attend.

"Most of you know each other, but I want to introduce Isabel Castillo, the clerk of courts who has recently favored Marge's diner and has assisted me with a great deal of research on this project," Nolan said.

"I'm eager to see why I've been checking all these properties at the courthouse." Isabel appeared stereotypical of a librarian as she sat with her hands together on the table, her silvery hair wrapped in a bun.

Clifton jabbed Nolan with his steel finger and nodded toward Isabel. "Gee, she sure is frumpy looking."

His wife overheard him and raised her voice, "Clifton Bell, as long as you're being critical, don't forget to tell your friend what happens when you fall asleep with your arm dangling down an open ice fishing hole."

Clifton's face reddened, and he sat down in silence. Nolan continued with the introductions.

"And of course our gracious host Aaron, who insists on helping us expand our waistlines with his fabulous desserts."

"I am Aaron Erdogan and welcome you to my restaurant. I am from Turkey where my family name means *brave warrior*. My new friend has a business idea where we will be challenged, and we must remain strong and open-minded. I don't know any of you, but since you have survived the troubled times we are in, I consider all of you my friends."

Be like me, "brave warrior." His open hand slapped his chest in a mock display of his surname. "You enjoy my desserts, and I want Nolan to guess the surprise ingredient in my tartlets."

Nolan completed the introductions of the other attendees to Isabel and Aaron, then proceeded to Aaron's test.

"Aaron, you have me stumped so far on this tartlet. I recognize the bananas and caramel, and of course your delicate touch with the pastry. I'm not surrendering just yet but will think about it while I continue to relish the flavor."

All the attendees except Jake and Isabel sat back in their chairs, their body language projecting their apprehensiveness. With his arms crossed across his chest, Clifton verbalized the emotions that most of the group was feeling. "Let's get on with this, Nolan. I've got fish to catch early tomorrow morning."

"I will make this as pointed as possible. First, I should share a little of my background. After all, I can't expect you to listen to any of my ideas if I have zero credibility. Some of you know I grew up here in town and left at the age of eighteen. After that, I finished college, eventually received a master's in business and became a consultant for what I considered medium-size companies, perhaps five hundred to five thousand employees. These organizations faced declining revenue, profits, or both. It was my job to make recommendations to turn them around. I was successful and fortunate to invest in a few restaurants in Atlanta. Food was always my passion, but I made my money by putting companies back on the path to success. When my wife got cancer, she became my only focus. I abandoned all my business activities to care for her. After she passed, I returned to work, only to discover my companies were in financial ruin, and my supposed partner had embezzled sizable sums of money."

Clifton cleared his throat and spoke up. "I'm just gonna ask what we're all thinking. If you were so good at saving companies, why couldn't you save your own?"

"I've asked myself that many times. The answer is we were too far gone. My partner had signed building leases, purchased restaurant and office equipment with outrageous monthly payments and terms, and most of my employees had quit. Truth is, I failed. It was my responsibility, and I should have been more mindful of my own finances. But I would do it all over again and cherished every moment I spent with my wife before she passed."

Silence gripped the attendees while many shuffled about in their seats, crossed arms, shifted their ball caps, or cast their eyes to the floor.

"Now let's get back to the present. You'll have to decide whether you trust me or not, and I'm fine with that. I believe you will all agree Erie is declining at a rapid pace. One on one, we have discussed the problems with the receding population, business bankruptcies or relocations, and the high unemployment. With all that happening, life for those who remain here becomes more difficult each year."

Marge spoke out, "I hope I didn't close my diner early just to hear you tell me things I already know."

"Madam, do not be rude to my friend," Aaron interjected. "He comes here to tell us a message of importance. We should listen."

Marge leaned forward in her chair, but Rose tugged her shoulder. She then frowned as Rose reached into her sister's handbag, opened a spice stick and slid it into Marge's gaping mouth.

"Please continue, Nolan. My sister just needed a fix, but she'll be fine now."

"So we all understand the city needs an idea that will not only keep existing business, but attract new ventures, residents, and even tourists. The concept must be sustainable over time, yet an inexpensive start-up, in view of our limited resources. I believe I have a plan to do exactly that, but it will take lots of hard work."

The crowd remained silent but peered at their host with keen looks of curiosity.

"The city has a beautiful port with views of Lake Erie, and a peninsula that extends into the bay as a natural tourist attraction. While the park on that isle is well maintained by the state, the city has never taken full advantage of its potential. In addition, we have a rich cultural heritage in Erie. Just here in this room, we have several nations represented.

Nolan pointed to Dimitri, "Turkey", then to Marge, "obviously Ireland," which got some chuckles. "My ancestors are from Poland," and he stepped toward Isabel. "Castillo? I should have researched that name. Italy?"

Isabel shook her head. "Not Italy but Spain. Actually, my dear Chico and I came here from Mexico, or Meh-he-co, if I pronounce my birthplace correctly."

Nolan continued. "And it is our ancestry and the picturesque setting of Erie that we should use as our foundation. Of course, we must find many more ethnic representatives to join us if we are to be successful and truly diverse."

Marge blurted out, "Sounds like we're going to have a church fair." She chuckled to herself and received an insolent glare from Aaron. "Okay, okay. I'll be quiet."

"I propose we create a theme attraction that will capitalize on our ethnic backgrounds and display our heritage. Of course, we'll need to expand far beyond the representation in this room. We can also utilize the natural lake setting and integrate the isle across the bay. We start small with our limited resources then gradually enlarge our village."

"Nolan, I'm probably a bit dense, so could you bring this down to my level?" Clifton asked.

"Sorry about that. My proposal has several phases. First, we use Aaron's restaurant to create a number of stations that sell a variety of ethnic foods—many restaurants in one. Turkish, Chinese, African American, Japanese, Brazilian, and so forth. We would need to modify The Landing to make this happen."

"You mean we would build an area like a food court at a mall?" Rose asked. "I don't see people coming to live here for that."

"Rose, this will be nothing like a food court at a shopping mall. Our group of food booths will only serve authentic cuisine of that country. And the restaurant is just the start. That's why Isabel has been checking the land ownership and zoning in this area."

"I have lots of information, but it doesn't seem to mean anything to me," Isabel said.

"After the food booths are open, we create additional areas that celebrate the cultural background of each of these nations at a specific time in history. What was life like for the Native Americans in this area? Why did the Chinese first settle in America? We create an environment that matches that time when each ethnic group emigrated here and depict their lifestyle in that era. We can sell products from each nation as well, then eventually, I'd like to see us make these products here in the USA. Best of all, we do it all right here on the bay front. We expand as our finances permit and involve other residents of Erie."

"I know you have lots of questions but let me continue just a while longer. We need to attract traffic away from that one road that goes onto the isle. In summer, I understand congestion is still terrible, and parking there is a problem as well. We can offer parking here at the pier and ferry passengers across the bay. I've learned you already have a ferry boat that provides tours of the harbor, and the owners should jump at the chance to increase their business. This would also force thousands of people past our attraction, and many will become our customers."

Evelyn frowned. "I think this is all good, Nolan. I truly do. But where are we going to get the money to do all this?"

"That's why we'll start with the food section. That cost should be minimal. But we would have to close The Landing during construction." Nolan peered at Aaron to observe his reaction, but his expression was unrevealing. "And once we open, we would close the diner and redirect those clients here."

"What? Are you crazy? I'm barely making ends meet, and you want me to close my diner then send my clients to this oaf?"

Nolan glanced at Aaron, who remained stoic.

"Each of you has the choice of participating or not. I am only bringing this proposal to you because I have learned to respect you. But stress has taken away your spirit; you have no zest for life anymore. Your apathy controls you and prevents you from becoming more successful. You all complain and wait for someone else, perhaps the government, the unions, or even divine intervention to breathe life into Erie. I'm sorry, but I don't see any reasonable chance in those options. You are all hard-working and intelligent people who have been victims for so long you no longer have faith in yourselves. You all have talents. This is only an opportunity. There's no guarantee it will work."

The attendees spoke to each other in low tones for what seemed like minutes, but Nolan did not interrupt.

At last, Aaron stood and addressed the group. "I have the most to lose, but for real, that is not much. Perhaps this will give my son a reason to stay and take my place." He paused and looked around the group. "For me, I am interested. I will try hard to look through the eyes of my friend because I am so close I cannot see."

Silence overtook the congregation, then Nolan resumed. "Isabel, please review what we've learned with your research."

She pulled a black spiral bound notebook from her purse. "None of this made sense to me before, but I know where you're going now. Let me see." She put on her reading glasses and continued. "Everyone knows about the snack bar at the pier. The Cai family has owned that for almost forever, per everyone's recollection. It surprised me to learn the city purchased the parcels from a gentleman named Walter Smythe just before the Civil War. When they purchased the land, the city granted a perpetual transferable lease for the use of that land for any business purpose of the family. In 1912, the records show the Smythe lease was transferred for 'good will and one dollar' to Cai Liu Wei. I found a newspaper clipping that referenced the transfer and the relation to a shooting contest won by Mr. Cai. That family leases the property from the city for one dollar per year, and the contract is solid. In fact, a perpetual lease is rare. The city has no right to evict the owners if it is being used for business, and they cannot raise the rent. And the best part, since the property is leased, there are no taxes."

The group was listening once again as Nolan interjected. "This is important because the current owners can use that building for any business purpose. There are limited zoning restrictions that could be imposed. I suppose there are some city ordinances that would allow the government to act if there were illegal or immoral activities in the building, but that's seems improbable. If we can get the current owner to become part of our plan, then we can target that building for our first expansion beyond The Landing."

Clifton added, "The Cai family still owns the meat and seafood market in town. Their son moved out of town last year, but their daughter Li Na moved back. She takes care of her aging folks and runs the market too. Scuttlebutt says she may not open the snack bar this year. The woman and I don't talk exactly—she nods at me every now and again. But us anglers talk."

Isabel resumed her report. "Then we have the shipyard, dry dock, and surrounding area. The shipbuilder went bankrupt in 1980, and the city foreclosed on the property shortly thereafter. Again, common perception is the city owns that property. But that's not true. It is owned by a Mr. Shongo. No one I spoke with knew anything about him, but the tax bills are being sent to a post office box in a small town in New York. The taxes are all paid. My guess is he bought it on spec but did nothing with the property."

"Thanks Isabel," Nolan continued. "That covers the center of the pier and the area just east of us. We also discovered some interesting items about The Bayview Restaurant and the western area. Isabel . . ." Nolan nodded for her to continue.

"The Bayview is about to be taken by the city for non-payment of their property taxes. But you probably aren't aware the restaurant building is only a small portion of the parcel. The building and parking lot occupy a minute amount of the almost seven acres."

"Seven acres!" Clifton exclaimed. "That's impossible. The boat slips come right up to the parking lot. And beyond that lies the rail yard."

"Well, let me show you." Isabel withdrew a manila envelope from her purse and produced a reduced copy of an old survey. "The parcel is oddly shaped, sort of like a reverse question mark." She laid the survey on the table and turned it toward Clifton. "The restaurant is at this dot on our question symbol. You can see the property shape narrows as it passes the boat slips, then gradually curves and expands. As it approaches the rail yard, it narrows again and curves down toward the water."

Clifton replied. "That might be the most useless piece of land I've ever seen. It's only thirty feet across at the widest point, not considering the land the restaurant occupies. I wonder how that was ever divided that way."

"The property records don't reference any reason for the plat allocation," Isabel responded. "It's possible the railroad got whatever they wanted and left the rest. The railroads still have a great deal of influence from old laws that allow them to acquire properties whenever they want. Railroads seize property under eminent domain and have done so for many years."

Clifton continued his observations. "Well, that rail yard was used primarily for delivery of iron ore to the forge plant. I've seen no activity there for a few years now."

Nolan commented, "I'm not sure this knowledge provides us with any options, but at least we know more details about the lots and ownership. The information about that snack bar could be most useful."

"And speaking of snacks," Nolan smirked at Aaron, "do you have a chestnut tree in your backyard?" Aaron appeared dumbfounded as he rested back in his chair and mumbled something in his native tongue. "I recognized the flavor from something my mother used to make. There was a chestnut tree in my yard when I was a young boy, and I gathered them off the ground each year. I recalled the taste from my childhood, but it took me some time to match that flavor with my memory."

"So, you have cheated again," Aaron accused. "And I misjudged you to be an honest man." He beamed with pleasure, yet his eyes displayed a twinkle of mischief.

Nolan turned back to the group. Their interest appeared heightened with more positive energy and buzz in the air.

"I know it's getting late, but I would like to learn how you all feel about the project right now. We need to move fast if we want to take advantage of the summer tourist season. I suspect you need more information to buy in, but I'd like you to take turns and share how you stand at this point."

Nolan looked at Evelyn, who had been silent through most of the discussion. "Evelyn, what do you think about this?"

She responded without hesitation, "I think it's a damn fool idea—reminds of that movie which was out several years ago. You know, the guy who built the baseball field in the middle of his corn." She paused and stood to face the group. "But by God, we have to do something. Neither the government nor the union cares one bit about us. And I'm sick of cleaning and eating the fish Clifton catches every day." She stared at her husband. "You've been making decisions for our family since the day we got married, Clifton. So, it's about time I had a turn." She extended her right hand, "Nolan, let's shake on this. Clifton and I are in on your plan so far. What do we do next?"

Clifton's face erupted with a huge grin as he watched Evelyn take charge.

"Well, we plan. We have lots of work to do to get the restaurant changed over, and I'm hoping Clifton can be our guide for that rehab. For the rest of you, I merely ask you to think it over. We'll have to draw up some legal documents regarding our little group, and I'll make a punch list of other items that will need attention. I'll also work up a budget before we work on something we can't afford to finish. I suggest anyone who wants to be a part of our group meet here next Monday at the same time." Nolan glanced toward Aaron. "If that's acceptable to you, that is."

"I should never open Monday at all. Two customers tonight." He held up his fingers.

"That is not enough to even pay the light bill. Of course, we will meet here. I don't understand the story about a baseball field and corn, but if that worked, this will be easy as pie."

"I'll put my pies up against yours anytime, oh, brave warrior," Marge said.

Aaron frowned, but before he could respond to Marge's challenge, Isabel rose from her chair. She stepped to the front of the group. "I can't use a hammer, but I have some money saved that I will consider investing as soon as you tell me more, Nolan." She too extended her hand for a vigorous shake.

Rose followed behind Isabel and likewise shook Nolan's hand. "I'm sorry I can't speak for Karl and me just yet. But I'll get him to come next Monday. I'll sort of fill him in before then."

That left Marge and Jake still sitting at the table. "Rose, you know this is all your fault."

Rose turned with a look of dismay. "How on earth are you going to blame me for the condition of Erie, Marge?"

"No, not that. This whole idea would have never come up if you hadn't thrown a fit about that bowling tournament. Nolan would have taken care of his business and left for home by now if you hadn't made us look so desperate."

"Now ladies, please don't start here," said Nolan. "Aaron still thinks we are a civilized group, and he may not let us back here if he thinks his china is at risk because of the two of you."

"Mr. Erdogan, I will teach you about baseball and the cornfield." Everyone stared at Jake, who was uncomfortable speaking before any group. "I have the movie at home. Maybe you can come over sometime, and we can watch it together."

Meanwhile, Jake's mother and aunt continued to glare at each other. Hearing her son's interest, Marge turned her head away from her sister. "I suppose I don't have much choice at this point. You've got this angel thing going, so I'll come next week to hear some more. You have any idea what you're going to call this place, assuming it works?"

Nolan beamed at Marge's expressed interest. "We may already have the start of a perfect name in The Landing. We are going to celebrate the heritage of our countries of origin on or about the time each group immigrated to the United States. That was a time of hope for each immigrant as they arrived. I suggest we take that one step further to match our current situation and name our project Hope Landing."

CHAPTER ELEVEN

Images and Icons

The start-up would need money no matter how frugal their plans. Nolan hadn't spent much since he arrived in Erie, but a few hundred dollars was not enough to seed a project of any magnitude. He spent his time away from the diner determining the value of his baseball memorabilia. His vehicle held his most valued items. A friend was holding some pieces, and another part of his collection contained baseball cards that were over fifty years old. Their considerable bulk would have overloaded his SUV, so he had secured them in a climate-controlled storage facility. He was uncertain of his plans for them.

Jake became Nolan's dedicated partner in the classification and sorting of the valuable objects. They worked together a limited amount of time each evening, since Jake was still in high school. Marge frowned at the hours Jake spent on the project and made certain he tended to his homework before he touched anything related to baseball. But Nolan also learned that Marge's gruffness was a façade. When Jake was telling her about a baseball autographed by Mickey Mantle, her glow didn't emanate from her appreciation of the item, but rather the happiness she saw on his face.

Jake was intelligent but needed schedules and direction. His organization was precise, and this explained why he was comfortable when he plated food for diner customers. The fare should be evenly spaced, quantities exact and arranged the same way on each dish. He would tell Nolan if there were too many peas on a plate, or the meat portions were unequal. Nolan wasn't about to count peas, but he changed his behavior to accommodate his junior assistant. It was easier for Nolan to place five asparagus spears on a plate versus an unknown quantity of peas, thus eliminating Jake's frustration.

Nolan greatly enjoyed sharing his memorabilia with Jake. The young man didn't know who Mickey Mantle was, but he focused on Nolan's every word. When Clifton stopped by to update Nolan on his progress, Jake would challenge him with a baseball trivia question.

Nolan unveiled two identical packages one evening to reveal his crown jewel to Clifton and Jake. He propped a pair of photos side by side against the headboard.

"While both photos appear identical, I assure you they are not. One displays the authentic signatures of Ted Williams and Babe Ruth. The other is a fake. Can you tell which one is real?"

Both photos were eleven-by-seventeen-inch landscape images of Ted and The Babe shaking hands. Both were in uniform with a stadium full of fans in the background.

Clifton and Jake studied them, and Jake picked one up for closer inspection.

"I'd be very careful with that, Jake. If any of these is real, it's worth a pretty penny."

"It's okay," Nolan said. "Jake is most respectful of the collection."

"I don't believe either of these is real, Nolan. They can't be," Clifton said.

"Why do you think that?" Nolan asked.

He rubbed his chin while inspecting the photo in Jake's hands. "Both Williams and Ruth are in uniform. They never played together. Ruth retired in 1935, and Ted Williams' rookie year in the majors was 1939—not a chance this is real."

"Your baseball history is correct, Clifton. However, you're not thinking outside the box."

"What the hell, er, heck does that mean? Sorry, Jake."

"You don't have to apologize, Mr. Bell. My mom says things a lot worse than that to Aunt Rose all the time."

"Yeah, well, I believe that, but you don't need to get a habit." Clifton peered at Nolan. "Now tell me what you got here. You know I'm not a thinking-outside-the-square kind of guy."

"All right, they never played together, but they were in uniform together. 1946. Ted Williams had returned that year from his military career during World War II. On the day before the All-Star game, there was an exhibition game in Boston's Fenway Park. Babe Ruth and Ted Williams were opposing managers. This picture was taken before the game, and then later a limited number were autographed by both players. Ted Williams signed quite a few more, but without Ruth's accompanying signature. Those signed by Ted Williams alone are valuable. This shot with both signatures is worth some big bucks."

"Wow, Mr. David. And you have two of them," exclaimed Jake.

"It appears so, Jake. However, as I said, one is a fake. Because of its value, I purchased one photo with only the signature of Ted Williams. I hated to damage it, but I did so for security. The photo with the forgery of Babe Ruth's autograph was displayed above my mantel, while I stored the authentic one in a safe. I brought them both with me for the same reason. When I would leave the room, I placed the forged copy in plain view, while I stashed the real one or often carried it with me."

"So how much cash you got tied up in all this?" asked Clifton. "And why are you carrying it all with you?"

"Believe it or not, the collection doesn't equate to a vast amount of money. We're almost done sorting and counting with a total approaching fifty thousand so far. But the Williams and Ruth photo? I've not had it priced since Ted Williams died, so I don't want to know. I would be tempted based on my recent financial problems."

Clifton didn't push further, but curiosity glimmered in his eyes.

"And guys, I hate to do this to you, especially you Jake. Please tell no one about this. Not even your mom." Jake appeared disappointed, as anyone would have been at his age. He may not have been the most popular kid in school and showing this off might at least broaden his circle of friends.

"All right, Mr. David. I can keep a secret, I guess." His shoulders slumped as he walked away.

"When the time is right, I'll let you show it to your mom and Aunt Rose."

He straightened his posture. "Boy, I sure will surprise them."

They finished as Marge called from the bottom of the stairs. "Nolan, your orders are getting backed up, and you've got a visitor."

They hastened downstairs to the diner where Isabel sat at a table.

"Isabel, please order some dinner, and I'll be with you as soon as I can. Dinner's my treat, and I should be with you by the time you've eaten."

Isabel had become a valued research assistant over the last several days. She accepted her assignments with enthusiasm, and her knowledge of city and county records was a convenient asset. She also used her internet access to compile the contact information that Nolan requested. He sat next to her and picked up a sheaf of documents.

"There's all the material you requested," she said. "Most of the data is basic directory information for the contacts you mentioned. I've given you home and business addresses, plus phone listings for those that I could locate, but I assume most have mobile phones only. I've also provided a list of the churches that I felt had sizable congregations, but some of those are guesses. The church list shows the proper title for the head of each denomination as well: pastor, rabbi, and so forth. I can't guarantee they are 100 percent up to date, but I should be close."

"Thank you very much. I suspect this may have eaten into your personal life."

"Personal life? I haven't had anything personal since I got a robocall that knew my name. You just keep on passing along your questions, and I'll get your answers as best I can. Now, you were looking for a historian of our area."

"That's right. Someone who can tell me about the ethnic mix here in town, and when countries had surges of emigration."

"Well, I've got your ethnic statistics in there. The 2020 census shows a clear breakdown."

She was right. The table displayed a subset of nationalities to a tenth of percent. *Never too much information*, Nolan thought.

"Your historian was easy to select. I asked a few people at the courthouse, and they all recommended the same person. He's a history professor at the college across from the courthouse, and he's also the president of the Erie Historical Society. He's getting up in years and has reduced his teaching to part-time this year. My sources say he's very sharp and should have the knowledge you need or can recommend where you could find it. His contact details are on the last page."

Nolan winced when he recognized the name of the historian.

"You'll also note the brief bio there on our mystery man, Mr. Shongo."

"You found him? I must thank you, Isabel, for doing an outstanding job for us. I know you are probably content with your job at the courthouse, but you have some genuine talent that could do you very well in the private sector."

"I don't need your flattery. Finding him wasn't that difficult. It's what I discovered that surprised me."

"So he's either in jail, a leader of industry, or he's dead. Those are my guesses."

"Option B and then some," she touched her phone and placed it on the table. "I knew the tax bills were being sent to a post office box in Salamanca, New York. That's a small town in the southern part of the state about two hours' drive from Erie. Here is the city on this map photo of the southern portion of New York State. I called my counterpart there in the clerk of court's office. As soon as I mentioned his name, she knew who he was."

Isabel paused and watched Nolan's expression. "He's the chief of the Seneca Indians." Isabel stated this with a broad smile.

"A Native American. I suppose that makes sense."

"And there's more. The clerk was thrilled to give me the lowdown on him. Everyone in that area knows Shongo. The Seneca Tribe has a big casino operation in Salamanca, and he founded that many years ago. The Senecas own the entire city of Salamanca. It seems the city founders built on land leased from the Seneca Nation. The government and the Native Americans have been bickering in court for years. Salamanca made national news about twenty years ago when the leases expired for many of the homes in the town. The Senecas threatened to evict the residents because the lease payments were far lower than reasonable for today's economy. This went on for years, and Chief Shongo was at the forefront of that fight. At last, they renewed the leases to everyone's satisfaction. He's a tough business executive and most consider him to be fair-minded."

"Well, he's a potential player in our group. He has the resources, and if our plan succeeds, his land value would increase significantly. I'd like to meet him if we proceed. I'm guessing he'll have a definite opinion."

Nolan thanked Isabel again, then she left. He still had several items on his list to accomplish before Monday's meeting, and Isabel's historian would force Nolan to come face-to-face with his past.

CHAPTER TWELVE

Freedom and a Prayer

It seemed perspiration discharged from every pore in Nolan's body as he approached the campus of Haven College. Visiting the cemetery was easy compared to what faced him this day. At least no one spoke to him from the graves. Today, he was uncertain if he could go through with this meeting. He carried one of his journals, a portfolio with Isabel's notes, and a list of questions.

It disappointed him to learn the tiny restaurant where he ate almost every meal after class was now a billiard hall. He located a park bench that overlooked the college entrance, plopped down and removed his journal. This was the location where his life had changed. He had read the passage so many times he could repeat the words without benefit of the paper. This time, he spoke aloud.

Journal Entry, September 21, 1989

I felt good about myself this afternoon when I left the police station, despite what seemed like a personal vendetta from that detective. He offered no apology but told me he stopped his investigation. Sly Cermak was dumbfounded he failed to uncover evidence to tie me to the crash scene. Mary's death was ruled accidental. He wouldn't admit I wasn't involved, nor did he volunteer to clear my name with Ellie, her family or the press. I again tried to tell him some kids had more information about the other drive, if he pursued it with the same passion he had come after me. I heard the stories myself, but couldn't pin down the driver's ID.

Sly also warned he would be watchful of my actions in the future, so I should be certain to act as a model citizen. He made it clear he would reopen the investigation at my slightest wrongdoing. All the while he spoke, he used his thumb to twirl a ruby ring on his right ring finger. He said I was free to leave the city if I wished. I felt like a character in a spaghetti western where the sheriff was running me out of town.

But I had no intention of leaving after that meeting. Sure, I had to always drive under the speed limit, never drink a drop of alcohol until I was of legal age and cross the streets only in the designated areas. That was fine, for I was sure Ellie Thompson and her family no longer had a reason to condemn me. Her parents prohibited Ellie from meeting me since my name was mentioned in the investigation. She could have protested and slipped away for a secret rendezvous. That's what I expected. But she didn't. She phoned just once and said we should stop seeing each other until "all this" was over. That was such a vague term. Was the funeral the end to "all this"? Or did she mean until the police ran out of people to ask if they were certain they didn't see me with Mary near the scene of the accident? Or did "all this" have more permanence?

I discovered the meaning of the phrase as I was springing up the steps to class. I felt her presence before I noticed her. Funny how that occurs with someone with whom you have a powerful bond. Sometimes you can feel their essence in a crowded room. I stopped so fast I almost stumbled on the stairs as I turned to scan the quad.

"Nolan," I heard her call my name, but I already spotted her long-legged frame and sandy hair amidst the other students.

"Ellie," I called with excitement as I bounded down the steps and was before her in an instant. But while I was expectant of a wel-

coming embrace, my feet skidded to a halt as she extended her palm toward me. Her expression was not of a joyful reunion, but stern and sorrowful. I knew what was coming before she even spoke.

"Nolan," she stammered a bit as tears streamed down her cheeks. I reached out for her, but she stepped back. "Please, let me say this. I have to tell you in person."

Her slender fingers smeared her eye makeup.

"Ellie, don't do this. You know I wasn't involved in that accident. The police cleared me today." I was hopeful the legal release would change her mind—that she hadn't yet heard the news.

Her voice was a faint whisper as our eyes met. "I believe you did nothing wrong. I always knew. But my mother and father won't forgive you—especially my mom. And I can't sneak around and cause more grief for them right now. They need me, and they're my parents."

"But El, let me speak with them. Give me a chance." I tried to reach for her again, but she turned to hide her tears. "I love you, Ellie."

She sobbed aloud, then shook her head and trudged away, her elegance marred by the uncontrolled shaking of her heartache. I stood helpless as I watched the woman I intended to marry stroll out of my life. She stopped after about twenty feet away, pivoted, and mouthed, "I love you."

Nolan replayed that scene countless times over the next few years. Most often he would scold himself for not running to her at that last moment. But then he would change his opinion, persuading himself that any action would have only made matters worse.

So, here he was, climbing those same stairs of Haven College. He withdrew Isabel's contact list from his portfolio and flipped to the last page. He stopped mid-stride as he stared at the name of the recommended historian: Father Andrew Belczyk. While the receptionist spoke to him, his pale and confused appearance was noticeable.

"Can I help you, sir?" Then, as she received no recognition, she went around her desk and touched Nolan's shoulder. He jolted and dropped his papers to the floor. "Sir, are you all right?"

"Yes, yes, I'm fine. I'm sorry about that." She squatted and retrieved his sheets, being the ever-courteous front guard of the administrative building.

Nolan composed himself and asked how he could find Father Belczyk. She buzzed a phone, advised Nolan that he was free, then handed him a visitor's badge and logged him in. Nolan was relieved he had two buildings to navigate before he reached his target, the former head of the orphanage.

As he stopped outside the open door, a soft-toned voice leaked from the office. Nolan peeked at a man who had grayed and added some bulk, but he was the priest whom he ignored for most of his time at the facility. No collar, no robes, just a simple white golf shirt with little contrast to his pale skin. The priest cradled the phone to his right shoulder while he scribbled notes on a yellow legal pad with his left hand. The priest noticed his guest standing there and waived him in, then pointed to a cracked-leather high-backed chair at the side of his desk. Nolan sat. The walls were crowded with photos of Erie history and a few of the priest in vestments, as he shook hands with dignitaries. They were people of power or influence, and two were ex-presidents of the United States. As he finished his call, the professor watched his visitor concentrating on a large black-and-white photo of the orphanage in the center of the wall behind him. Their eyes met and locked for a long instant before the priest rose and extended his hand in greeting.

"How can I help you, Mr. David?"

"Oh, you know me?" Nolan stammered a bit. "Oh, of course, I get it. The receptionist from downstairs, she ... uh ... must have announced me, that's how you know my name."

"Relax," said the priest, "you wanted to see me?"

"Oh, yes, I remember all too well. Anyhow, Father, I was told you are the leading authority of the history of Erie, and was hopeful you would share some of your knowledge with me."

"Please don't call me Father; it's just Andrew. I haven't been an active priest since that orphanage closed almost fifteen years ago, and I began my second career here at the college." He met Nolan's intense stare, then continued. "Is there a particular time or incident that is the basis for your need?"

"Yes, Father," Nolan replied, then corrected, "I mean Andrew. Yes, there are many eras that attract my curiosity. I'm researching a project where it would be helpful if I knew the primary years a particular nationality emigrated to America, and the details of the lifestyle they faced upon their arrival."

Andrew didn't immediately respond, so Nolan continued. "For instance, I know the heaviest immigration era for the United States occurred in the opening of the twentieth century. But I also recall a significant Irish population was already present by then, at least in the larger cities in the Northeast. Therefore, I'm searching for details of those years of heavy immigration and the living conditions they faced. What type of food did they eat? What did they wear? What was their very basic day-to-day lifestyle, including their political and economic achievements?"

"A curious project indeed," he said. "But why come to me? Most of this information is available on the internet. Few people rely on the old methods of research these days."

"A very valid question, and one with more than one answer. First, I'm pressed for time. Online research is the quickest route for most information, but I doubt I'll locate specific data. I'll get statistics for the United States overall, but I need more. I'm interested in the soul of these nationalities as they adapted to their new environment. What challenges did they face? What type of work did they do? How were they accepted by the existing residents? Those details are difficult to locate without speaking with a knowledgeable human, and I'm told you are that person."

"I'm flattered and curious about the nature of your project."

"How much time do you have today? I can either provide the mini-version or explain in detail depending on your availability."

"Time is no longer a concern for me. I need to administer a final exam at seven this evening but am free until then. If you're willing to buy me lunch, I will listen to your plan and decide if I believe it has merit."

Nolan glanced again at the photo of his former home, held his gaze for more than a few heartbeats, then returned to look at the priest. "I will tell you now the project provides a spirit of hope for the citizens of Erie. I can explain further over lunch."

"You have me intrigued. So, we shall go to a place rich in local history, the perfect setting for such a discussion. Let's take a stroll to Paddy's Irish Pub."

CHAPTER THIRTEEN

Faith and Begorra

Paddy's appeared as if it had been in a time warp for the last 150 years. The paint on the exterior brick was faint but still displayed "Opened in 1875." The interior décor was drab with wood floors that long ago lost their luster, and a tin-plate ceiling stained dark yellow from generations of smokers. An oak bar stood perhaps seventy-five feet in length with a suggestion of prior elegance as it curved around to prevent access to the spirits. The mirror behind the bar covered the entire wall, reminiscent of an old western beer parlor. All the establishment needed was a sheriff with a holstered six-shooter to greet the patrons. The tables, chairs, and barstools were all wooden, and it seemed miraculous the saloon had not burned like a tinderbox from a misplaced hot ash.

"If we're going to discuss the history of Erie, there is no better place than Paddy's." The professor ordered a Kohler beer on tap, and Nolan recognized the name of the brewery which had been a mainstay in the city so many years before.

"I'll join you, Father. I thought Kohler's went out of business a while ago."

"You know more of our history than you admit. The original brewery did indeed shut down, but a local started a microbrewery, and the Kohler logo is once again dear to the tastes of beer drinkers in Erie." He tipped his glass in salute. "To old friends," he said.

"Old friends?"

"Anytime we speak of history, we discuss old friends." He spread his arms and rotated in his chair. "Paddy's is full of their spirits. This bar was the center of activity for at least a century. With the proximity to city hall and the shipyards, politicians and industry leaders of Erie made this a popular watering hole."

The menu did not feature bangers and mash or other Irish fare, so they ordered traditional American favorites of burgers with fries. While they waited for their order, Nolan summarized the Hope Landing project. Father Andrew absorbed the explanation without being too inquisitive.

"So you can see, a historian familiar with the area is necessary. For our plan to have a fair chance, we need information regarding the eras when certain nations had significant emigration to the United States, and then to Erie. We must learn of their culture, employment, and way of life in those years. Those details will guide us toward a realistic depiction of how the immigrants survived."

The priest sat back in his chair and lifted his glass to request a refill. "But, from what you are telling me, the lifestyle portion is in the second phase of your plan. I can't offer you any advice on the native foods of each country."

"So, you see no need to help us now since you believe we'll fail, is that it? Seems I'm renewing my fight with the Catholic Church."

"Excuse me? Not at all. You misunderstood." The priest took a tug at the draught beer and peered into the amber glow in the glass. "This is the best advantage of not wearing a collar. People may know I'm a priest, but if I'm out of uniform, they grant certain leeway of their judgment. Now, allow me to clarify my comments."

Andrew used his fingers to emphasize his points. "One, you have no help from the government, and neither want nor expect any. Two, your capital is limited. And three, you've no definite method to attract customers."

"Sounds about right. However, our idea is new, and I believe we have the talent to get this off the ground. Please come to our meeting this Monday night, and you'll learn a great deal more."

"Monday night . . . hmm," he rotated his hourglass shaped container of draught beer while he thought. "I'm in a golf league on Mondays, I'm afraid."

"Our meeting doesn't start until ten at night."

"In the cover of darkness, the secret society shall meet."

"Quotation?"

"It is now," he responded with a grin. "Even a priest cannot resist all temptations. I look forward to hearing more of your plan, so I shall attend." He took a long pull of his beer. "Now, let me provide a primer on the immigration of the Irish since we are sitting in one of their pubs. But we'll have to make this an abbreviated version, for if I have a third beer, I may attract the attention of someone who will post this on social media."

Nolan withdrew his pad and took notes as the professor spoke.

"The Irish arrived in the United States in two waves. The first was before the Revolutionary War, generated by a great famine in Ireland around 1740. Of course, they arrived along the East Coast and settled in the major cities such as Boston, New York, and Philadelphia. They were Protestants from Northern Ireland, so they caused nothing but problems upon their arrival."

Nolan stared with raised brows. "Is that the official version of the Catholic Church?"

"I can see you have doubts, as you indeed should have. I wanted to add some levity to history since most students pay closer attention that way."

He continued, "Their lifestyle adapted to the cities in which they lived. Some became noted politicians and were important to our government's foundation with the Declaration of Independence. Indeed, there were many Irish who fought in the Revolutionary War."

Andrew took a long sip from his draught.

"After that war, Americans migrated west and drove the indigenous away from their homelands. I don't know when the first Irish moved to Erie, but by 1851, when our city was established, a significant percentage of our population was of Irish descent. Many of these Irish came to the United States during that second wave, when the potato famine of 1845 killed over a million people in Ireland. Perhaps another million immigrated to North America, with half of them landing in those same cities. Jobs were scarce, thus requiring the Irish to search for work beyond the major cities. Some followed the railroad, worked in the coal mines in Pennsylvania, or along the ports of the Great Lakes. Others tried farming again and found potatoes grew well in the climate and soil of this area.

"The Irish faced many of the same prejudices other nationalities have endured upon their arrival and expansion in our country. The Ku Klux Klan was already active by then, and the Irish Catholics in the second wave became one of their primary targets. In addition, the residents did not consider these Irish as true Americans and resented them taking their jobs for lower wages. Does this sound familiar to you?"

"Very much so; the same is occurring now with the influx of undocumented immigrants."

"This discrimination is a developed pattern of American behavior. History has repeated itself so often that we can expect our reaction to be similar when the next nation has a sharp rise in their population here in the US." Andrew finished his beer.

Nolan glanced at his phone's time display. "I appreciate the lesson. Your knowledge will be important to our little group if you decide to join us. Plus, your presence will add some credibility as we start the specific plan."

"Ten o'clock is almost past this old man's bedtime, but I'll see you on Monday."

Nolan drove toward the cemetery to freshen the flowers at his parents' gravesite. The temperature reached seventy, and even though a stiff wind blew in from the lake, the air held that aroma of life starting anew in spring. Now, this was baseball weather.

He picked up the several silk arrangements he ordered earlier in the week and made his way toward the cemetery. He was upbeat and looked forward to spending a bit of time with his family.

However, he became a bit agitated as he approached the graves. The flowers he placed there a few days ago were nowhere in sight, and he didn't quite understand what could have happened to them. The wind? Perhaps. He rested the pot of silk red roses and white carnations atop the marker. They cost way too much, but he was trying to pay back years of denial that his parents ever existed.

He drove by Mary Thompson's site on the way to the cemetery office and noticed those white lilies were gone as well. That made no sense at all. Who would steal flowers from a cemetery? Flower bandits? He was certain other graves displayed fewer blooms as well.

The caretaker at the administrative office had the decorum of an embalmer. He was tall, lean and dressed in dark gray slacks, and a black turtleneck sweater under a charcoal-gray sport coat. His oval face was accented by a white mustache too thin to compliment his appearance.

"Can I help you, sir?" His low voice matched his appearance, and he fit the stereotype for his role.

"I know this is an odd question, but have you had a problem with thieves stealing flowers in the cemetery?"

"Thieves? What do you mean, sir?"

"If you are not aware of it, then I hate to be the one to break the news. But there seem to be many flowers missing out there." Nolan nodded toward his parents' graves.

He didn't respond at all, so Nolan continued to report the crime. "When I was here several days ago, the cemetery looked great. You know, as well as a cemetery can look. Flowers and blooming plants were everywhere—all types and colors. But today, there seem to be fewer. Even those I placed on my parents' marker are missing."

The custodian appeared annoyed.

"Sir, did you place fresh blossoms on the grounds?" The corners of his mouth turned down, and Nolan recalled the Mother Superior's frown as she informed him the rules barred him from the girls' wing in the orphanage.

"Why, yes, of course. What difference does that make?"

"You're not from around here, are you?" He didn't wait for a response. "Because if you were, you would realize you may not place fresh flowers anywhere in the cemetery until after Memorial Day."

"What kind of crazy rule is that? So, you just had a massive crackdown, and the flower police confiscated hundreds of mischievous flowers? Wait until the other people see this."

"The people who come here appreciate the rules, mister. You're allowed artificial flowers between Labor Day and Memorial Day. After that, we require fresh flowers or plants. Every Easter, we have an increase in families who bring live flowers and plants. Our caretakers spent considerable time this morning removing them." He paused, then pointed his finger at Nolan. "Your *fresh* flowers were among the ones confiscated. We have these rules to maintain the proper appearance of the cemetery."

"I just put a vase of silk flowers on a grave. Do you mean in a few weeks you're going to just throw it away?"

"Whose grave are you visiting, sir?"

"What difference does that make? Are there certain privileges to the upper class even after death?"

He shook his head in dismissal. "So, you're one of those."

"One of those? One of those what? Living people? Caring people? Or logical people who know when a rule is bullshit?" Nolan stopped as he realized he had become engaged in a shouting match with an administrator of a cemetery. He bolted from the office and peeled his tires as he left the rule enforcer behind. He hoped there was not a security camera, since he was certain it was a violation to lay rubber in a cemetery.

CHAPTER FOURTEEN

Blink Softly

Nolan located Cai Li Na packing boxes at the pier's snack bar. That is, he thought he found her. As he slowed past the building entrance, he noticed a figure in blue jeans and a denim jacket with tufts of straight raven black hair protruding from a ball cap. The bright interior lights revealed her taping a corrugated box. By the time he exited his vehicle, the door was still open, but the carton and she were nowhere in sight.

"Ms. Cai?" He called her name again a bit louder and edged inside. The tiny room was the size of a walk-in closet, abundant with canned goods and signs. A large stainless-steel freezer occupied an entire wall.

The door to the kitchen area stood open. He paused a moment and listened. The waves of the bay sloshing against the concrete breaker behind him drowned out all other sounds. Nolan eased toward the doorway and took one step inside. A grill, sink, and countertop were to his left. Then, he turned his head in the opposite direction to the sight of the double-barrel of a shotgun just a few inches from his cheek.

"No quick moves bad boy or they'll have to ID your body from fingerprints." Her voice was calm and in control. "Did the city send you? I told them I needed a few weeks to get my stuff out of here."

"No, ma'am. I came to talk with you about some ideas to pick business up in this area." He didn't move a muscle. He didn't even blink.

"How d'you know I'd be here? I told no one I was coming here tonight." She held the shotgun steady, her left hand cupping the barrel with her right middle finger on the trigger.

Nolan spoke with caution, wondering if he could jerk his head back and make it out of the room and around the corner of the building before she made him a statistic. "Clifton told me. He knew I wanted to speak with you, and he saw you coming in here earlier."

After several seconds of silence, "I don't know anyone named Clifton."

"Damn, the angler with the artificial hand. He's always out there by the walleye. You've seen him, I'm sure."

More silence.

"Okay. You want to talk with me, prove it. You take one step back into the supply room and start talking. If I hear your voice fading or you run, I'll give you the Superman test."

Faster than a speeding bullet? Not him, Nolan thought. He stood motionless as he summarized the plan for Hope Landing. He even calmed down after a few moments as he spoke with enthusiasm for the group. Shadows moved in the kitchen, then Li Na's figure emerged, shotgun slung at her side.

She just stood there listening, never interrupting nor changing her facial expression. He concluded with an invitation to the group's meeting later at The Landing so she could meet the others and learn more. He still hadn't moved his feet while he studied her. The long shotgun extended from the floor to the center of her chest. At last, she hoisted the weapon and set it atop the counter.

"Well, you're a little late. I told the city this morning I wouldn't renew my lease this year, and they could have it. I don't have the time with the meat market and caring for my folks. My dad's in bad shape, and he's more important to me than this old snack bar."

"I'd like you to come to our meeting. Perhaps you'll change your mind. Or at least pay the lease and wait to see how the project does. If we're making satisfactory progress by midsummer, then you can join."

"Doesn't quite work that way. What's your name?"

"Call me Nolan. David's my last name."

"Well now, Mr. David, you don't understand how my lease is set up with the city. It sounds like you've done some homework, but there's a flaw in your plan. I paid the lease at the end of last year like always, but that's not the problem. You see, for me to stay here, I must use the building for commercial purposes. The wording is plain as day. If the building sits vacant, then I forfeit my lease."

"The building isn't vacant in the winter. You're just closed for the season."

"I know, but the city isn't buying that right now, and I don't have enough money to fight it. I got a letter from the court a few weeks ago, saying if I didn't open the snack bar by Memorial Day, the lease would be void, and they would assume occupancy. They also told me the terms of the lease stated the business must remain active. Even if I opened, I would just postpone giving up the building until later this year. I don't see any reason for me to get all excited about reviving this area, since there's no way I would last the winter."

She stared at Nolan in a peculiar manner, then tilted her head. "You can move you know."

He peered at her and chuckled to himself as he relaxed. "Forgot you set the shotgun down."

"Besides, I never took the safety off." Her cynical smile was her first facial expression.

"Please come to the meeting, Li Na. Perhaps there's some way we can work this out. At least give it a chance."

His words again received no response. For at least a full minute, silence drifted between them.

"What time's your meeting start?"

Nolan glanced at his watch. "Ten o'clock—about one and a half hours from now."

"I'll see if I can get back. I didn't get much packing done and need to get home to check on my dad. There's a fair chance he'll be asleep. If he's doing all right, then I'll consider coming, but don't count on me."

"That's all I can ask. Take care of your dad. Nothing is as important as family."

CHAPTER FIFTEEN

Giggles and Wails

Nolan wandered throughout the dock area, familiarizing himself with the layout and structures. The Bayview had a picturesque location with waves crashing against the concrete pier, a mere thirty yards from their main entrance. The available parking was minimal, unless one utilized the street's parking meters. There's nothing like the inconvenience of running out to feed the meter in the middle of a relaxing dinner to discourage repeat business. The exact property boundaries for the restaurant were not visibly marked, but Nolan reviewed the survey as he walked. The plat map showed the borderline kept to the left of the gravel road that snaked west to the abandoned rail yard. That narrow band of land appeared useless. Having completed his casual walkabout, he made his way back to the warmth of The Landing.

There, Father Belczyk finished his meal and observed the arriving attendees. He was sipping a glass of red wine as Aaron approached.

"Magnificent dinner. I will tell my friends in the parish office and am certain to get you more customers."

"Thank you, dear Father." Aaron put his arm on the shoulder of the seated priest and turned to the attendees. "Now that Father Andrew has joined our family, I am sure God's blessings will lead us to prosperity."

"If this priest is so powerful, why didn't he help us before now?" asked Marge, seated at the next table with her son, her sister, and Evelyn.

Marge. Oh, dear God. Please don't be your cynical self for these few hours. Nolan thought.

Rose reached out and slapped Marge's arm. For a moment, it appeared the two would end up wrestling on the floor. As Marge pivoted to Rose, Evelyn grabbed their wrists and shook them. "You both behave, or I'll muzzle you, so help me God. Now, that's a religion you can count on."

Marge pulled her arm free from Evelyn's grasp and turned away with a pouting expression.

Aaron spoke with tenderness, "Father, I apologize for her behavior. I believe she is of the age when a woman becomes moody, and her hormones change. She is likely experiencing a hot flash."

"Hot flashes . . . listen you old goat, I'm young enough to be your daughter, but I thank Jesus at least he didn't deal me that deck of cards."

Aaron pointed to the kitchen. "Nolan, I'd like a word, please, in private."

Nolan followed.

Once behind the swinging door, Aaron said. "You didn't tell me you invited a priest."

"Is that a problem?"

"No, no. But I want to invite my Imam to our next meeting. It will help to have Allah on our side as well."

"That's a great idea. The more support we receive, the better off we are." He felt an awkward moment between them. "I'm sorry I didn't think of your beliefs sooner."

"Don't be foolish. You wouldn't know I am Muslim any more than I would know your religion. What's important is I respect you as a new friend and am an excellent judge of character."

The group's numbers had increased since the last meeting. Rose had brought Karl, who roamed about, gazing at photographs of Turkey scattered on the walls. The attendance pleased Nolan since the evening brought a chilling rain. The thermometer hovered in the low forties and a brisk wind off the lake made it feel colder.

The breeze gusted into the restaurant as the door opened, and Cai Li Na strode in a deliberate manner toward their tables. Her entrance silenced the barbs between Aaron and Marge. Nolan introduced her and inspected the crowd.

"I've placed an outline of the plan in front of each of you, complete with the construction sketches for the first phase, along with a cost estimate. Please look those over while I talk. I included the top dozen populations of the world. If we're targeting visitors, our market should include those countries with the largest communities, and these choices will also provide us with a variety of cultures."

Rose's husband, Karl, spoke first. "This remodel looks pretty basic. There're ten stalls and a shared kitchen. I'm not much on food prep, but that seems like a nightmare."

Clifton responded. "I'm going to open another entrance to the pantry to create a circular traffic flow. That will help some."

"I thought everyone would have their own equipment for cooking," said Aaron.

"That's phase two," said Nolan, as he picked up a stack of papers. "Jake, could you give one of these document packs to each person?"

He sprung out of his chair. "Sure thing, Mr. David."

Nolan pointed to the opposite side of the space. "The second phase, as shown in the handout, will happen in the south section of the restaurant, which is larger and can accommodate twelve larger units, with room for cooking equipment and plumbing. Each vendor will have a limited menu but can rotate food selections as much as they wish. Once that area is functional, we'll dismantle the temporary stalls and replace them with more seating."

Marge spoke up. "How long to build, and how much money?"

"Once I get the building permits," said Clifton, "I'll have raw product built for phase one within a week, plus another week for painting and any other surprises that come along. That includes the cut-through of the pantry which will take a full day."

"That's a very ambitious schedule, Clifton." Nolan admitted. "You did a great job with this layout. It appears very functional. The kitchen use issue can be a major problem but will be easier to accept if it's temporary."

Evelyn stood. "Let's get back to Marge's question. How much cash do you need to finish the project? For each phase."

"I've discussed this with Clifton," Nolan said, "for materials only, phase one will be about twenty thousand. The second phase will need labor costs, and that will shoot the estimate up to about two-hundred fifty thousand."

A soft murmuring spread throughout the room.

"I'll discuss this plan with each of the vendors and hope some will pay for their own equipment up front. For those who cannot, we'll need to offer some type of financing."

Marge folded her arms across her chest. "How long?"

Clifton answered. "Timewise, I'm projecting seven to ten days per booth, depending on the specs of each. That's phase two, which is where we need to be as soon as possible."

Karl raised his hand. "At seven to ten days per booth, that's about three months. That will put us at the end of summer. That doesn't sound like good timing."

"I agree." Clifton peered at Nolan, then went on. "But right now, there's me and maybe one other person. I had to base my estimates on the facts."

"Well, I'll be glad to pitch in," said Karl. "I can't take off work right now, but once I finish this project at the office, I can take some vacation time and work with you on the second phase. We've got to be open by the Fourth of July. At least that's how I see it."

"That's not going to put a hurt on your bowling time, is it Karl?" Clifton asked.

Karl accepted the light jab and glanced at his wife. "No, Rose has persuaded me to not bowl in the summer league, so I'll be able to work on this every evening." His mate nodded with a grin.

Karl looked at his best friend. "I know, Clifton, but don't say it. Rose talked me into helping, but I'm glad she's finally excited about somethin', even if it's a damn fool idea. Sorry, honey."

Nolan was inspecting Clifton's budget calculations. "Say, it appears you might be short on labor cost."

Clifton looked down at the ground and hesitated. "These are mostly material costs. I'm not working anyhow, so I'm not losing any wages. I hope to get a friend to help and pay him a few bucks plus some beer."

Nolan shook his head and glanced at Evelyn. "Clifton and I don't have much money to put into the project. We talked it over last night, and he and I will volunteer as much of our time as possible."

Jake bolted up from his seat. "I can build, Mr. Bell. I'll be your helper, and we can save more money."

Marge stuttered. "I don't know . . . I mean . . . Clifton would love to have your help, but you know I can't let you . . . I'd approve, of course, but the principal would never allow it."

"It's the end of the year, and we're not learning anything new anyhow. I'll bet if I explained how important this is, the teachers would let me take the tests now then skip classes 'til school's out."

Clifton interjected. "Jake, I'm sorry, but I need someone with experience. You've never worked in construction, and while I'd like to have your help, I don't have the time to train you. Maybe after we get this first part done, we can bring you on as an apprentice. How would that be?"

Jake sat with a thud so hard he challenged the chair's craftmanship. "I build ships, Mr. Bell, and you've seen them. And I never make a building mistake." He finished with emphasis as he crossed his arms and bit his lip, pulling away from the light touch of his mother's consolation on his shoulder. Fierce determination remained in his eyes.

Nolan raised his hands to get the group's attention. "I feel it necessary to point out that Clifton's costs are for the build-out alone. We need to budget lost income for Aaron and Marge while their restaurants are closed. We will also need working capital for supplies, equipment for the stalls of our initial work group, plus marketing and advertising. I'll start off by saying I have a collection of baseball memorabilia that I will sell, then contribute the proceeds."

Clifton snapped his head, and he stood up from the chair. "You can't do that Nolan. I've seen how much you take pride in all those items. It's taken you years to accumulate your stuff and selling it for us is not acceptable." Evelyn reached out and held Clifton's prosthesis.

"Sorry, Clifton. It's not your decision. You want to work for free, and I don't care for that," Nolan said. "It seems like we're all going to give up something if this project has any chance of success. I hope to raise fifty thousand when I sell all the minor items. I have a few pieces which have the potential of totaling another six figures, which we'll need as we progress. We haven't even budgeted for advertising, licensing, and initial inventory. Believe me, the money will go fast. Of course, when our first two phases are successful, then we'll seek outside funding for phase three."

Isabel stood, her tiny frame wobbling, and she pressed her knuckles against the table-top for support. "I thought about this all week, and what my late husband would have done. We always regretted not taking any chances. We were married forty-three years and never even had a real honeymoon." She removed a wrinkled check from her purse and handed it to Nolan. "You better take it and cash it, young man. I threw it away twice, including once with the coffee grounds. But I think my dear husband delivered me a message when the garbagemen forgot to pick up my trash yesterday. So, here's twenty-thousand dollars. I might invest more, depending on how the project's going."

"Isabel, I'd like to count on your talents and contacts to help us with the proper licensing and permits."

She responded in a meek voice. "I'll be happy to do whatever I can. My job's been boring these past years with the population decline, so I look forward to the change of pace."

"I think I know the message from most of you remaining, but would still like to hear from you. Marge?"

"I don't have anything to give, but I believe in you. I don't know how I'll ever give up my diner and work in here with this jackass," she nodded toward Aaron who beamed at the reference, "but I'll try."

Jake popped up after Marge. "I can sell my ship collection, and you can't stop me, Mom." He once again slammed his husky teen-age body into the chair, and Marge rolled her eyes.

Rose nudged Karl, and he stood. "We're not as bad off as Marge, but truth is, we aren't very good savers either. I've got some money in my retirement plan at work that I can tap, but it's not much. Rose and I will talk it over and give what we can."

"Father Andrew, I'm interested in your comments now that you've heard more of our plan and met our group," Nolan said.

"Well, I'm quite impressed. Of course, I can't pledge any money from the diocese, but I will be glad to assist with your historical que-ries. I will also discuss your intentions with the bishop, although I doubt he will open the coffers of the Catholic Church. Still, I have some influence and have one suggestion he may approve of. I'll let you all know at the next meeting—if I'm still invited."

"We each have a valuable role to perform, and your histori-cal perspective is as much a key as our working capital," Nolan responded.

Aaron stood and rested his clenched hands in front of him. "I am sorry I cannot contribute any money. Instead, I give my restau-rant, my heart, and my sweat. I think my son, Kadir, will come to the next meeting. Now, I serve dessert, and I request a volunteer to help. Miss Marge, would you be so kind? I will show you my kitchen where we can become familiar."

Marge's gasped at the awkward invitation. "I'll be glad to help you, old man, if you don't become too familiar."

Aaron's pace seemed more energetic as he led Marge away.

Every couple or individual had spoken except Li Na, who con-tinued to sit with her pensive expression.

"Li Na, I'm sure you have questions, and I'm not asking for a commitment. But, we would all like to hear your thoughts. Your little snack bar might become a significant part of our plan."

She stood and addressed the group in her soft tone. "As most of you know, I returned to Erie to care for my aging parents and my ailing father in particular. I also manage our meat market, and I've seen all your faces there. Thank you for your business. I don't know how my little snack bar can mean so much to so many people, but you have my interest. It will come as no surprise our market is not as profitable as it once was, and my father's medical bills are depleting his savings. I'd like to continue to come to your meetings and learn how I might help more."

She projected her right arm and demonstrated a powerful grip in her handshake.

"And by the way, I'm glad I didn't shoot you."

"We've got lots of work to do before we meet again, and we can use Isabel's funds to purchase initial materials. I'm handing out this budget projection as well.

"I'm going to pursue others who might be interested in booth space, so I ask each of you to think of people in the community with restaurants or food=related services. Father Andrew, I'm hopeful you will introduce me to some other leaders in the community who may also lend their support. You and I can meet to discuss the details."

"Are you planning to have a Chinese section?" Li Na's steady voice interjected.

"Why yes, of course."

"I am searching for something to interest my father, and this may lift his spirits. The hot pot method of serving Chinese food is quite popular and easy to prepare. I'll discuss this with my parents."

"Consider yourself part of the team, Li Na."

"By the way, I've been meaning to ask you about that contact from the city," Nolan said. "Did you ever speak with anyone or was the letter your only contact?"

Li Na withdrew a letter from her hip pocket. "It's written like a simple form letter from the city manager, but I received a phone call from Ashley Pershing."

"She's on the city council?" Evelyn asked.

"Yes. I thought that was odd, but figured it was something related to the city bankruptcy. At the time of the call, I intended to surrender the snack bar, but didn't care for the tone of the conversation. She was pushy. She said keeping the lease meant staying open year-round."

"That was the only contact?"

"No. The next day, I got a visit from a cop who reminded me of the tall guy from the *Munsters* TV show. Not Herman, but the big, quiet guy."

"Lurch," Jake said.

"That's it. This cop has the same forced smile. Said he was an ombudsman for the city and came to answer all my questions. Now that I know what you are planning, I wonder if the city wants a piece of this."

Everyone in the room shifted a bit uneasily.

Nolan spoke up. "Before we finish the meeting and serve dessert, I want to establish a target date for opening. We know we'll have some snags, but we should be functional on the week before Memorial Day with our grand opening on that holiday weekend. If you agree, please raise your hand."

They lifted their arms in unison. This was the time for Aaron to reveal his dessert challenge, but Marge and he had not returned. The sound of giggling emanated from the kitchen, and it was pleasing to hear Marge wasn't at Aaron's throat for a change.

"Hey, you two," Nolan called out, "there's a bunch of hungry people out here."

Light giggles were followed by Aaron and Marge charging together through the double doors of the kitchen. The group awed in unison as Aaron pranced with an enormous dish of a chilled delicacy. Marge strolled next to him, carrying bowls and a serving spoon.

"I present cinnamon ice cream with noodles served with chocolate mousse and a mystery ingredient." His smile was devious. Marge spooned generous portions of the dessert, and Jake finished his portion before everyone else was even served.

The ice cream was rich and delicious. Nolan swirled a tiny spoonful around his mouth.

"Aaron, you disappoint me. This poses a weak challenge." He grinned with the confidence of victory.

Aaron frowned as he looked at Nolan's dessert, then his impish grin returned.

"Saffron," Nolan boasted, but Aaron chuckled and shook his head.

"My friend, that would be much too simple. True, saffron is in the ice cream. But come now, do not think I'm a fool."

Nolan then tried a scoop of the chocolate mousse, furrowed his brow, and stared at Aaron. The secret taste was strong but complimented the chocolate well. Nolan shook his head.

"Aaron, you may have me. I'm guessing it's some type of special Turkish flour you imported just to cheat me."

His chest puffed out as he proclaimed victory. "Your guess of a rare flower from Turkey is close, but not good enough. I flavored the mousse with salep, a special Turkish beverage used for the finest occasions."

Nolan laid his spoon down and wanted to spit out the concoction and run to the restroom. But no, Aaron would not serve what Nolan was thinking.

"What? You stop eating now? You're a poor sport?"

Nolan whispered, "You didn't use fox testicles in the mousse, did you?"

Aaron roared with laughter so raucous that everyone stopped eating. "Testicles of a fox," he bellowed as he doubled over with glee.

Marge's Irish temper came to a rapid boil. She wound up and slapped Aaron across the face. "Fox testicles? You fed us fox testicles? I'm going to feed you your own damn testicles, you Turkish pervert."

"No, no, no," he shouted back.

"You lied to me," Marge's voice was now at full volume as she stood toe to toe with Aaron. "You told me the secret was a drink from Turkey, not testicles. I should have known. All men lie. You lied about your age too, forty-five. How stupid do you think I am?"

"He said fox testicles," Aaron said, pointing at Nolan. "Salep is fox testicles in Arabic. My language shares many words with Arabic, but in Turkish, salep is the tube of a beautiful orchid. We make a special liquid to use for baking or drinking at a festival." He focused on Marge.

"You made me look like a fool," Marge said. "You can have your dessert and your project. I knew this would be a waste of time and money."

She bolted from the tables and yelled, "Jake, get our coats and meet me at the car." She charged through the door and ran into the night air. Aaron called out to her, but she was outside in an instant. Rose ambled toward the exit. A dull thud was followed by the sound of a wailing wild cat as Rose burst outside.

"Marge!" she screamed in panic.

CHAPTER SIXTEEN

Secrets of Love and Money

The entire crew crowded into the emergency area of Erie's hospital near the Bayfront. It was fortunate the medical facility was a few city blocks from the pier, and the ambulance had arrived on the scene within a few minutes of Marge's scream. They milled about, awaiting a visit from a doctor to provide them with a report on her condition.

No one in the assemblage knew what had happened. They all ran from the restaurant and found Rose kneeling at Marge's side, who wailed, as she lay with her legs sprawled on the cold asphalt. A youthful police officer had somehow already arrived at the scene, and the flashing blue lights added to the feeling of chaos and fear for Marge. She must have been struck by a car, but the police cruiser was the only vehicle at the scene.

Rose hopped into the ambulance with Marge and was now somewhere behind the scenes of the emergency room. Jake sat staring into space with his feet rocking back and forth. Aaron paced like a caged lion, mumbling something in Turkish. He was either praying or blaming himself for the tragic accident. Nolan was sipping on a steaming cup of coffee dispensed from a machine for one dollar. Even though he selected extra cream, extra sugar, and extra coffee, the liquid still tasted like boiled water with sugar and a touch of paste.

"Excuse me folks," Nolan said. "I still get queasy if I stay too long in a hospital—bad memories, you know, so I'll be back. Just need some fresh air."

Clifton stood outside the emergency room exit, involved in a very animated discussion with a young man in a grey-plaid sport coat with suede elbow pads. The stranger appeared not much older than Jake, and he was jotting on a pad as he asked questions. The pair noticed Nolan and approached him.

"My invisibility cloak must be low on batteries," Nolan said.

"Huh? Oh, that's a good one. I'll have to remember it," said the visitor. "Hi, I'm Jamal Moore with the *Erie Gazette*. I understand you're the person in charge," he glanced at his notes, "Mr. Nolan David."

The group needed advertising, so perhaps this wasn't all bad, Nolan thought. The reporter's white shirt was crumpled and too big for his frame, with a wide gap between his buttoned collar and his neck. His paisley tie clashed with the plaid coat, and he would appear more presentable in baggy jeans and a T-shirt.

"Do you plan to sue the city, Mr. David?"

Nolan raised his brows, and his forehead skin wrinkled. "Me? Why would I do that?"

Nolan looked at Clifton, who opened his mouth to speak, but the journalist reacted first.

"For Mrs. Kelly's accident. Since a city vehicle hit her, I'm assuming the police have offered to pay her medical expenses. Has someone from EPD contacted you? Have they issued an apology?"

"Young man, I'm sorry, but I don't know what you're talking about. You mean the police car hit Marge? By the way, for the record, it should be Ms. Kelly."

"Thank you, sir. I heard about the accident on my scanner. I'm surprised the officer isn't here checking on her condition. He must be back at the station filing a report. I am hoping to interview him. What's the extent of Ms. Kelly's injuries?"

Rose and a middle-aged woman attired in hospital green-and-white lab coat entered the guest area, and Nolan rushed back inside. The reporter followed, but Nolan held out his hand.

"Access limited to family and friends. Sorry."

"But . . ."

"No buts. In this case, the public doesn't have the right to know." The columnist looked like a puppy told to stay when all the fun was in the other room.

Rose appeared with red eyes and tear-stained cheeks but was nodding and spoke up before the doctor. "This is Dr. Madeleine Jenkins. Marge is going to be all right but needs surgery, and she'll explain."

Dr. Jenkins spoke with monotone softness, likely honed from years of providing families and friends with good and bad news—no emotion, merely the facts. Nolan's memory flashed back to a terrible day not too many months before. The setting was similar, but he was the sole recipient. "Your wife's tumor is very aggressive, and the cancer has spread to multiple organs. Her body has not responded well to treatment, and there are no other suggestions we can offer beyond pain management and making her as comfortable as possible."

This time, the diagnosis was not as catastrophic. "Marge sustained two fractures in her upper left femur where it meets the pelvis and is known as a hip fracture. Since she is young, we will repair this by placing five titanium pins to join the areas of fracture. I expect her to make a full recovery with proper care and physical therapy. The pins will allow her normal movement, but she will require a second surgery perhaps a year or two from now to remove the pins. In time, her body will replenish the bone marrow where the pins were once located." The doctor paused and scanned the group who were beyond earshot. "She has no other injuries, so is very lucky in that regard. She is under a mild sedative but is conscious. Marge has requested her son Jake and Mr. David to come back to see her. We will take her for surgery soon, so your time will be limited."

The doctor turned and Rose, Jake, and Nolan followed. The reporter called Nolan's name as the automatic door closed behind them.

Marge looked pathetic and in obvious pain as the trio entered her room. A nurse explained transport to the OR was on the way, so their visit would be brief.

"The doctor says you were real lucky, Mom. I know everything will be good," said Jake.

Marge reached out and weakly ruffled her son's hair. She forced a weak smile, opening her right arm to embrace Jake. He cried, and she whispered in his ear, then patted his muscular shoulder, and he stepped back.

"Nolan, I want you to take care of Jake for a few days. The doctor tells me I should be out of here in two or three days, and Rose will stay with me afterward."

Rose nodded in agreement and wrapped her arms around Jake as he wiped his eyes with his sleeve. The teen brushed her hand away as was his habit of limiting physical contact.

"Nolan, please go by the diner and put a sign on the door that we are closed due to family illness. Bootsie's number is on the wall by the phone in the kitchen. Tell her I'm sorry and don't know when we will open again." She was fading as the sedative took hold. "And make sure Jake goes to school. He doesn't need to sit in this hospital and watch over me."

An attendant entered and announced he was Marge's transport. Jake and Rose embraced her one more time, but she was already asleep.

The three returned to the waiting area to find the balance of the group on the edge of their seats or pacing about the room. Rose assured everyone that Marge would be fine, and they all promised to help care for her during her recovery.

"Rose," Nolan said, "do you have any idea how this happened? Who hit her?"

"Best I can tell, the police car was making rounds in the neighborhood, and Marge ran out in front of him. He wasn't going very fast, or she could be much worse. He radioed for an ambulance before he even got out of his car, which explains why they got there so quickly."

That explanation appeased the crowd. The group broke up, acknowledging the late hour and their need to get some rest before rising for work.

"Clifton, before you go, what did that reporter want?" asked Nolan.

"Oh, you know. He's the ambulance chaser type. I gave him some story about your idea, and he got all excited. I think you'll see more of him."

"I want the press coverage, but not sure this is it. I suspect he's wanting to cover the accident and say nothing about Hope Landing. Thanks for talking with him."

Then Karl, Father Andrew, the Bells, and Li Na left.

Aaron sat beside Nolan and confided he would prefer to take Jake to the diner and stay the night with him. He had mentioned this to Jake, who refused, and insisted he remain at the hospital.

Aaron hoped Nolan could help persuade the young man to agree and emphasized his plan was the best for all.

Nolan persuaded the teen by telling him his mother trusted him to post a sign, and Aaron would drive him home. He didn't accept that well but agreed to leave if someone called when his mom was out of surgery. That was a satisfactory compromise. Rose had taken a break to check out the snack bar. Only Isabel and Nolan remained in the family waiting area.

"Isabel, what are you still doing here?"

"I wanted to ask something if I may." She had a way about her that seemed much too polite to be real.

"Of course, Isabel, what is it?"

"Are we still going ahead with our plan?"

"Why would you ask that, Isabel? Have you changed your mind? Or do you think we can't succeed without Marge?"

"No, it's neither of those. It's well, I'll just have to say it. I know you and Marge aren't an item, at least I don't think so. But I've got the feeling you're doing all this for her and Jake."

Nolan rubbed his forehead with his palm as Isabel continued.

"You know, because you feel sorry for them. Please don't tell anyone I said that."

Nolan folded his hands in front of him, closed his eyes and raised his head as if searching for the right words.

"Isabel, please believe me when I tell you what we are doing is for the good of us all, and Erie. That's my motivation and am also paying back an ancient debt to my parents. No need for you to know about that right now. I feel sorry for everyone who lives here. Marge's unfortunate accident may force each of us to take her place for a short time, but I have faith our team is up to the task."

Isabel hesitated and looked about the waiting room.

"What else, Isabel?"

"Well, I'm sort of surprised Aaron left. We need his restaurant to make this work, and if he pulls out, then our plan is dead as far as I can see."

"What's going on, Isabel? I assure you Aaron is a solid part of our team. Why would you think otherwise?"

She hesitated again and glanced around, looking cautious of who might be near. "Without Marge, I'm afraid he may not be as enthusiastic, that's all."

"Isabel, it's two in the morning, and we're all exhausted. Please be clearer because I don't understand your lack of confidence in Aaron."

"You men always need everything spelled out. Haven't you noticed how he picks on her with that playful expression? He's sweet on that Irish lass, as he calls her."

Nolan sat back in his chair and looked pensive.

"I'll talk with him, but I'm sure you're wrong. I mean, perhaps not about Marge, but about Aaron's commitment. This Marge thing, wow, that throws me, but I guess I'll have to be more observant."

Rose joined them with her own cup of tasteless coffee, and Isabel said her farewells. Rose notified the volunteer at the desk of their location, so they'd hear when Marge was in recovery. That would be about three more hours and allowed some time to catch a nap.

Nolan fell into a deep sleep but awoke with a jolt and discovered himself alone in the room. His rapid steps showed his concern as he scurried to search for Rose. He found her near the elevators, speaking with a towering senior-aged officer in uniform.

"Oh, there you are," said Rose. "This is Lieutenant Hutchinson. He's explained the city has insurance for this type of accident and assures me all of Marge's medical bills will be covered. It will relieve Marge. They may even pay for lost wages."

"That's terrific news, Officer." Nolan shook his hand, "Sorry I missed all the details."

"The lieutenant's going to come by later today and get her signature on a few documents."

"Of course," Nolan said. "How did that accident happen, Officer?"

"It's Lieutenant. I'm afraid the report won't be filed until we speak with Ms. Kelly."

"I see. But we're all curious. I'm certain you understand."

"I'm not familiar with the facts of the case. My role here is to advise the family of the insurance coverage so they may relay that to Ms. Kelly. If she has any concerns or problems with the process, I'll serve as the liaison for the city to make sure she receives proper treatment."

"I see. Great." Nolan looked the man up and down his torso, then squinted. "Excuse me, Lieutenant, you say you're not involved with the investigation. It strikes me as odd that you're delivering this message in person at three in the morning. Don't you have an assistant who can do this? I say that with all respect. After all, you're a lieutenant, and rank must have some privileges."

"We take all incidents involving our officers and citizens as very serious, Mr. David. When I learned of this unfortunate accident, I insisted on coming to the hospital to demonstrate our concern."

"Well, then I'll leave you two to finish up, and I'll go raid the vending machines," said Nolan.

Nolan felt uneasy about the night's events. The accident involved a young police officer, and now a senior official made a middle-of-the-night visit to speak with Rose. Nolan sensed the police would have known Marge was in surgery, and it would have been more prudent to interview her in the morning.

When he returned with a protein bar and imitation coffee, Rose was settling back into the lounger.

"Rose, did you tell the lieutenant my name?"

She narrowed her eyes and placed an index finger to the corner of her mouth. "Why no, I didn't. We never spoke about you. He woke me, and said he wanted to speak with me, so I followed him out here. That seems rather odd, now that you mention it."

"Yeah, odd is a good label for it. I'm willing to bet he has all our names, but I can't figure out why. Catch some shut-eye, Rose. I'll wake you when we have any update on Marge."

Nolan wandered the halls and paced by the nurses' station for the next few hours. One of the aides even allowed him into the employee kitchen, where he was treated to a genuine cup of brewed coffee. He returned to his aimless patrol with an added caffeine boost in his step. A nurse told him Marge was out of surgery but would be in recovery for about an hour before they could see her. Rose was in a deep sleep as Nolan left the area.

His mind touched on all those events persuading him to leave Erie, and he wondered what Detective Cermak's role had become in the city. Nolan blamed him for turning Ellie's family against him and still held that grudge. He didn't regret his life after Erie. He never would have met his soulmate if he had stayed. The detective mentioned he was sort of retired, but Nolan planned to ask Isabel if she recalled his name from her work at the courthouse.

A different nurse approached Nolan. "Sir, Ms. Kelly is being moved to a temporary room now and can see family members. Are you related?"

"Well, no. But she added me to some list before her surgery."

"Oh yes, sorry. One of the other nurses pointed you out to me."

Nolan woke Rose and told her the good news. He next phoned Jake and informed him he was on his way to pick him up so he could visit his mother. Nolan asked to speak with Aaron, but Jake said he was really busy, and he would tell Mr. Erdogan about the call.

As he approached, the diner's lights and customer activity surprised him. Jake ran out and opened the door before the vehicle came to a full stop.

"Whoa, Jake. I don't think your mother would be pleased if both of you were in car accidents in less than twelve hours."

"Is she okay?" He buckled and was ready to go in an instant.

"Your mother's fine, Jake. Rose is visiting her now, and the nurse will take you back to see her. She'll still be tired and sore, but very glad to see you."

Nolan looked through the rear window and noticed everything appeared normal as more cars pulled into the lot.

"Jake, didn't you put a note out front like your mother asked?"

"Mr. Erdogan said he didn't have a restaurant anymore until Mr. Bell finished the construction, so he was going to help Mom out by running the diner until she got better. Isn't that great? But we're not supposed to tell her. He wants it to be a surprise."

"Another secret. If there's anything Erie has plenty of, it's secrets."

CHAPTER SEVENTEEN

Perfectly Clear Confusion

Nolan awoke just before seven and grabbed a cup of coffee from the kitchen. Aaron was preparing the breakfast orders and whistling a happy tune. The diner was bustling with activity, with two new staff members.

"Aaron, you're sure you want to do this? I mean, this is a noble gesture, but the hours are grueling. I don't suspect Marge will be able to work until we have Hope Landing up and running."

"I opened the diner because it's the right thing to do. Customers from here will go to our Hope Landing when we open, so we must keep them. I hear them talking about the project and are asking questions."

Nolan poured himself some coffee. "Yeah, we could use spreading the word around town."

"Now, you meet my son and his future bride. Kadir . . ." he raised his voice as a handsome man in perhaps his mid-twenties entered the kitchen, followed by a petite and graceful young lady.

"Nolan David, I introduce my son, Kadir and his bride-to-be, Caitlyn."

"Please call me Kade," he said while they shook hands. "And this is my fiancé. She prefers to be called Cat." Her hand was gentle, and her handshake reflected her shyness. Aaron's son bore a close resemblance to his father.

"My father's told me very much about you and your plans. Cat and I are looking forward to the next meeting." He grinned at

Aaron. "He hasn't been this excited about anything as long as I can remember, so we are both eager to help."

Aaron added, "We have worked out our shifts so Kadir and me will share cooking in the diner. Cat was working with us before, so now she's part of our team here. And Nolan, you should know the name *Kadir* means powerful. And *Caitlyn*, not Cat, is purity. With them on our side, we will be full of success."

Before Nolan could ask any more questions, the imposing figure of Bootsie blocked the door from the kitchen to the dining area. Her voice boomed, "You think one of you three cooks could find the time to fix those two orders I put up? Or do you just want to chat at a table and I can cook and serve too?"

Bootsie's career as a server had always been limited to places like the diner or Waffle Palace where her aggressive comments would be tolerated. She was a hard worker, but if she had a thought, it was voiced. A few days ago, she wanted to cut a patron off from the all-you-can-eat fish fry. The woman requested a fourth helping, and Bootsie told her that if the goal was to bankrupt the place, she was well on her way. While the woman was complaining to Marge, Bootsie slid an overflowing order of fish in front of her and said, "You keep on eating like that, and you'll be bigger than me in no time at all, honey." The accent may have been on the "honey," but a brawl almost broke out.

Marge lost a customer, had to comp the meal for the woman and her husband, and told Bootsie she would be back at Waffle Palace in an instant if she opened her big fat trap again. Bootsie took it all in stride, but she toned down her comments afterward.

"Kadir will take over now, and we can go to visit Miss Marge," Aaron said. Nolan wondered how this Irish lass felt about Aaron, because this Turk sure seemed excited about visiting someone in a hospital.

"Let me take a shower, make one phone call, then we can leave. Why don't you round up Jake and I'll be ready in thirty minutes?" Nolan asked.

"Jake left very early."

Nolan stopped in midstride. "What do you mean Jake's gone? Marge asked me to be responsible for him. Did he go to school?"

"No, he went to visit Miss Marge. He said he could not sleep, was worried, so he walked."

"Damn." Nolan said. "I don't think Marge will be happy about this. She told me to get him to school, and she didn't want him hanging around the hospital. I planned to let him rest today and get him back to school tomorrow. She's going to fry our asses, Aaron. I hope you're prepared for that."

He grinned and Nolan thought Aaron didn't understand the gravity of the problem, or he was looking forward to Marge's spirited counseling.

"While I'm getting ready, can someone look through today's *Gazette* to see if there's anything on the accident?"

Kade replied. "We already have; no mention at all. It must have been too late to get in the paper today."

"Probably. Thanks for checking." He scurried upstairs, showered and changed. He next called the baseball memorabilia dealer to sell his collection. This buyer had a reputation for fairness that was unmatched in the industry. Besides, he was very familiar with the collection and had wanted Nolan to sell it to him on several previous occasions, so this would be faster and more lucrative than shopping around. Nolan learned his fifty grand asking price was possible, but the dealer expressed concern with the condition since Nolan had transported it a fair distance. Nolan agreed to email him an entire list with his individual price estimates to aid the negotiations on the next call. With that process initiated, Aaron and Nolan were on their way.

They cracked open the door so not to disturb Marge, but she noticed the movement and waved her hand for them to enter. She looked pitiful. Rose was snoring in the lounger, but Jake was not in the room. Nolan groaned.

"How's the pain, Marge?" Nolan asked.

"It's not all that bad. The meds keep me groggy, but if I lie still, I'm just a little sore. I had a rough time a few hours ago when the pain in my leg was killing me, but it turned out it to be a muscle spasm. The doctor told me those would come and go for a day or two until I could get up and move about more. Why don't you both go to another room and borrow a couple of chairs?"

Rose awoke and lifted herself out of the lounger. "That thing kind of possesses you once you get settled. One of you can sit here; I need to stretch my legs." Nolan tried to get her attention, but she was still half asleep.

"Aaron, you grab the chair. I can only stay a short time. Got to run some errands for Hope Landing."

Marge focused on the door. "Where's Jake?" Her eyes lifted and caught Nolan's with that "don't you even think of lying to me" look. "Is he at school?"

Nolan responded before Aaron could admit they had no idea. "Yes, he went to school. He was late. Sorry, my fault. He wanted to visit you, but I told him he had to go to class."

Marge raised her eyebrows, but the answer slipped past as she tried to brush her hair with her fingers.

"My, I should have had Rose help me get more presentable. I must look like a scarecrow with my hair all knotted like this."

"We have a saying in Turkey, Miss Marge. 'A goddess possesses natural beauty and looks even more radiant in times of trouble.'"

Marge blushed while Nolan rolled his eyes.

"Well, you two don't need me as a chaperone, so I'm headed to make some copies at the library. I'll be back as soon as I can."

They both ignored Nolan as he slid away. He found Rose, as expected, in the cafeteria. She hadn't seen Jake either and wanted to accompany him on his search. She would go back and tell Marge she needed to get some fresh air, then he would pick her up at the main entrance.

"What's with those two?" she asked even before she could buckle up. "If he pulled that chair any closer, it would become an extension of the bed."

Nolan smiled and waited a few seconds.

"Damn. You mean? Jesus, Mary, and Joseph, it's about time. No wonder she's had a bee in her bonnet the past few days. I figured it was nicotine withdrawal. This explains why she had me toss out her supply of spice sticks. She doesn't want her breath to smell like forty cloves of garlic."

"Any idea where we should search for Jake?"

Rose thought a moment. "Let's try the arcade up the road first. Jake can get distracted, and he may have stopped there on the way to the hospital. If he's not there, I'll call the school. I need to tell them about Marge anyhow, so they'll mark his record in case he's got any tests coming up—end-of-year you know. By the way, that cop came by again earlier this morning."

"Hutchinson?"

"Yeah, same slimeball. He wanted me to leave while he talked with Marge, but she said no way. So, he apologized for the city, told her all medical bills would be covered, and she would get compensated for lost work time at a thousand dollars a week until she got clearance to return to her job. But, and here's the slimy part, if she gives up the diner, then she has to pay it all back. He said the insurance company would determine the money was accepted with fraudulent intentions, and she would have to refund all payments plus interest."

Nolan processed every word from Rose. "Wished I'd been there to hear him," he said.

"Of course, he was so smooth that it sounded very routine. 'Just paperwork, ma'am' and all that malarkey. 'We don't mean to imply anything' he said. And there's Marge, still all doped up from surgery."

"Did Marge sign the documents?"

"Hell, no. I kicked his butt out of there. I told him it was too soon after surgery, and her mind wasn't clear yet. He emphasized this was a very attractive offer. Well, I made enough noise that one of the nurses came in and asked him to leave."

Nolan parked in front of the arcade. "Rose, you did the right thing. I don't know what's happening, but your judgment was correct. I'll run in while you call the school. In the meantime, think of another place to look, because I don't think Jake's here."

He glanced at his side mirror to make sure he could exit safely and noticed the approaching police car that slowly passed. He stepped onto the street and jogged into the arcade.

A few minutes later, he was back outside and headed for his SUV. He noticed a police vehicle parked about a block away but couldn't tell if it was the same one which he saw a few moments earlier. He hopped into his car and shook his head. "Jake's not in there, and no one's seen him."

Nolan reached and touched the side of a camera mounted on his windshield.

"What's that?" asked Rose.

"It's a car dash camera. It was set to record activity in front of me, so if I get into an accident or a ticket for running a red light, I have a recording. That might help me later in court if I need it."

"What did you do to it?"

"I think we have company. The police are parked about a block behind us, and I flipped the camera to record through the rear window. Just a hunch."

"You're not recording me, are you?"

"Don't worry, Rose. It might capture you if you were in the back seat, but I want it to catch what comes up our butt." He studied the image in his rearview mirror. "Did you call the school?"

"I played it cool. I told the office Marge was recovering in the hospital, and they were relieved that she was improving. The secretary already called the diner, and the office already knew about Marge's accident, so they figured Jake was with her."

"Rose, I believe I know where Jake is. We'll be there in a few minutes." He hung a U-turn and headed toward the pier. The SUV had traveled a few hundred feet when flashing blue lights came up behind them, and one gentle squeal of the siren suggested he pull over.

"Rose, say nothing, and I mean it." Rose slouched in her seat.

The officer was young and full of testosterone. Nolan was meek and respectful. He answered more questions than seemed normal for a routine traffic stop.

Nolan glanced at the Officer's name tag. "Officer Goodwill, is it?"

"Ah, yes sir."

"Aren't you the officer who was first on the scene of that accident last night? Outside The Landing Restaurant?"

The young officer stammered. "Ah, no sir. I don't think so."

Nolan grinned as he took the ticket. "Sure, it was you. I'm sure of it."

"Listen, mister. Let me have that ticket back and I'll turn it into a warning."

But Nolan slid the ticket above the visor. "Say, Officer Goodwill, if that's your real name, I have a feeling we'll have an opportunity to chat again real soon. Don't forget to tell your boss you gave me a ticket."

"Shit!" said Goodwill and kicked a pebble as his shoulders slouched on his walk back to his car.

"What was that all about?"

"No time to explain now, Rose. We need to find Jake. They were on their way again, proceeding at the twenty-five miles per hour limit allowed by the city.

"I'm willing to bet Jake's at the pier helping Clifton." Rose still sat there like a scolded child. "Rose, I'm sorry I spoke to you that way. Police just rub me the wrong way, and I have some history with the ones here in Erie."

"Apology accepted, and I think you're right. Jake will be with Clifton." She was still pouting a bit. After all the disagreements that she had with Marge, she had learned resilience.

As they passed the hospital and drove down the hill toward the bay, Clifton's black pickup was visible alongside the building. Nolan felt confident about finding Jake here, and before they even stepped outside of their vehicle, Jake stood curbside.

"How's my Mom?" Perspiration soaked his T-shirt.

"She's doing well, Jake. But you gave us a scare." The innocence in his eyes held no inkling of any wrongdoing. "You told Aaron you were walking to the hospital. What happened?"

"I went to the hospital, Mr. David. My mom and Aunt Rose were sleeping, so I figured they needed to rest. The restaurant was not far, so I thought I would work down here for a little while and then go back. I guess I lost track of time."

He hung his head, but then he brightened. "I was a real help to Mister Bell. He was glad I was here. Come on in, and he'll tell you."

The interior of Aaron's Landing restaurant was in shambles. Tables and chairs were piled high to the ceiling, and lumber was stacked to the right of the entrance. Clifton appeared exhausted.

"How's Marge?" he asked between deep breaths.

"She doing very well," Rose replied. "She has her own personal male attendant."

"What does that mean, Rose?" asked Clifton. "Do you and your sister always talk in this secret code?"

"You'll figure it out later, Clifton. But she's doing as well as she can be after the surgery," Nolan said and nodded at the obvious work they had accomplished. "You've created a very organized mess, Clifton."

"We created the mess together. And I'm glad Jake was helping. I forgot about this preparation phase. It's the hardest part of the job. We've been toting equipment and lumber all day. I sure was glad to see him when I pulled up this morning."

"For the record, to all of you, our story is that Jake went to school late. Marge wouldn't approve of him skipping school to be working down here, and you all know that. Now, I think Marge will cook my goose if Jake doesn't show up all clean and smelling good at the time he would visit after school. Can you spare him in a little while, and we'll have enough time to pull this off?"

"Mr. David?" Jake asked. "I can't lie to Mom. I'll tell her the truth and let her stare at me like she always does when I do something wrong."

Jake was one of a kind. Nolan knew little about autism but guessed Jake's penchant for honesty was related to his special ability.

"Let's see what happens, Jake. I won't ask you to lie. I'll take the heat if it comes to that. We'll show up at the time she's expecting you, and she may not even suspect anything."

"Clifton, why don't you use Jake for anything you need his broad shoulders for, then we can leave in about fifteen minutes?"

"Perfect. C'mon Jake, let's move that tall shelf out of the pantry, then you can go."

Rose and Nolan sat on a bench overlooking the bay, but Nolan was staring back at the scene where Marge was struck last night.

"Did Marge tell you anything about the accident?" asked Nolan.

"I'm glad you brought that up," Rose said. "I was going to tell you, but I got all tangled up in the story about that lieutenant."

"Well?"

Rose turned toward Nolan. "This won't make much sense, but here goes. Marge said that when she ran out of Aaron's, a parked car surprised her when it started up and revved its engine. She was angry and ran straight across the street, but the car pulled out from the curb, and they sort of ran into each other."

"So, is Marge saying that the police car was waiting in front of the restaurant?"

"Not quite. She said the car came from left of the entrance."

"Watching us," Nolan replied.

"That's why it doesn't make any sense," Rose said. "I'll ask Marge again, and she'll have a different story."

"Rose, I've learned that whenever something happens in this town that doesn't make sense, there's a very odd reason and I think I've figured it out."

"Figured what out?"

"The accident. That young officer back there was the one we saw last night outside the restaurant. I think he was watching us, but no one was supposed to see him. Well, he panicked when Marge ran out the doors. He must have tried to pull away but instead ran right into her."

CHAPTER EIGHTEEN

Poison Darts

Nolan gazed at the landscape portrait of the orphanage while he waited for Father Andrew. He estimated the image predated his stay by several years. The building and grounds appeared better maintained than he remembered, and the black-and-white photo quality gave the enlargement that grainy look.

"I miss the old place," Father Andrew commented as he stood at his office entrance.

"I can imagine. You must have spent a good percentage of your career there." Nolan moved to the guest side of the desk, not wanting to appear as if he'd been caught with his memories hanging out.

"Over thirty years in all. It was my first assignment out of seminary, and the bishop sort of forgot about me."

"So, you didn't enjoy your stay at the orphanage?"

"Quite the contrary. But the post was not one most priests relished. Parish life could be rewarding, and most Catholics in that era admired the priests and pastors. I was the administrator of over one hundred children who had either lost their parents through a tragic accident or illness or were abandoned with no relatives who wanted them. Many had serious emotional difficulties. Nightmares were most common."

He paused and caught Nolan's eyes as he stood across from him. "I was very proud of each of their accomplishments. Some have become very successful, and I'm satisfied I had at least a small hand in their development." He extended his fingers so the tips brushed the top of his desk. "But there are just as many that never recovered from their ill-fated beginnings. In those cases, I very much hold myself responsible."

"I wouldn't beat yourself up. I've learned that people who care are their own worst critics and never take enough credit."

"Well spoken, my young friend." He extended his arm toward the leather guest chair.

"Andrew, I've listed my selections of the ethnic origins I would like to have represented in our project." Nolan slid a copy of the handwritten list before him. "I picked twelve, thinking this might allow us some flexibility when we encounter interested parties."

Africa
China
United Kingdom
Mexico
Native-America
India
Japan
Brazil
Puerto Rico
Russia
Indonesia
Ireland

"Most interesting," the professor commented.

"As you may remember, we're prepping for eight units in phase one. So, this gives us even more leeway in our recruitment of the owners of those units. I'm hopeful you can spread the word in the community as well as target some individuals of influence."

Andrew rubbed his chin as he continued to study the countries.

"There are a few surprises here, I must admit. But the list makes sense once I give it some thought."

"Such as?"

"Erie doesn't have a significant population of Chinese for one. And the Hispanic community is seasonal. Many of them work on the potato farms or vineyards during the harvest months and then vanish afterwards."

"If Hope Landing is going to be successful, we've got to think globally. I chose these nations because of their sheer numbers and presence in our country. I'm trying to bring a larger footprint to Erie."

"You're right. Too many years here have limited my perspective. Now, Native Americans? We have a few, but they will be difficult to locate, and they must have the resources available plus be interested."

"I'm counting on your powers of persuasion and leadership in the community." Nolan grinned, then continued. "I believe the inclusion of Native Americans will identify Hope Landing as more of a historical village versus an amusement park. After all, how can we have a park dedicated to the ethnic origins of America without including those present when the Europeans invaded?"

"Interesting viewpoint, and I agree. In fact, we had a rather significant discovery here in Erie about four months ago. They unearthed skeletal remains during the expansion of the library near the marina. They were identified as Native Americans and were dated over three hundred years old. The site was believed to be a burial ground, but by the time the news was leaked of the find, the entire area was already under a concrete foundation for a parking garage."

"Any idea what tribe may have lived here?"

"Seneca Indians had a stronghold on a significant portion of New York State, extending to parts of Pennsylvania, Ohio and bordering areas. The way they handled this discovery upset me because of the mystery surrounding the tribe that lived in the Erie area."

"I love a good mystery. What sort?"

"A small settlement of Native Americans lived in this corner of the state as peaceful farmers. Any trail of their existence disappeared shortly before the Revolutionary War. The most common belief is that the expanding Seneca Nation conquered this group and absorbed the survivors into the dominant tribe. But another theory says traders coming down from Canada spread an infection of smallpox that wiped out the entire village. I would have very much liked to inspect that burial site before the contractors destroyed it."

"Which theory do you believe, Andrew?"

"The Seneca Indians had a government structure ahead of their counterparts. They recognized the need to work with the colonists, whose numbers and weapons were becoming too overwhelming to defeat. They joined a coalition of neighboring tribes to form the Iroquois Confederacy, which paused the expansion into their territories. In addition, they negotiated for ownership of property in return for an agreement of non-hostility. In fact, the Senecas still have rather substantial land holdings not far from here in New York."

"Salamanca, New York."

"Well, yes, that's part of the area. How do you know of Salamanca?"

He explained the information Isabel had discovered about Mr.

Shongo and his ownership of several acres near the bay. "He's on my list of potential investors. I suspect he has an interest in Erie, or he would have never purchased that shipyard."

"Good luck with that. He has a reputation for not being easy to deal with."

"I have an idea of how to approach him. I believe he'll bite."

"But tell me, if Erie is in such difficult financial shape, why did they decide to spend money on the library enlargement? I'm certain that was a worthwhile cause but seems ill-spent when you consider the city's current crisis."

"That decision created a bit of controversy. But the city didn't spend one dollar of local taxpayer money on that addition. Federal and state grants funded the entire project for educational development. City council representative Ashley Pershing was behind it, and she'll use that as an example when she runs for mayor. She insists there are many grants available that Erie should take advantage of but are not. She cites that as only one."

"Interesting, and she might have a point. I suppose if someone understands the system, perhaps there are grants available. What do you think about her chances of winning?"

They both jumped as a voice blared from the phone on his desk. "Father Belczyk, are you there?"

He punched a button to reply, "Yes Tami, but I'm still in my meeting."

"I figured that, but the clerk of court is on the line and insists on speaking with you—says it's urgent."

"I'll speak with her. Thank you for interrupting me."

He pressed another button, and Isabel's voice was even louder than Tami's.

"Father, have you any idea where I can find Nolan?"

"I'm right here, Isabel. What's wrong?"

"The city's about to take possession of The Bayview for back taxes. I learned a letter is going out today, and if the bill isn't paid in full in thirty days, then Erie owns Bayview Restaurant."

Nolan's head hung a little as he asked, "How much are the taxes?"

"You're not going to like this. Are you ready?"

"Sure, why not? Tell me."

They heard her gulp before she blurted, "Just shy of forty thousand dollars, including penalties and interest."

Father Andrew whistled and looked at Nolan.

"Isabel, I appreciate you tracking me down with this information." He paused for a few seconds. "I have two immediate questions for you."

"No, I don't have an extra forty grand," she said.

"Hilarious, Isabel, but that wasn't one of the questions. First, do you believe there is any chance the owners will pay that bill?"

"No way in hell, excuse me, Father—forgot you were on the line. The restaurant didn't even open last year. The owners retired and moved to Florida. They've tried to sell. Even if they have the money, I don't think there is any desire to keep that building."

"Next question: was The Bayview isolated out for this tax issue, or are they among a large group of other buildings that are being targeted?"

"From what I understand, the answer to both parts is yes. The city's financial problems have caused the assessor to send out harsh letters to quite a few commercial and residential property owners who are behind in their taxes. However, Bayview is the one instance where the demand is for 100 percent now. Everyone else is being requested to contact our office for negotiation of a payment plan."

"But not The Bayview?"

"Nope," she said. "Maybe the city administrator knows the owners have left town, but it still doesn't seem right. Erie needs money, so I understand pressuring those who are behind on their taxes. However, seizing property will not bring one cent into the town coffers."

"I agree. I have one more special request," Nolan said. "Would it be out of the ordinary if you contacted the owners of The Bayview prior to mailing that demand? Sort of feel out their intentions, then advise them the letter is on the way?"

"I can do that. Their contact information is right here. I'll get back to you."

Andrew disconnected the line, and the pair stared at each other. The priest spoke first. "To answer your question regarding Ms. Pershing, she will win by a landslide. The term of the current mayor is over, and he cannot run again. Pershing's the Democrat nominee, and a Republican has not been in the mayor's office in almost fifty years."

"So much for the two-party system here. Do you think she has genuine concern for Erie? Or is it personal?"

After a bit of silence, Andrew spoke. "Based on rumors alone, she's in this for power and money."

Nolan's attention seemed to drift away as he stared at the picture of the orphanage.

"Do you still want me to continue to solicit for the restaurants?" Andrew's question returned Nolan to reality.

"Why?" Nolan asked. "Sure, the tax issue is a minor setback. Somehow, we'll get through this."

"Well then, I have some additional news I hope you'll receive better than Isabel's call." He clenched his hands on the desk and met Nolan's eyes. "I am now assigned to Hope Landing, if you'll have me. As you know, I planned to retire, but when that happens, I'm at the mercy of the parish office for money. I discussed your project with the bishop this morning, and he agreed I would still serve the church by working with your group. I put a bit more of a Catholic spin on your plan, wanting the bishop to see the cause and donate some funds. But the best I could do was get a three-month postponement of my retirement."

Nolan shook his hand as he welcomed him onto their team. As they bid their goodbyes, Isabel phoned again and was back on the speakerphone.

"I don't have wonderful news this time either. Mr. Ingleman, he's the owner of The Bayview, passed away last week. His widow has Alzheimer's, and she is being transferred to a long-term care facility. One of her friends was picking up some personal items for Mrs. Ingleman and answered the phone. I'm afraid the tax bill will go unpaid."

"Any children, Isabel? Who's in charge of the estate of Mr. Ingleman?"

"That's a dead end, too, pardon the pun. There was a will that named the Mrs. as the executor, but if she was unable to perform her duties, then it was to be their son Harold. But no one in Florida knows where dear old Harold is. They couldn't locate him for the funeral, and the friend told me the Inglemans never even mentioned they had a son. I'll try to locate him on the internet, but don't expect a miracle unless Father Andrew there has one up his sleeve."

Andrew spoke up. "I'm afraid the diocese has not granted me that power yet."

"There is one other incidental item I want to mention," Isabel said. "The city is preparing to announce major staff reductions. The mayor and council are arguing about the extent of the cuts, and the departments that will be affected."

"Is your position safe?"

"I work for the county, so I should be all right. Plus, I have more seniority than most anyone at the courthouse. Unless they shut us down, I believe my job is stable."

As he headed back to the hospital to check on Marge, his mind touched on all the difficulties that were arising. He was much more confident a mere twenty-four hours ago that Hope Landing would be a rousing success. They needed to step up their timeline and find more liquid capital, or this would become a resounding failure.

CHAPTER NINETEEN

Extra! Extra!

The joyous whistling and humming of a stout Turk who appeared to float in front of the grill, greeted Nolan in the morning. Nolan didn't have to interrogate him to know the source of his positive outlook.

"I missed you at the hospital last night, Aaron. But Marge is progressing well, don't you think?"

"She fights like a tigress. She is very strong indeed." Nolan was curious about how their day together went but allowed him some privacy. He knew the facts would leak soon enough, when Rose and Evelyn got a whiff of Marge's attitude.

"Is Rose driving Jake to school today? We dodged a bullet yesterday."

"No. We agreed Rose and Jake would go to the hospital a while ago to see the doctor when she makes her rounds. Then, Kadir will pick up Jake for class. No chance for an escape today."

Nolan snickered and picked up the *Gazette*. As he searched, he smiled. "Well, at least she's not on page one." His scanning fingers paused at a small section headlined, "Police Blotter."

FLEEING WOMAN STRUCK

"An Erie woman sustained minor injuries when she ran into a police vehicle near the foot of State Street. The officer driving swerved but could not avoid the collision. The pedestrian darted into the front of the car, which stopped to determine why she was running.

She was identified as Margaret Kelly, 38, of Erie. She is being treated for her injuries at the Medical Center and is expected to make a complete recovery. The official report indicates the officer was on patrol in the area and was startled by the fully clothed female who appeared to be fleeing from a nearby building.

The mishap is still under investigation, but no charges have been filed. Toxicology results have not yet been returned."

"Holy crap," Nolan exclaimed. "Fully clothed?" He lifted his eyes to peer over the fold. "Aaron, there's an article in the paper about Marge."

"Oh?" he looked up from the grill. "Please read it to me."

"Promise me you'll remain calm."

He didn't promise, but Nolan read it anyway. After he finished the brief piece, he received a colorful education of the Turkish vernacular. Aaron's tirade lasted only a few minutes, since there was no one present to take the opposing view.

"I agree, Aaron. Now please stay quieter this time while I phone our young reporter."

Nolan withdrew the business card from his wallet and dialed the mobile number for Jamal Moore. He expected any reporter hungry for news would answer at any hour. He was correct. After many rings, a drowsy voice mumbled.

"Jamal Moore? Good morning. This is Nolan David." He paused a moment for the reporter to recognize his name and wake up.

"Yes, er, sorry, sir. I had a short night. I didn't think you'd be calling to thank me so soon."

"You sure are a treasure, kid. You mean you suspected I would call to express my appreciation?" No one could be this stupid, Nolan thought.

"Of course. We got some good feedback, but it was after midnight. I hoped you didn't mind me identifying you by name."

"Jamal, what the hell are you talking about? And what do you mean by your reference to Ms. Kelley as fully clothed?"

He chuckled. "Oh, that. I didn't write the article. I mean, I wrote the original copy, but my boss trashed that story and replaced it with that swill."

"But it's your byline."

"If the story has anything to do with the police, I get the in-print credit. My editor tells me the more the cops see my name in print, the better chance some of them will leak information to me."

"I suppose that's possible, but the article's misleading."

"Nothing I can do about it now."

"What were you talking about a few minutes ago? Why did you think I'd be calling if it wasn't about this police blotter trash?"

"Why, the blogs, of course." The reporter now sounded wide awake and enthusiastic. "The Erie blog, Mr. David. I wrote all about Hope Landing from my interview with Clifton Bell at the hospital. It wasn't until late last night that I finally posted it, but we got hits and comments right away. I'll need to go check it now. I didn't expect people to call you so early this morning. Did anyone mention they heard the radio show? They must be excited."

"Radio? You have a radio show too?"

"Blog radio. It's sort of like radio on demand."

While Nolan chatted on his phone, he noticed the large to-go order Aaron was preparing.

"Jamal, listen to me for a minute before you get way out of hand.

No one has called, and I'm not sure they would know where to find me. I'm not listed in the phone book, you know."

"Gee, I know that. I've been checking you out, but I need a face-to-face interview to fill out your bio for the blog. Can I come right over?"

"Come right over? You don't even know where I am. I could be in Canada for all you know."

"You mean you're not at the diner? Clifton told me you stayed there with Mizz Kelley, and that's what I put in the blog."

"He told you what? Don't you have to confirm your information with another source before you print something?"

"Well, no. This is just a blog. We don't have to confirm anything. Don't you know what a blog is, sir?"

"Of course I do," Nolan said. "But you must have some sense of social responsibility, don't you? You can't create posts without verification. I stay at the diner alone, and Mizz Kelley has another residence where she lives with her son. We have no romantic connection."

"Oh, that's okay. I would never enter a story like that in the blog without a source, and I quoted Mr. Bell for his statement."

"Well, Clifton's going to need a medic when his wife and Marge get a whiff of this story." Then Nolan glared at Aaron and slapped his palm against his forehead.

"Jamal, this is serious. You need to retract that statement before Mizz Kelley sues. Your information is erroneous."

"I'm sorry, but I don't need to retract it."

"Yes, you do. You don't understand implications like that can destroy her reputation."

"Please relax, sir. I already logged onto the site and deleted the entire reference. See? I don't have to retract anything. Blogs are so easy. We already have fourteen comments from last night. Now, about that interview—"

"Not now," Nolan said. "I'll agree, but not one about me. I'll answer all your questions about Hope Landing, but I'm not the story."

Nolan set an afternoon appointment to allow some time to check damage control and return to the negotiations for the sale of his memorabilia.

After listening to half of the conversation with the reporter, Aaron spread his arms wide. "That didn't seem to go well."

Nolan explained everything would be fine but couldn't answer his questions about the article in the *Gazette*. With all the discussion about the blog, he forgot to pursue the news column. Nolan made a mental note to address that later.

It was too soon to call the dealer about his collection, so Nolan prepared to check on Marge. Aaron handed him that to-go breakfast Nolan had watched him prepare, laden with bacon, sausage, hash browns, scrambled eggs, and a biscuit.

"That's not necessary, Aaron, but I appreciate your thinking of me. I'll take a cup of coffee with me."

"Coffee, oh yes." He returned with a Styrofoam cup plus a handful of single serving creams and sugars.

"Aaron, you don't need to wait on me like this. I know my way around the diner."

"You? All this for Miss Marge." Nolan grabbed the sack full of food, shook his head, and left the diner.

When Nolan entered the hospital lobby, Rose was pacing and waving a folded newspaper.

"Fully clothed? Reason for her behavior? What the hell is this supposed to mean? What did that juvenile delinquent reporter say? Aaron told me you talked to him." She was firing questions on automatic and was totally loaded.

He set Marge's breakfast and coffee on a table in the lobby and gripped her shoulder. "Rose, sit."

She sat but continued to bite her chapped lower lip. He calmed her, then informed her about Clifton's statement regarding him and Marge living at the diner. Her eyes widened, then returned to their normal state when he explained the information was no longer on the blog.

"Marge doesn't know about any of this." She nodded at the newspaper in her hands. "I've been afraid to tell her. Evelyn's up with her now and has seen the paper, but I'm sure she would have called me if she knew about the blogs."

"I'll tell Marge about the news article after she eats this breakfast for four that Aaron prepared."

As they rode the elevator to Nolan talked to Marge's floor, Nolan asked, "How does Marge feel about Aaron? 'Cause I got to tell you, he's fallen for her like a landslide."

"She griped about him all morning. Said he was doting over her all afternoon and made himself a real bother with the nurses. She also complained he had the intellect of a squashed flea. So, I think she's crazy about him."

"Yeah, I agree."

Marge appeared much better just one day after surgery. Color had returned to her cheeks and was augmented by some light makeup which Rose must have applied.

"Doctor tells me if I can get up on crutches tomorrow, then I'll go home." She kept looking behind him at the closed door. "Thank God you didn't bring that Turkish pervert with you. I couldn't get rid of him yesterday after you disappeared. What's he up to anyhow?"

"Aaron? I have no idea." He held up the paper bag. "He handed me this food to give to you, then said he was busy."

"Hmm . . ." Marge looked again over Nolan's shoulder. "He has nothing to do now that Clifton is working in his restaurant. That's all I heard about yesterday, trust me."

"Uh, maybe he went down to Hope Landing to help Clifton out." Nolan replied.

"He wouldn't last five minutes there. I doubt the fool knows the difference between a hammer and a screwdriver."

She continued to complain about Aaron while she devoured every scrap of his terrible meal.

Nolan prefaced the reading of the *Gazette* article with the good news about the favorable blog comments that were being received. He also downplayed the location of the piece and by this time, she was getting anxious and told him to just "read the damn paper." So he did.

"Could you please explain that to me?" Marge scrunched her nose as she looked at Nolan. "I think my pain pills have made me groggy. I don't understand what you mean. Did you say fully clothed?"

"We don't know why that's in there. I suppose we can't argue the point since it's true, and we don't want to imply you were partially or otherwise clothed."

"I get that. But how can they print that? It doesn't make sense."

"The power of the press, Marge, or in this case, perhaps it was the influence of the police. I'm not sure."

She maintained her serenity, and it was obvious the pain pills contributed toward her melancholy spirit.

"I've replayed that scene a hundred times in my mind, and I believe I surprised that little shit of a police officer. As soon as I busted out of the restaurant, he started his car and those headlights came on. The beams blinded me, and I ran faster. I didn't know he was a cop. I raised my arms to block the brightness, and he plowed right into my side. That's why my arms didn't break or have a mark on them. I can't wait for that lieutenant to come around again waving those papers, because I'll shove them—"

Rose palmed her hand over Marge's mouth to muffle the end of her less than eloquent comments.

"I checked with the insurance clerk downstairs earlier today, and she said the city insurance will be charged for all of Marge's costs here," Rose said. "She couldn't verify her rehab would be covered but admitted it would be most unusual if they denied physical therapy under these circumstances."

Nolan excused himself, then returned to his room above the diner to make his dreaded call to the dealer. Of course, he had to provide a detailed report on Marge's progress to Aaron, who was so distracted by the news that he botched two orders. Bootsie exercised her diplomatic skills by referring to her new boss as a blind jackass.

Nolan's reluctance to sell his collection seemed normal. After all, he had taken years to select each item, get a reasonable price, and then maintain his items in pristine condition. Now, in the duration of a five-minute phone call, almost every treasured item would be gone.

He thought of his deceased wife as he often did whenever he

tried to make a painful decision. He pondered what advice she would have offered in this situation. She would have said, "You're thinking of donating all your hard work, plus over fifty thousand dollars to a group of relative strangers. Is that what you want to do?"

Nolan thought he would have lowered his head and remained silent, which would tell her he had already decided. Then she may have said, "You know I will support your decision. Someday, maybe someone besides me will appreciate all you do."

He proceeded with his call. The dealer, Moe, surprised him with a no-haggle approach to his asking price of fifty thousand. They agreed Nolan would pay shipping and pack the collection himself. The dealer offered to pay half upon arrival of the shipment, then the balance after he completed his evaluation. He estimated this would take thirty days. Nolan requested an advance of 10 percent, which was needed for proper packaging and shipping.

Nolan then told him about the thousands of cards stored prior to his departure, with a value of twenty thousand more. Moe wanted the cards, doubted the value, and didn't want his store inundated with over 100,000 baseball cards. They both knew the cards didn't take up that much room, but the dealer posed the space issue as a fair objection to discount the price. The final agreement was fifteen thousand, with Moe paying for the shipping from Atlanta.

"You seem desperate for cash, Nolan. This isn't like you at all. Are you all right?"

"Yeah, I'm fine, Moe. I had some recent financial issues, but I'm working on a new project now that could turn all this around. You know how it is. Spend money to make money."

There were a few seconds of silence on the line before Moe spoke again. "Have you given any more thought to your big-ticket piece?"

They both knew his reference. "Well, I am thinking about it. I'm still working on the budget for this project and have some large investors who are interested. If they come through, I won't even have to consider the picture any further." Nolan didn't want Moe to think he was in dire need. He trusted this dealer, but the word of his financial desperation would spread through the collector community and would affect the eventual price.

They ended their conversation, and Nolan was as comfortable as possible with the proceeds. With that settled, he needed to escape from his room. Even though his collection contained all inanimate objects, Nolan felt penetrating eyes following him, accusing him of betrayal.

CHAPTER TWENTY

That Thing You Do

Jamal Moore and Nolan met in the rear of a cigar store located a few blocks from the *Gazette* office. The shop served premade sandwiches to patrons of the nearby buildings and had three tiny square tables crammed in a corner. The reporter was again wearing that paisley tie with the plaid sport jacket, but at least his shirt fit better this time.

"I meet people here because it's quiet and close to the *Gazette*."

Nolan met his gaze and glanced at the two remaining vacant high-tops. "So, you don't have an office."

"That too."

The interview flowed well, and the reporter took copious notes along with a voice recording with his phone, which he had placed on the table. Nolan learned the blogs were not products of the newspaper, but were instead the reporter's personal sites, so perhaps the postings were less influenced by the paper's editors. Jamal seemed to care about the city, although his ambition for the big story was his primary motivation.

They spent almost an hour talking about Hope Landing and the group's expectations. Nolan made it clear this was a team development, while he minimized his leadership role. Nolan wanted the citizens of Erie to have a sense of pride and ownership in their project. Every time Jamal tried to focus the interview on Nolan, the answer emphasized the local citizens. At the conclusion, they were both satisfied.

"Now, if you're all done asking your questions, then I have a few for you." Nolan tapped the phone, "But this won't be running."

Jamal raised his eyes and turned off the recorder.

"You submitted copy, and someone changed it. Is that correct?"

"Yes, sir. Although it's not that unusual. If we're tight on space, then sometimes my stories change big time, or are even trashed. On other occasions, Fitz will tell me I missed the tone of the article, and he'll rework it."

"What happened this time?"

"The latter for sure. Fitz, that's my editor, checked my story with the police, and he was kinda harsh with me. He said I didn't get any of the facts right, and he had to write it from scratch. I tried to argue with him, but he has a short fuse."

Nolan leaned over the table and whispered. "Think about this next question for a minute before you answer."

The reporter nodded and moved up on his seat.

"Did Fitz make contact to confirm your story, or did he receive a phone call?"

"I don't know for certain but let me explain. I took an incoming call from some lieutenant who I had never heard of before and transferred it to Fitz. So, while the caller asked for him, the guy might have been calling back from a message Fitz left earlier. I can't be sure."

Nolan pondered this for a moment. "The lieutenant—you never heard of him? Isn't the police beat yours?"

"Oh, that's my turf all right. I even asked Fitz about the guy, Lieutenant Hutchinson. That was it. Fitz said he thought the cop retired last year before I became the liaison with the department, and now he's back on some special assignment."

Jamal tried to pick up the tab, but Nolan told him to save his money to get a tie that matched his jacket.

Nolan next drove the short distance to the pier to check on Clifton's progress. He was glad to see a few more pickup trucks parked near the restaurant and guessed a few of Clifton's friends stopped by to help. He should have brought beer, since that seemed to be accepted as the universal gratuity for all construction workers. Isabel had come through again as he noticed the building permit stapled to a nearby wooden utility pole.

He heard a circular saw whirling its familiar sound from the rear. Clifton was finishing some rough cuts and ignored Nolan's presence for a few moments. Then he lifted his safety goggles and wiped the sawdust from his cheeks.

"Nolan, you owe that little reporter a case of Kohler for whatever he put on the internet."

Before he could answer, two young brawny men exited the restaurant and stepped into the alley.

"And here are a couple of reasons now." He pointed at the pair as they walked toward them. "Nolan, I want you to meet Sean Dugan and Jerry O'Dea."

Nolan shook their huge paws and thought he recognized them. When Sean stomped his boot to free some sawdust, this clicked in Nolan's memory.

"I think you guys come to the diner. I recognize you from the morning of the snowstorm, coming in and shaking the snow off your boots."

"Could be us. We eat there now and then. Food's good, and we get plenty."

Nolan believed that was Sean, although they could pass as

brothers. These were the guys who he pegged as lumberjacks on the first day he stopped at Marge's place.

Clifton explained the surprise. "They were on the internet last night and saw we were starting the work on Hope Landing. I didn't tell you, but I filled that young fella's ears with all sorts of propaganda about our project, and he put it all on a website."

"Speaking of propaganda, did you perhaps tell him I was staying with Marge at the diner? Like we were an item?"

He laughed. "He didn't print that, did he?" Nolan returned a hard stare. "Well, I'll be damned." He looked again at Nolan's frown. "What? I figured it was a good side story to the accident. Got it all tied in to you and Marge with this budding romance and the new project for the city, and Jamal was all over it."

"Clifton, what you don't realize is Marge has a real guy she's fallen for, and if either of them gets wind of this, especially Marge, she'll beat you unconscious as soon as she's able."

"I didn't know that. Whoever it is will run for cover once she unveils that fiery temper of hers."

"Well, the guy seems to be enamored with that fiery temper and loves to light it. It's Aaron."

"Man, I didn't see that one coming. But I'll have to get caught up on that gossip later. I want to use these boys as long as I have them. Plus, there's another worker inside." He gripped Nolan's shoulder for an instant and looked serious. "Nolan, I should tell you something else before you blow a cork."

"That doesn't sound too good. What's wrong?"

"Nothing is wrong. But Jake is in there."

Nolan raised his eyes to the clouds as if searching for divine intervention.

"Great, now Marge will kick both our asses."

"But Nolan, the kid is great. He walked here from school after Aaron's son dropped him off. That's like four miles. And he's been helping all day. He's inside now with Jane."

"Jane?"

"She's the other surprise. Found out about us the same way as Sean and Jerry. They came here looking for work, Nolan. I told them they were volunteers for today, and if we could pay them after that, they had to speak with you."

"Fair enough." Nolan addressed Sean and Jerry. "I'll go in and meet Jane, then we can get together for a few minutes and talk."

Nolan found the petite but agile Jane overseeing Jake as he drove nails into the beginnings of a stall frame. Her jeans and denim jacket did a poor job of disguising her natural beauty, with tufts of her jet-black hair revealed at the sides of her ball cap. The pair introduced themselves while Nolan observed Jake at work.

"The young man is like a machine," Jane remarked.

"I don't believe he's ever handled a hammer before," Nolan said.

"That's what he told me too," she smirked. "Of course, he also told me I was doing it all wrong. I assumed he was a smartass punk, but he looked so serious, like he was giving me pointers. When I asked him what I was doing wrong, he told me my spacing was irregular and messy. Can you imagine that?"

"What did he mean by that?"

"See the way he's selecting the next spot for his nail? He rubs his fingers along the grain of the wood like he's measuring, then wham. Every one of those nails is three inches apart. I measured them once, and I'm not challenging him again. It's like he has an app in his fingers."

They watched as Jake continued his display of craftsmanship. "He's a special young man, that's for sure," Nolan said. "He builds model ships, and I believe he's transferred his techniques from that small scale to what he's doing now."

"Well, he's a natural carpenter, no doubt about that," Jane replied.

Nolan was eager to share this discovery with Clifton and Marge, but Marge would have to wait until a better time. When was the proper moment to tell his mother they had contributed to his skipping school? Nolan decided there were other priorities that needed attention, and the right opportunity would present itself.

Sean, Jerry and Jane were not pleased with Nolan's initial offer of what he considered a fair wage. They wanted him to post the job through the local carpenters' union, and they would make sure they would get the assignment. The carpenter's rate was thirty dollars per hour and Nolan backpedaled. He explained he could pay seventeen dollars an hour, no benefits, and they would be responsible for their own taxes. He also told them if they finished the project by the end of the week, each of them would receive a one-hundred-dollar cash bonus.

"I'm fine with whatever you guys decide," said Jane and walked back to work.

"Well, we're not fine. If we get such a shitty wage, then we've got to get double time for anything over forty," said Sean.

"Won't do that, guys. If I agree to that, you'll drag your feet and put in lots of overtime to get paid more. I need you to care for the project."

"We want to help, but we want decent pay."

Nolan was in a pickle. He needed carpenters, but he was working with a frugal budget.

"All right. I'll go twenty an hour, no OT. That's the best I can do on phase one. We can talk again when the first part is done."

The brothers grumbled but shook Nolan's hand and went to report to Clifton.

After Nolan felt he had negotiated to avert a crippling strike of national proportions, they all agreed to continue working, and the trio invited Nolan to join them at Paddy's Irish Pub after they finished for the day. Nolan was up for it and looked at the progress Clifton and his crew had made. He was most impressed. The stalls were taking shape, and he could visualize the building filled with customers.

As he moved about the restaurant, an odd sensation overcame him. On occasion, he had a similar sense after his wife's passing. But in each of those incidents, he perceived her essence was near, and sometimes even detected her very scent. However, this was not a replica of those events.

Nolan had always been more sensory than most. He remembered the special people in his life who had their own spirit labeled in his mind. His mother and father had that imprint of parents, yet each projected a unique element which he sensed more than visualized. A handful of close friends, who had been dear to him for years, contributed their own unique impressions to his memory.

He then recognized the exact vital components of this person from long ago and spoke her name aloud before he even realized it. "Ellie" Nolan called out but didn't turn. He told himself he was drifting into old memories.

"You can still do that—know I'm in a room before you see me."

He pivoted to the sound of her voice and faced the beguiling smile of Ellie at age eighteen when her penetrating emerald eyes pierced his heart again.

CHAPTER TWENTY-ONE

Barbed Reunion

Nolan was awestruck as he stared at Ellie. Memories rushed through him as snippets of time projected on a tiny viewfinder: the day they met, their first kiss, the faux wedding at their senior prom, her sister's death, her final words of goodbye, that erogenous essence of Ellie at his side. And now, someone was calling his name to distract him from those pleasant visions.

"Nolan, are you okay?"

He heard that voice, *her* voice, and refocused. He then realized he was standing in front of Ellie again after almost three decades. His mouth needed to move, to say something, anything to acknowledge her while he composed himself.

"Ellie, you haven't changed a bit." He heard the vowels and consonants combine to form words, but swallowed hard when he realized he had spoken them. With thirty years to plan his first words if they met again, Nolan vocalized one of the weakest replies in conversational history.

She laughed at him, which merely created more visions of good times projecting across that damn viewfinder in his brain. Nolan needed something to jolt him back to reality.

"Nolan, I've got crow's feet, a double chin, plus I'm at least ten pounds overweight. But I'll accept the compliment just the same." She smiled again, and the viewfinder began anew.

"Mr. David," Jake approached with a look of concern, "are you all right?"

"Of course."

"You look kinda green. I ate a live tadpole one time when I was little and got real sick. My mom said I looked green, and you look that way now. You didn't eat a frog, did you?"

Nolan burst with laughter and patted Jake on the back to assure him he was indeed fine and used Jake's remarks to settle himself. He introduced Jake to Ellie but still sensed an aura about her that warned him to not get too close. Her wedding ring served as an active repellent.

"El, let's go outside so we can avoid the hammering and dust."

Nolan led her through the front to dodge the curious stares of Clifton and his men in the alley. They walked with a loud silence between them to a bench across the street at the front of the vacant Bayview Restaurant.

Nolan sat a few feet from Ellie, aware he wanted to embrace her. Nolan thought even if he just cried with her about his deceased wife, he would feel so much better. That was the type of relationship they used to have; lovers understood the best way to mend each other's hearts.

"How did you know you'd find me here?"

"The Erie blog mentioned this project started by this charismatic man of mystery. The guy had been in town a short time, yet had become the center of controversy, attracting the interest of the police and some local politicians. I had a strong feeling it was you."

"Thank you very much for coming. I mean that." Nolan felt an uncomfortable gap in their conversation. "I'm assuming you didn't come to drive nails, so can I buy you dinner?"

The dazzle in her eyes seemed to diminish, and Nolan recalled that sparkle always lessened right before she delivered disappointment or bad news.

"No, Nolan, I can't stay. I came to help though." Her thumbs rubbed her fingertips while she paused and took a deep breath. For a moment, he thought she was going to leave, but she continued. "That is, if you'll accept me for who I am now."

Nolan's face couldn't hide his disappointment at the dinner rejection, but he grasped at the chance of spending more time with her. "Ellie, believe me when I tell you no matter how you wish to pitch in, your offer is welcome." He looked at her ring again, dwelling on it for as much as thirty seconds. "Yes, I'll always respect you for who you are."

Her reactive smile sent a chill up his legs.

"I'm a marketing consultant, Nolan. Based upon the limited information I learned from the blog, I think Hope Landing has merit. But you'll need more than that little twerp's blog and some flyers to attract enough people to make this a success."

"So, how do you know the eloquent Jamal Moore?"

"I represent quite a few businesses in Erie. If someone sends him a complaint, legitimate or otherwise, he posts it. When I approach him, he deletes the reference like it never existed. I was not too polite when I told him his thoughtless editorial policies would invite any terrorists group to post their rhetoric with no objection from him. Don't get me wrong—his blog is informative and a meaningful resource for the folks in town. But the kid needs to use his brain now and then."

"I agree. I've had a similar encounter with his zealousness for one-source information, with the same reaction of immediate deletion, as if that solves the problem in its entirety." Nolan realized he was speaking with Eleanor, the marketing consultant, and no longer Ellie, the teenage babe. "Ellie, I must admit our liquid capital is very limited. As much as I want your services, I doubt we could afford them."

She gazed at the workers packing their tools in the trucks across the street.

"What are you paying them?" She nodded toward the crew.

"Well, our total labor cost to date is zero, but we have a payroll coming up."

"I suspected as much. Nolan, you always could inspire people. I remember watching kids in high school accept you as their leader for no reason at all. My sister, Mary, idolized you. You're energizing the base population. So far, it's happened at a slow pace, but it will escalate. Believe me, it will. And like you attract those who believe in you, there is also a guaranteed percentage who will despise you. This time, I want to ride this to the finish, and I won't listen to what others think."

She glanced at her watch. "I have to go home. How about you tell me every detail of your plan over lunch tomorrow?"

They agreed to meet at the diner midday, and Nolan really needed a drink to settle his anxiety.

As he drove to Paddy's, the past flooded his consciousness. This time, his recollections were of all the pleasant times of high school dances, dinner with Ellie's family, and long conversations beneath an immense oak tree. His deceased wife again came to mind, and Nolan wondered about her guidance. She made it very clear prior to her death he should seek another companion, remarry, and enjoy life. He never doubted the sincerity of her remarks. But, he's had difficulty letting go of their relationship. Nolan didn't know if he could ever find a moment of happiness with someone else.

As he parked near Paddy's, he was ready for a beer and the comradery of friends. He located Clifton, Sean, Jerry, and Jane at a corner table, and they were already a drink ahead of him.

"Clifton, where's Jake?"

"I dropped him off at the hospital. Don't worry, he cleaned up and changed his clothes. I wouldn't be shocked if he tells Marge what he did today. That boy has a problem with honesty. He was so happy when I left him; I know he'll blurt out every detail as soon as he sees his mom. So, you better sit here and drink with us where she won't come looking."

Nolan knew Marge wasn't about to leave the hospital but also knew her tendrils were far reaching with the aid of the telephone. He ordered a round for the crew and was halfway through his first beer when Isabel entered, shuffling toward their table. Nolan dragged over an empty chair.

"Isabel, what's wrong? You look pale."

As she lifted her head, her reddened eyes reflected recent tears.

She sat and clutched at her handbag that she rested across her lap. "Oh my, I haven't been in a beer garden since before my Armando died. I'll have a draught. Please."

Nolan didn't see any sense in asking Isabel which of the fifty-seven flavors of beer she preferred. He ordered a light ale and set it before her. She took a hearty gulp, and Clifton shrugged as his eyes met Nolan's.

"Okay, Isabel. Give. Tell us what's going on or you're cut off from the bar."

"I don't think you can do that, Nolan. I believe the bartender has that responsibility."

Nolan rubbed his temple with his fingers, wondering why

women had to be so difficult when one was looking out for their best interest.

"All right, relax. I'll tell you." She grimaced and spoke with a whisper. "I lost my job today."

Of all the things that had sped through Nolan's mind prior to her announcement, this was not even on the topic list. "Isabel, how can that be? You're one of the senior personnel at the courthouse. What happened?"

"I got a whiff of a rumor at lunch, but I didn't think much of it. On occasion, I share a table with a district judge, and he told me some job cuts were in the wind, so I should watch myself. He'd heard my name mentioned, but he wasn't too concerned because of what you said. I've been there over thirty years." She wiped a tear from the corner of her eye with her napkin, then continued. "At three o'clock, I got a message to report to a room on the second floor, and there sat the city manager and one of the county commissioners. Now keep in mind I work for the county, so I didn't expect this problem with Erie would affect our staff at all. However, when I saw the city manager in there, well, I knew my goose was well done."

"What was their reasoning for your dismissal? Were you fired? Laid off?"

"They eliminated my job. The commissioner explained most of the county revenue comes from the city, which I already knew. Since the city of Erie cannot contribute their normal taxes and appropriations to the county, my job was being eliminated as a full-time position. They'll staff the clerk of court's office with a part-time person. They gave me severance and of course, I have my retirement pay and Chico has his VA disability, so my finances are okay. It's a shock, that's all."

Nolan thought of her twenty-thousand-dollar donation. "Isabel, I'll return the money that you gave us. We'll make it somehow without it. I can't cash your check now. I feel responsible for you losing your job."

She swatted the back of Nolan's hand. "Nonsense. I think they did me a favor. I've been so bored in that office over the last few years but had no reason to retire. But now I do. I can spend more time helping you and Father Andrew, or whatever else you need an old woman to do."

"Isabel, are you sure you don't want your money back?"

"Oh, I want my money back all right, and a lot more when Hope Landing is successful. Until then, I'm fine."

"They released how many others from the courthouse today? Any idea?"

"Nolan, that's why I came here tonight. I didn't come to have you feel sorry for me, but you should know this. I was the only person who was let go. And the fact the city manager was present at the time of my termination was most odd. He has no authority in county government—none. He was there to make certain that the commissioner did it right, I'm sure of it. The entire process was much too formal. Don't worry. The buzz among the girls at the courthouse is that all my snooping attracted the attention of the wrong people. Now, can you please be a dear and fetch me another beer? Not a light this time, okay?"

The evening became even more interesting when Jamal ambled to their table. He grabbed a seat and heard about Isabel's unexpected departure from county government.

"I'll get this up on my site tonight. We'll show these people they can fire Isabel, but they can't stop freedom of the press."

"Jamal, I've been meaning to talk to you about your attitude with that. You know there is some responsibility that goes with the management of your blog. Your editor at the paper doesn't publish every story, does he?" Nolan paused but restarted before the reporter could respond. "Of course he doesn't. He has responsibilities to the community to print confirmed information of interest to the readers. If you're publishing a blog dedicated to the citizens of Erie, you should have that same accountability."

The reporter seemed attentive.

"Your blog may have started as a personal venture, but it has expanded to include serious comments about issues important to the folks who call Erie home."

"I'm aware of the impact of my blog. But I'm not about to do anything different after my editor told me today to back off on my stories."

"There's a pattern here I'm certain even you can see. What did your editor say?"

"We had a man-to-man chat, at least that's what he called it. He monitors my posts from time to time to see how my writing and talents improve. Fitz was laying it on thick—even had me believing him for a few minutes. The paper is considering adding my own daily column about the social activities in the city. Then he said of course, I wouldn't have time for the blog anymore and acted like that was a damn shame."

"And how do you know he wasn't telling you the truth?"

"Ha, that's easy. When I told him I could do both, he became insistent that stopping the blog was a condition of the job offer. Then we argued, and he told me my blog pissed off the wrong people. He was getting complaints about me, and I had to change or stop my blog right away."

"So, what was the bottom line? Did you agree?"

"Hell, no. He said if I didn't remove it soon, he would have to further evaluate my performance at the paper. He about told me I was going to get fired."

"Did Fitz mention who were the wrong people? Any names? Any hints?"

"Not really. I figured it has to be related to that Hutchinson guy somehow, but don't see the link."

"Well, I've got to give you credit. At least you've got some integrity, and that makes up a little for how you dress."

"What's wrong with my clothes, man?"

"If there was a shelf life on style, your wardrobe would have expired years ago. But let's not get into that now."

It was almost nine o'clock, and Nolan still hadn't eaten but drank plenty of beer. If he still had that cruiser on his tail, it guaranteed him a DUI.

"Young Mr. Moore, you're about to drive me to Marge's diner, and I'll buy your meal. How's that sound?"

"Sure. Just let me finish my beer."

Nolan grabbed the mug from his lips and slid the half-filled glass across the table.

"You're driving, so you're cut off. We can't take any chances. And we shall have a long talk, young man. I have a feeling you know more than you realize. I need you to be patient and alert."

They slid out the door, down the hall from the restrooms and into the alley behind Paddy's. Nolan sent the reporter for his car while he peeked at his SUV parked across the street from the main entrance. There was an unmarked police vehicle sitting three spaces behind him, but it was empty. The creaking springs of the side door alerted him, and he sank behind the dumpster. Dull black shoes thudded past him toward State Street. The footsteps stopped, then padded off and faded. Nolan took a chance and bolted away in the opposite direction.

Nolan cornered at the next street and knelt. As he looked through the cracks in a picket fence, he noticed a young blond man entering the alleyway and proceeding toward him. Nolan recognized him as the young officer who had ticketed his recent U-turn, but he now wore blue jeans and a white T-shirt. He aimed his phone camera through the gaps and pressed record. Nolan hadn't spotted him in the crowded bar. Still, he was positive the cop was following him as he captured the incident. The officer approached, stopped at the corner, and then turned toward Paddy's. Nolan hurried away from State Street and eluded his tail.

He circled back to the main drag but several blocks away from Paddy's. Within a few minutes, Jamal noticed Nolan and pulled over to the curb with his window down.

"Where'd you go? I gave up on you. I was on my way to the diner, guessing you hopped a ride with someone else."

"Just drive. It's my turn to ask questions." He slid into the car, and soon they were at the diner.

It didn't take long to get the reporter on track with useful information. Jamal didn't know why the city manager would have involved himself in Isabel's termination but had gathered more background on Lieutenant Hutchinson.

"He was more active before I came to the police beat. The guy who taught me the ropes at city hall told me Hutchinson screwed up somehow and was almost kicked off the force. But he was so close to retirement, the union stepped in and saved him. In fact, he got the softest assignment on the force, as ombudsman for citizen complaints."

"This guy who trained you, where is he now?"

"Duane Zuccola. He retired and bought this nifty cottage near Hogs Head, North Carolina. I called him earlier, and he gave me the lowdown on Hutchinson."

Nolan laughed, "I believe it's Nag's Head, not Hog's Head, but we can work on your geography later."

"What's Hutchinson's relationship with Ashley Pershing?" Nolan recalled the letter from the city manager's office regarding the snack bar's lease, and the subsequent follow-up call from Pershing's office.

"Oh, they're real tight—good friends, I guess. I was at city hall today and saw Ms. Pershing with the lieutenant on one side of her and the former chief of detectives on the other. Matter of fact, you must know him, because he told me the other day to tell you he said hello. It slipped my mind—too much going on."

"Former chief of detectives, you say? What's his name?"

The reply came as if this was just another name. "Cermak. His first name is Sylvester, but few people know that. Most call him by his last name, but I've heard a few refer to him as Sly in conversation."

Many years of anger boiled inside Nolan. The detective who had ruined Nolan's reputation thirty years ago was still on his case. He had progressed a great deal in Nolan's long absence and was eager to show his influence. But Nolan David didn't return as a scared teenager, and this time, he would stay. It was his turn to direct the offense and find out who killed Ellie's sister.

"Jamal, I don't want you to run out on me, but I have a bad feeling about all this. You can't mention this in your blog, but somehow, that trio is connected to a decades-old homicide, and I'm not leaving this city until I uncover the truth."

CHAPTER TWENTY-TWO

Bewitched and Bedazzled

Father Andrew arrived at the diner early the next morning with a progress report. It saddened him to learn of Isabel's unexpected freedom from employment. He even agreed with her comments that her dismissal may have been a blessing since she had become rather stagnant in her job.

Andrew had secured agreements for two additional units at Hope Landing, with a third appointment scheduled for later that day.

"This was easier than I expected, and my collar paid dividends. The daughter and son-in-law of a bishop of a sizable Baptist church will take the African American slot. She owns a small catering business with the church as her primary customer. Beyond that, I don't believe she has many customers outside the church community. But she's enthusiastic, and the bishop will front the money for the equipment. That one is locked in and golden."

Nolan appreciated some good news for a change.

"A second person has also joined us and was obtained through my diocese contacts. We have a rather sizable Russian population in town, and many attend Eastern Orthodox services. Their bishop and I haven't always agreed on past issues, but he saw this as a sort of olive branch and latched on. There was a diner in town years ago, Dominick's. I'm not certain you would remember it."

"I have a faint recollection. I believe it was close to the downtown area."

"Correct. Erie was a growing city then, and Dominick's was at the last stop of the trolley line. When progress replaced the rail with bus transportation, Dominick's choked. They hung on for many years, but when the patriarch of the family, Dominick, passed, so did the restaurant. Dominick's grandson just graduated from a community college with a degree in hospitality and would like a chance at Hope Landing. He seems capable and will borrow the money for start-up costs. So, he's in place for the Russian sector."

"I'm impressed. You've done a helluva lot of work in a short time. Oh, sorry about the hell part. I'm not used to hanging around a priest."

"Calm down. You've forgotten the language I survived that came out of the mouths of you orphan children."

"Andrew, that means we're almost full—only two more to go. In fact, we could always open with a blank space or two and perhaps attract someone later."

"We may have the UK booked as well. I mentioned I have an appointment later this afternoon, but I wanted to get your approval before I made a commitment on this one."

Nolan shook his head, willing to accept the priest's decisions based on his superior results. "You don't need to check with me on anyone, Andrew. I've got plenty happening in the political arena I will brief you about."

"You need to hear this, and yes, you may have a problem with this person."

Nolan sat back in his chair to listen.

"Do you remember Mrs. Bennett?"

The cogs in Nolan's brain didn't catch and provide a match right away. Then, he remembered the English ingredient, recalled a round face and stern voice, and someone slid into view. Nolan recalled her adding food to his plate with a loud splat and a hearty, "Move along, young lad." *Of course*, Nolan thought, *Mrs. Bennett was the cook at the orphanage.* "When did you realize who I was?"

"Well, you gave it away yourself by staring at those photos in my office. Then, of course, your name change was not creative, merely dropping your last name. I was fairly sure by the end of your first visit. By the second time we met, I was certain."

"Why didn't you say anything?"

"It wasn't my place. You had issues with your past, and I didn't want to be responsible for further complications. But, when I realized Mrs. Bennett would be such an excellent fit for the English piece, I knew we had to have this talk."

"You hold no grudges, Father?"

"So, now it's Father, is it? What happened to Andrew?" He raised his voice and leaned forward in his chair. "Listen to me, Nolan Kaminski. I've always believed you to be a person of honor with a brilliant mind. Just because you pulled a few childish pranks on me wouldn't be a reason to alter that judgment." He paused for a moment, then continued in a softer tone. "Death to those you care about the most seems to haunt you, and I regret that. But you've survived through at least three occasions that I'm aware of, and the residents of Erie need you. To be quite honest, I need you too. You're giving this city life again. People like Isabel and I are filled with despair from watching the slow demise of our beloved town. You're providing us a chance to dream again, and when you reach retirement age, a purpose to get up each morning becomes mighty important."

He still projected a tone of anger as he pointed his index finger at Nolan.

"Now, Mrs. Bennett hasn't had a steady job since the orphanage closed over fifteen years ago. I'm willing to ante her up-front costs if you have no objections."

"Like I said before Andrew, I trust your judgment." Nolan extended his hand, but the priest sidestepped him and gave a firm hug.

"Please tell Mrs. Bennett I look forward to seeing her again," Nolan said. "And Andrew, I never imagined we would be friends, but I'm glad I returned to Erie, even if it was just to learn how you feel about me. Thank you."

Nolan was summarizing recent events when Isabel joined them.

Andrew reached out and touched her shoulder, "Sorry about your job, Isabel."

"Don't raise your voice so loud, Father. I've got a headache from last night's festivities."

Andrew and Nolan both snickered, but she looked bedraggled.

"Do you know those boys had me pouring salt on my hand and drinking shots of some odd-sounding liquor?"

"Tequila?" Nolan asked. "Did Clifton allow that group to give you tequila shooters?"

"I believe so. I remember nothing after the second one until I woke at dawn all tucked in my bed wearing the clothes I wore last night."

All three of them giggled while Isabel sipped at her black coffee. Then she slid a small sticky note toward Nolan.

"But I've been hard at work this morning already. You have an appointment tomorrow afternoon with Mr. Oteliani Shongo at his office in Salamanca. That's his address, and I don't recommend tardiness. However, bring plenty of patience. I understand he sometimes will keep people waiting in his office for hours to test their reactions. Take a book."

"Thank you, Isabel. You have indeed been busy." He tucked the note in his shirt and noticed the time. He had two hours until his luncheon with Ellie.

"Regarding Mr. Shongo," Isabel continued, "I need to share some background details I uncovered. He is very proud of his ancestry and his accomplishments with the Senecas. The name 'Shongo' is a tribal name which originated on the Cattaragus Reservation in the late 1800s. That location is very near the current city of Salamanca. Also, his first name is Oteliani, which means 'one prepared' and is traceable to that same era."

"You are truly remarkable. Thank you, again."

"I have two other pieces of information for you. First, Marge is being released today and has a contract out on your head."

"Ah, Jake. I forgot about that mess. She should have no difficulty getting an arrest warrant. Tell her to call Ashley Pershing's office, and they can radio the car that's usually nearby."

She scowled, then Nolan remembered she was not yet privy to his cat-and-mouse game with Sylvester Cermak and the Erie police. He provided the quick overview in his softest tones out of deference to her hangover. "The dash cam has a limited memory, so I download and save every recording which has images of my being followed. It seems I am rarely alone."

"And does all this have anything to do with an attractive female who visited you yesterday?"

He sighed. "It has nothing to do with her at all, but time will tell." He knew by their open eyes and closed mouths that both were waiting for more details, but none would be forthcoming. He moved the conversation forward.

"You said you had another item, Isabel?"

"Humph, secrets, is it?" Nolan remained silent.

"Very well then, secrets it shall be. Do you hear that, Father Andrew? I lose my job of thirty years for this fellow, and he doesn't trust me with the details of a brief visit from a woman who Jake describes as a witch."

"A witch? Where in God's name did he get that idea?"

Now she was the one giggling. "Why, it's very simple. Jake said she must have been a witch, because she cast a spell over you. He said you followed her out of that restaurant like you were in a trance."

Andrew and Isabel laughed at Jake's analogy, while Isabel blurted out in the middle of her laughter, "I've got to tell Aaron."

Nolan raised his arms in surrender to them both. "You have me. I'm busted. Can we please move on to your other matter of business? Or was that it?"

"Oh no, I have more. I'm uncertain if this is good or bad news, but news it is just the same. I spoke again with the folks down in Florida who are caring for the widow of The Bayview owner. They were going through some of her mail and discovered a letter from dear son Harold, but they didn't know how to go about reaching him."

Andrew interjected, "No return address? No phone listing?"

"There was a return address all right. Young Harold is at one of those extended stay facilities run by the federal government outside Portland, Oregon. He's almost to the middle of a ten-year sentence for sales and distribution of illegal drugs—to minors, nonetheless."

"That boy had fine parents, too," Andrew said. "I remember they bragged about how creative he was while he was in school."

Isabel expounded. "Creativity was his strength, but common sense was his downfall. I spoke with the night sergeant out there in Oregon. I needed Harold to know his daddy was dead and his mother wouldn't recognize him by the time he got out. I learned this young fellow had a perimeter of sweet corn surrounding a trailer where he cooked crystal meth. The tall corn stalks shielded the trailer, and he sold the corn and meth at a roadside stand. A school bus driver got suspicious when so many students insisted the bus pull over so they could buy some corn for their parents for dinner. Such was the finale of his creativity."

Rather than feeling sorry for the young man's fate, Nolan's mind was churning on how they could turn this to their advantage.

"Isabel, are you up for a road trip?" He explained his plan, and both Andrew and Isabel believed they had at least a fair chance of success.

CHAPTER TWENTY-THREE

Roll 'Em...

Ellie arrived right on time, and Nolan led her to a quiet table in the far rear corner. She wore a conservative light green business suit and carried a leather portfolio.

"My, you look like you belong in *Fortune* magazine. I'm now positive we can't afford your services."

Her lips raised in a delicate smile as she selected the seat across from Nolan. He held every expectation she would at least sit next to him, but the sight of her after so long gave him a unique sense of fulfillment. He couldn't complain about the seating selection.

"You continue to bring up the cost, Nolan, so allow me to clarify this for you. It may shorten our meeting." She spoke with almost an abruptness in her tone. "You and I have ancient history together, and we can talk about that sometime. I feel bad about the circumstances under which you left, and for not believing in you. I was wrong."

"Ellie—" She held up her hand and he quieted.

"Please allow me to finish." She glanced away, took a deep breath, then stared point blank at Nolan. "As I was saying, I should have supported you and made certain my parents and that detective knew I trusted and believed you. I didn't speak out, and the entire episode went too far. It damaged your reputation. I can't fix that now, but I'm going to work on your team as your marketing director and won't accept a penny for my services. I'll pass along any expenses at cost and operate within the budget we establish. There, I said it."

He remained trapped in her eyes and processed her words like a delayed satellite feed.

"Nolan, there's one more thing you should know about me." Another pause, followed by a radiant smile, "I'm very good at what I do. My customers stretch from the Cleveland Metropolitan area east to Buffalo and then south to Pittsburgh."

"Uh, I have no doubt about your competency. And I accept your terms. You've given this considerable thought, and the team and I are most appreciative."

Bootsie accepted their lunch orders without a word, which was a special blessing. After Ellie ordered, she picked up her portfolio and moved to Nolan's immediate left.

"This will make it easier to explain some options I've considered."

Her move opened a field of vision inside the restaurant which allowed Nolan to see the young police officer from last night's activity at Paddy's. He wore the same dull shoes and jeans, but a different tee-shirt. His jacket was slung over the back of his chair, and he slid his arm down, held it still for a second, then raised it back to the table. He did this every few minutes when Nolan realized he was taking photos.

"Ellie, I need to interrupt your captivating voice for an important announcement."

She paused with pen in hand. "Nolan, you are still weird. Has anyone mentioned that to you before?"

"A few hundred times, but that's not the subject. Please don't stare, but there's an undercover police officer to your immediate left who is taking snapshots of us. I'm sure he doesn't have the welfare of Hope Landing at heart, so let's continue while I think of a way to resolve the problem. You may proceed."

"You don't believe I can just pick up where I left off."

"Of course you can. I'm positive you've been interrupted on countless occasions in a presentation and this is more casual, so it should be much easier."

"If you didn't expect me to react, why did you tell me in the first place? Does that make sense to you?"

"Yes, it does. I was concerned passion would overcome you and you needed to kiss me, for old times' sake. I didn't want that weak moment displayed on the front page of the *Gazette*."

"Kiss you? I'm a married woman who hasn't seen you in thirty years."

"All the more reason to make up for lost time, but I can control myself if you can, Ms. Thompson."

She set her pen down and folded her hands. "First, my married name is now and has been for many years Parucci. Now, we can continue this in a business-like manner, Mr. David, or Mr. Kaminski, however you prefer I address you. Or I could leave now, so you and your secret agent buddy can have at each other."

Nolan patted her hand, "Please continue, my love, I mean Ms. Parucci."

"Mrs. Parucci."

"Yes, I'm sorry."

Their banter ceased, and she returned to her presentation. The detail she had prepared for the meeting was impressive. Her ideas were bright and ambitious, plus Nolan believed she could transition them to reality. If Hope Landing could get off the ground, he felt their chances of ultimate success were pretty decent.

Nolan placed his laptop on the table where they both could view the screen. He reviewed the overview of their team members while they ate and informed Ellie of his pending appointment with the leader of the Seneca Nation. This prompted many questions about his meeting strategy, and he got winded from telling her he would figure that out when he got there. She wasn't thrilled with his, "it depends on Shongo's attitude" approach.

"What time are you leaving for Salamanca?"

"Oh, I'm not certain. I've been told it's about a two-hour drive, so if I leave at noon, I'll have plenty of time."

"I'll meet you here at nine tomorrow morning, and we'll strategize before we go. That will allow us adequate time to see his casino and get comfortable in his environment."

"Okay, boss." he replied. She then told him what to wear, but he didn't tell her none of her mentioned items were in his limited wardrobe. He wouldn't dare interrupt her; it was a pleasure just watching her lips move.

He set his keys on the table. "I'm going to bait our secret agent spy if you could do me a tiny favor."

She raised her brows.

"I am going to the restroom. If I'm followed, go to his right jacket pocket. His phone is in there. Push the tip of this little gizmo into the side of his phone, and the SIM card will eject. Pocket it, then text me when you're back in your seat."

"You want me to steal a part of that police officer's phone? Really?"

"Yes. He's taking photos of us, and I'm concerned they'll show up somewhere in the newspaper or on the internet. I don't think Mr. Parucci would be pleased."

"My husband knows I'm meeting with you. We're doing nothing wrong."

"The facts don't always matter. You should know that by now. The accompanying story may imply otherwise, and I won't allow that to happen. So, please do this, or I'll take his phone and drop it into our deep fryer."

She grinned. "See what I mean? You make people do things totally out of character." She rubbed her eyes, then shook her head. "As much as I'd like to witness the phone-in-the-fryer move, I'll try to do as you ask."

She picked up the key chain. "Why would you carry around that pointy thing? It looks like you could stick yourself."

"The fellow at the computer repair store gave this one to me. He used it to reset my notebook and told me it's a common tool for removal of SIM cards and resetting smart phones."

He scrawled his mobile number on a napkin, slid it in front of her, then stood and strolled toward the men's room. As he suspected, the inexperienced cop wasn't about to lose him again and followed: Advantage—home team.

The blond man entered while Nolan was washing his hands, and he walked to the urinal. Nolan glanced at him, turned away, then snapped his head back toward him.

"Hey, you look familiar," he said, stepping from the sink. "Do you come here often? To the diner, I mean. I've only worked here a few times. Fish fry Friday?"

"No, I, uh, never been here before."

Nolan waited, then the man zipped his pants and went to the basin.

"Damn. I know we've met. Recently, too. Any ideas?"

"No, sorry," he replied as he turned on the tap water.

Nolan slapped his palm to his forehead. "I got it. You're that cop who gave me the ticket for the U-turn. That's it. You know, I should have told you then. I'm new in town—Georgia plates. I was sort of in a hurry, trying to locate my boss's teenage son. Wasn't thinking. Probably a little late now, but is there any way I can get an exception for being an out-of-towner? You mentioned you could change that ticket to a warning, and I sure would appreciate that. Officer Goodwill. Right?"

"Sorry, sir. Once the ticket's been issued, there's nothing I can do." Nolan was standing in front of the paper towels, so the man shook the moisture off his hands.

Nolan's phone buzzed in his pocket, and he stepped aside. "I'm sorry to be in your way."

The man brushed past him, and Nolan followed.

Ellie nodded but kept her deliberate expression. They finished their meeting, then reviewed their timing for the next day. As they shook hands, she released a small slender item into his palm, and they both displayed deceptive grins of success.

Nolan's vehicle was loaded with his shipment to the memorabilia dealer, so he stopped at a Pony Express. His inexperienced tail passed the store, then pulled to the curb. Nolan approached the car, cranking his thumb and fingers together, so he would lower his window.

"Listen, I've got several boxes to tote inside, and I could use your help. You'll have to wait out here for me anyhow, so this will save us both some time."

The officer's face reddened with embarrassment, and he hesitated.

"It's okay. I won't say anything to Sly or Hutchinson. You can follow me again when I leave."

The young man stepped out and assisted Nolan without a word, looking relieved when the last box was on the counter.

"Thanks, buddy. I can save you some time, or in case you lose me. I'm driving to check in on Marge Kelly now, but my visit with her should be short. After that, I've got a meeting down at city hall, so if you want to take a break or run an errand, you could catch up with me then."

The officer's eyes flared in anger, but he never opened his mouth or approached Nolan.

As Nolan pulled out from the Pony Express, his assistant stevedore was right behind. Nolan pressed his luck a bit by accelerating to forty. He waved at the rearview mirror, and the officer replied with a solitary finger.

After he parked in front of Marge's, he popped the mini disk from his dash cam and slid it into his shirt pocket. He grabbed his laptop, then went up the porch stairs.

Rose answered the door, rolled her eyes, and nodded over her shoulder.

"Welcome to the love shack. Are you here to see Mr. or Mrs. Happy?"

He knew Rose could often communicate at a different frequency, so he tilted his head and squinted.

"The two of them have been complimenting each other since Marge got back from therapy a couple of hours ago. Aaron almost got tossed out of the building because he shouted at the therapist. He said she was working the poor girl too hard. Jesus, Mary, Joseph and all the saints. You've got to see this in action, or you'll think I'm bullshitting you. We have the most handsome man in the world chatting with the most beautiful woman, or the most intelligent male with the wittiest female. You get the idea. Follow me."

Nolan grabbed her elbow to slow her. "Rose, Isabel told me Marge was rabid about Jake missing school. Where is he?"

"Some woman in a hard hat picked him up and took him to the pier. She was an odd bird—said she needed Jake's magic fingers, but I didn't tell Marge. Jake and Marge cut a deal, so I think you're off the hook from permanent damage."

Marge was resting on her sofa with pillows stuffed about her every curve. Aaron sat on a folding chair, reaching with a cloth and wiping Marge's forehead.

"Marge, do you have a fever?" Nolan asked.

"Wow, look who's here," Marge said. "No, I have a slight headache, and Aaron has made it so much better with his delicate touch."

"Aaron? Delicate? I would ever use those words in the same sentence. But listen, I can't stay for long. I've got a police officer on my tail outside, and I want to get moving before he loses his patience. I stopped in, hoping you would have an extra memory stick."

"The police?" Marge asked. "I've heard you've led a rather exciting life while I've been laid up."

Nolan nodded. "It's been quite interesting. I suggest you have Rose call Isabel before she leaves for Oregon, and she'll bring you up to date."

Aaron asked, "Why is Isabel going to Oregon?"

"Long story. She'll be glad to tell you all about it. I'm sorry I let you down with Jake, Marge. I can give you some excuses but none good enough."

Nolan expected an outburst, but Aaron spoke next.

"We talked about the boy, and he'll go to school tomorrow, then help Clifton on the weekend. Jake has a generous heart and only wants to help."

"Very well said. You have such a way with words." Marge patted Aaron's knee while Nolan shook his head and sighed.

"About that memory stick, you know, those little rectangular pieces you can use to export photos and such off your computer."

"Do you mean thumb drives?" Marge asked.

"Bingo," Nolan replied.

"Aaron, honey, could you please be an angel and go back to my desk? There should be two still in the packaging in the top left drawer."

"Be right back, Sugar Babe."

Nolan opened his laptop and downloaded the video from his dash cam onto the thumb drive. He asked Rose to organize a meeting for next Monday night and to include all the new team members. He then bid his farewell and returned to his car.

Nolan waived at the unmarked car. The cowcatcher grill was inches from Nolan's rear bumper, and the blond cop tapped the side panel outside his window in a nervous rhythm.

"I apologize." Nolan yelled over the revving of his engine. "That took longer than I expected. Next stop, city hall."

He entered the government building with a jolt of exhilaration. He introduced himself to the young lady at the front desk. She smiled and waved her fingers at someone behind him, "Hi Pete. Why are you out of uniform?" Nolan didn't bother to turn around.

It took Nolan a few minutes to convince Buffy, which just had to be her name, to call the city manager's office and announce he was there to see him. She started to provide directions, but he stopped her. He turned and saw his shadow pacing the lobby while staring at his feet.

"Hey Pete," he shouted, "would you guide me to the city manager's office?"

Pete moved past with his shoulders slumped, and Nolan followed him down the hall and up two flights of stairs.

"I won't need you any more today, Jeeves," Nolan said. "You may have the rest of the day off."

Pete scowled and trudged down the steps.

"I'm afraid I don't know who you are, Mr. Nolan," said the city manager when Nolan entered. "I assume you're a citizen concerned about that ridiculous bankruptcy rumor coming out of the mayor's office."

Nolan smiled at the slender milquetoast of a man. "You are correct, sir, but with a slight twist. Perhaps it would be best if we had another person present for my remarks."

He raised his eyebrows, "Such as?"

"Perhaps the city has someone who represents the citizens in these matters—an ombudsman of sorts?"

He nodded and picked up his phone. "You're in luck. I saw our ombudsman a few moments ago and believe I can get him to join us."

Within a minute, Lieutenant Hutchinson entered and glared at Nolan.

"Please have a seat," Nolan pointed at an armchair, and Hutchinson sat without ever taking his eyes off him.

"Now, let's get down to business, shall we?" Nolan asked. "I have a rather serious complaint to lodge against council member Ashley Pershing." He paused while they peered at each other. "I believe she's abusing her office as a representative of the citizens of Erie."

Hutchinson turned as if to speak, but Nolan continued. "I've come to you both today, because I would prefer this be dealt with in confidence. A reporter with the Erie *Gazette* has contacted me concerning this matter, but I believe there's no reason to escalate an insignificant item such as this. You know how the media blows everything way out of proportion, don't you gentlemen?"

The city manager was nodding, but Hutchinson was grinding his teeth.

"Could we perhaps bring Ms. Pershing into our meeting? I'm most confident if she hears of my complaint, she'll have a very simple explanation, and I can advise the *Gazette* there is no story to print."

The city manager picked up the phone, but Hutchinson lifted his hand, "I'll see if she's available." The big man left.

The room remained silent until Nolan heard the clicking of footsteps that grew closer until Hutchinson, a frowning Ashley Pershing, and the distinguished Sly Cermak entered in unison.

"Ms. Pershing, it is an honor to meet you at last." Nolan reached out to shake her hand, but Cermak blocked his path. "I feel no need to introduce myself since you've seen many photos of me in the past few days."

She glared at Cermak.

"Sylvester Cermak, my, I must compliment you on your choice of undercover officers. Pete has been most cordial to work with today. I recommend him for a commendation for the help he provided unloading my vehicle at the Pony Express. He's a fine young man."

Nolan glanced at the tall lieutenant. "Before we begin, could I bother you for some water?" No one moved, then he added, "Please?"

The city manager opened a small black refrigerator next to his desk and withdrew a plastic bottle of water.

Nolan sat, and the others followed suit. "I'm so glad we could all gather this afternoon."

"Kaminski, what the hell are you're doing here?" said Cermak.

"I'm here to answer that question. I don't know what type of scheme you all have. Until today, I didn't care. I've watched your young beagle follow me around, taking pictures and keeping you up to date on my activities. I don't care what happens to me. But today, your scout was taking photos today of a friend of mine who is off limits."

He reached into his shirt pocket and withdrew the SIM card from Pete's smart phone. "All I wanted to do was help the town get back on its feet. But I understand whatever is good for the people who live here will jeopardize your plans. And now I care about whatever the hell you are doing. You could have left me alone."

He dropped the tiny SIM card into the bottled water. "I suspect Pete will need to service his phone."

Cermak spoke through gritted teeth as his thumb twirled a ruby ring around his right ring finger. "You're going to regret coming here."

Nolan stood rigid but looked each person in the eyes as he held the memory stick in his fingertips, then stopped with Cermak. "You can let us proceed with our project, and I'll stop digging into whatever you've got. I already have some videos. But Sly, I finally realized you have a personal stake in the death of Mary Thompson all those years ago. I don't know how or why," he said, taking one step toward the detective and looking him straight in the eye, "Yet."

CHAPTER TWENTY-FOUR

Lady Luck

The stone mason told Nolan the monument would be done soon, but it would still be a few weeks before he could make the installation. The groundskeeper would not permit any unnecessary ground disturbance until after Memorial Day, but at least he agreed to push Nolan's job ahead of others who developed patience in the afterlife.

He found the stone mason's staff easy to work with, so Nolan asked for their help with his search for the sites of his relatives in the cemetery. The mason's assistant was most willing to get the information and commented the cemetery caretaker could be difficult at times. Nolan gave her all the names and approximate dates of birth and death to assist her. He might get a chance to maintain those family gravesites after all.

Nolan drove the short distance to the cemetery, then rested in the warmth of his vehicle near his parents' grave. He closed his eyes and watched his father point to the sky.

The bright colors and loud booms were better than the boy imagined as the hues reflected off the still water of the bay. At times, the explosions lit up parts of the downtown buildings, and the clock atop the bank illuminated for a second longer.

As always, the fireworks were over too fast. Young Nolan held his father's hand as he guided him through the crowd toward their car. He had become one of the tallest kids in the third grade, so he almost kept up with his dad's stride.

They sat in traffic for a long time as they made their way down the only road off the isle. The trio rode in style in a 1958 Edsel Citation convertible, bright turquoise with cream-colored upholstery and whitewall tires. She was a beauty, even though she was an official antique. His father returned waves, nods, plus the occasional tap of a horn. He beamed with pride as they inched along the congested route.

His father and he worked out a routine whenever they met someone with the car. The stranger would compliment Dad on how good the Edsel looked, and his dad would say, "She's kind of like a slot machine."

Then, he would nod at his son and ask, "Why is that?"

Nolan would reveal his broadest smile and say, "Because you have a lot of fun, but you put all your money into her."

At last, they hit the four-lane and were on their way.

The yellow neon lights greeted them as they turned into the Whippy Dip, and Nolan got a fifty-cent chocolate ice-cream cone. His father explained they were splurging after he earned double time pay working at the factory on a holiday. Nolan wasn't sure it was worth him missing his ball game, but he enjoyed the advantages of living the good life, even if it was just for a time. He felt odd about the feelings he had all day that something bad was going to happen, and he was glad they were almost home.

Young Nolan concentrated on licking the melting treat to prevent drips as much as he could. A fifty-cent-er was a real challenge. His mom and dad were giggling again as she slid over in the bench seat, and his father wrapped his arm around her. They passed the corner grocery as he held his ice-cream cone tight, bracing for the bumps over the railroad tracks. Nolan heard the loud whistle of the train for a split second before the impact flung his frozen treat onto the upholstery, then he woke with a scream.

He was drenched in a cold sweat from the usual nightmare and moved away from the car to move about. The crisp morning air refreshed him, and he was about to leave when a familiar voice spoke from behind.

"I thought I told you to stay away from my daughter," was the unmistakable cadence of Mrs. Thompson.

"Oh no," groaned Nolan. "Don't tell me you're pointing that gun at me again."

Nolan turned his head and there stood Ellie's mom, leaning against the rear of his SUV, aiming the bobbing gun at him.

"Mrs. Thompson, you know you're not going to pull that trigger."

"I warned you, so it would be fair to shoot you for bothering Eleanor."

Nolan pivoted toward her with a gradual motion.

"Don't turn around and don't move. I'm trying to decide."

"Now, Mrs. Thompson, you must realize Ellie approached me," he said. "And she's helping me on this project to help get some tourism into Erie."

She nodded and slipped her gun into her coat pocket. "She told me. And I admitted I'd feel better if you were dead."

Gaps of several seconds spaced her sentences.

"She would hurt again if I killed you. So, I won't. At least for now. But I'm watching you, Nolan Kaminski," she wheezed. "You should know I can always change my mind."

With the help of her cane, Mrs. Thompson plodded away. Nolan had some extra time, so he searched a few more cemetery rows for the surname of Cermak. He doubted the cemetery records would offer any assistance with the limited information Nolan could present, even with the aid of the stone mason's assistant. With a glance at his watch, he gave up his quest and drove back to the diner.

Ellie grimaced when she noticed Nolan's wardrobe: blue jeans, a yellow rugby shirt, and white tennis shoes. Nolan had even washed and pressed the clothes, including washing the sneakers. But after he explained his encounter with the former detective, she turned supportive and encouraging. She suggested they leave the diner before Jamal arrived to quiz Nolan about the prior day's incidents. This was not the type of news story she wished would boost public awareness of Hope Landing.

She pushed Nolan out the door and into her hybrid. During their drive to Salamanca, Nolan briefed Ellie on the events with The Bayview and the reason for Isabel's trip to Oregon. He was summarizing the progress of the project's construction when she pulled off the highway and into a parking space at a shopping mall.

"Ellie, listen," Nolan said, "it's embarrassing for me to admit this, but I can't afford to buy a new wardrobe right now."

"I know a little of your recent financial hardship. You're not the only one who can play detective, Mr. David, or Kaminski. Since Father Andrew and that detective know your identity, I don't get the reason you maintain the ruse."

"I'd been thinking, too. See, the problem is I sort of became Nolan David after I left Erie. I've reacted to that name for more years than I did as Kaminski. I just need some time to decide."

"Fine," Ellie said. "I'm glad that's why. I thought you changed it because you ran, and I sense that won't happen again."

Ellie stepped from the car into a brisk wind, but Nolan remained and stared through the front windshield.

"Let's not argue," Ellie said. "I'm buying you some more presentable clothes as a marketing expense. Hope Landing can reimburse me when they're able."

"It's not that, El. I didn't run from Cermak. After I left, I changed my name because I was ashamed of losing you and angry at my parents for putting me in that position."

She closed her door with a crisp snap, then walked to the passenger side and extended her arm toward the mall.

"I know we need to have all these discussions, Nolan, but not until after we meet with Mr. Shongo. Right now, I'll use every minute to learn, plan, and focus. Improving your appearance is the next step. So, lift that firm butt out of your seat, and let me see you walk with that confident stride that once drove me crazy." Her eyes dazzled again, and Nolan knew he had no choice but to follow her orders. He thought it felt damned good.

After a rapid bout of shopping and an early lunch, Nolan emerged in conservative business attire: simple black Oxford shoes, light gray slacks, a white long-sleeve shirt and a navy-blue sport coat. The sole concession Ellie granted was the button-down collar did not encompass a tie. Nolan assured her he would pay her back as soon as he got the money from his memorabilia collection.

The pair arrived in Salamanca two hours before their appointment, but per Ellie, the timing was perfect. She insisted they become familiar with the town and casino prior to meeting the person who owned much of the county. As always, Ellie Parucci had done her homework, sharing her knowledge of Salamanca, the Seneca Nation, and Oteliani Shongo, as they drove about the area.

Salamanca projected a clean and vibrant atmosphere—a significant twist from the fading aura of Erie. While the town was small, the surrounding images displayed magnificent views of small mountain streams and an abundant forest that was the beginning of Allegheny State Park. Resting in a shallow valley, the sounds of the city were so energetic that each footstep on a sidewalk seemed to generate a soft echo.

At 2:45, Ellie led Nolan to the second-floor offices of the Golden Deer Casino. A youthful assistant with raven hair braided to the middle of her back, accepted Ellie's business card, then requested they relax in the waiting area. Ellie declined the offer of beverages for each of them, ignoring Nolan's glare. One interior wall of the suite contained a large display window with a view that overlooked the active casino. This at least provided a diversion while they waited, since the room held no magazines, brochures, or reading materials of any kind. It seemed obvious visitors were meant to observe the gaming tables, to boost their desire to gamble and become part of the ambiance.

Nolan became impatient after fifteen minutes passed, then opened his mouth to speak to the young woman behind the desk. Ellie laid her soft palm atop his hand, and he stopped. She blinked and nodded at the view of the slot machines.

"I was only going to . . ." Nolan said.

"We discussed this, Nolan." Her voice was like a caring embrace, with more words implied than she ever vocalized.

So they sat and observed the increase of activity in the casino below, as the afternoon progressed. One hour after their appointment time, they received an update.

"Mr. Shongo is detained and requests your patience."

"Thank you," Ellie said. "We appreciate your hospitality."

Nolan lifted his brows at Ellie's comment, then asked, "Did Mr., ah, Shongo indicate about how much longer he would be?"

Nolan picked up the slight frown of Ellie's disapproval of his question before there came a reply.

"Mr. Shongo would have told me to share that information with you if he knew." She paused and inquired again if they would like a beverage. "We have a full bar available if you wish. Besides water and soft drinks, we have beer, wine, and of course, every type of liquor."

"We'd be most grateful for some bottled water, please," Ellie responded.

The assistant slid out of the room and returned without a sound.

"Relax," Ellie whispered. "Isabel warned you this is part of his strategy."

They sipped their bottled water and turned to gaze at the card tables and slots below. After Nolan took several long glances at the assistant, Ellie spoke in a low but firm voice.

"Nolan, must you ogle that young girl? It's rude and demeaning."

"Ogle? No, I'm not. Well, at least not like that," Nolan said. "Her facial features remind me of someone, but I can't place her."

"Well, stop it."

At five, the assistant announced she was leaving for the day but assured them Mr. Shongo knew they were waiting and would return.

"Would you like to listen to the audio, or do you prefer I keep the speakers turned off?"

Ellie and Nolan glanced at each other, neither wishing to admit their ignorance, but Nolan spoke.

"We're afraid we don't know what you mean."

"Oh yes, this office is insulated for privacy, but sometimes Mr. Shongo or our guests enjoy the sounds of the casino below. Here . . ."

She twisted a knob, and the room filled with the chimes and melody of the hundreds of gambling machines, interspersed with some whoops of victory from lucky patrons.

"You can adjust the volume if you wish, with this control behind my desk. No one will object."

"We appreciate your thoughtfulness," Ellie said, "but perhaps silence is best."

"Of course," the young lady said, "and here is our break room." She opened a door to reveal a full kitchen, complete with all the major appliances, and a handsome stainless-steel bar with an adjacent wine cooler. "I'm not suggesting you will be here all night, but you are welcome to help yourselves to any of our selections. I wish you a good evening."

She then exited and bounded down the stairs. Nolan checked the door.

"We can leave, but we can't get back in. The door will lock behind us if we go out."

"So, our chief knows that if we leave, we have abandoned our chance to meet with him. Clever," Ellie said. "One of us could leave, and the other let them back in, but I'll bet it's not quite that simple either."

"There's another door at the bottom of the stairs, and I'm guessing it has the same system. Our options are limited," Nolan said.

Ellie smiled, "Never thought we would be together like this. This is all very bizarre, Nolan David Kaminski. But I would expect nothing less if I created the script myself."

So they waited. Nolan paced while observing the crowd who walked through the gambling area, knowing he could identify the Native American when he approached. Ellie fidgeted and picked every microfiber on her suit that seemed to mar its perfection. The hours ticked by.

At last, Nolan stopped his pacing, and Ellie followed his eyes into the casino. An entourage of businessmen made its way through the crowd. Four hearty men with serious expressions surrounded an elder in the classic diamond shape for his security. An unmistakable silver-haired Oteliani Shongo strode with a broad grin as he waved at his customers, wishing good luck against his own slot machines. He was admired as the leader of the Seneca Nation, but also a legend for his acts of wisdom and chicanery that outwitted the best legal minds of the state of New York. His reputation for bizarre public behavior added to his popularity. He once attended a formal dinner at the governor's mansion and arrived in nothing but a loincloth. He changed shortly after his appearance but caught everyone's attention.

But now, his attire looked as if he was returning from a legitimate business meeting, with a lariat necklace resting atop a ribbed tuxedo shirt and a black suit that appeared like it had been tailored for him yesterday. His formal wear contrasted his rugged and tanned skin. The group disappeared beneath the offices, and this suggested there was a secure entrance to the second-floor office.

Ellie prompted Nolan on some key points of discussion, as they crammed for the presentation so critical to the success of Hope Landing. They were so focused on their task that neither heard a door open or shuffle of a footstep, but the bulk of an odd shape had indeed joined them.

Ellie covered her mouth as she released an eek of surprise, first noticing the beige moccasins in her peripheral vision. Her eyes rose across the white suede slacks secured at the waist by a thin strip of rawhide that touched the muscled abdomen of their host.

Chief Shongo held his arms folded over his bare chest and projected a look of stern distaste at his guests. Ellie's eyes fixed on a magnificent Native American headdress which appeared natural on his frame.

Nolan extended his hand in greeting and said, "Mr. or Chief Shongo, I'm uncertain which you prefer, I take your appearance as a positive sign for our discussion."

"And why do you say that?"

"Very simple," he replied, "no war paint."

CHAPTER TWENTY-FIVE

Lonely Teardrops

Oteliani Shongo transformed to the quintessential business executive, as he listened to his guests describe the reason for their visit. Immediately after his shock appearance, he changed into beige slacks, a brilliant red polo shirt and casual loafers. For over two hours, his questions probed into every segment of Hope Landing as he displayed genuine interest.

"I have respect for your plan and enthusiasm and appreciate your intention of involving the Senecas. While you have not yet asked for financial assistance, I expect we have arrived at that point. However, you must understand my skepticism. The private business sector and the government have a poor history of the benevolent treatment of Native Americans."

He paused and slid a copy of a newspaper clipping about the discovery of tribal graves during the library construction.

"In addition, recent activities by officials of Erie have again shown your lack of concern for our heritage."

"The library expansion," Nolan said.

"Yes, our history speaks of a tribe of our people who were stricken by a disease that left no survivors. They could have sent for help, but would have infected many more of the Senecas, so they did not. We owe the survival of the Seneca Nation and perhaps the Iroquois to this tiny group. Yet your city council ignored the discovery of their burial ground and never even notified the proper officials. Now, you ask me to aid this city."

"I have just learned of this offense which involved one of the city's council members," Nolan said. "But I assure you, Hope Landing is not connected with that contingent of government. In fact, our project seems to have become a target of this same group."

Shongo rose from behind his desk and strode to peer out over his casino.

"The city of Erie has interested me for many years, because of the mystery of our lost brothers. I will consider your proposal overnight, and we shall reconvene in the morning."

Nolan glanced at Ellie, knowing she had a family which expected her return. She held up her cell phone and waved it.

"We appreciate the considerable time you have given us," Nolan said. "Is there any other information you will need to help your decision process?"

"Not at all. You've been quite thorough. Now, you will both stay here at the Golden Deer as my guest, including dinner. Unfortunately, I cannot join you. But since you are somewhat of a gourmet, Mr. David, I am interested in your review of our restaurant."

Ellie and Nolan traded glances a few times as Shongo spoke.

"I sense some discomfort with my invitation. If you are thinking of driving to Erie and returning in the morning, I am absolute in my request you stay. The temperature will approach freezing tonight, and ice forms across the roads from the snow that melted throughout the day. Now, I will arrange for adjoining suites if that is satisfactory."

"Oh, that won't be necessary, Chief," Ellie said. "I mean, we need separate rooms, but they don't have to adjoin."

The chief bid them a good evening. Nolan volunteered to get a table at the restaurant, then wait for Ellie to take care of her obligatory phone calls.

After she returned, they toasted a job well done and were confident of their morning meeting. Nolan informed Ellie that Isabel had arrived in Oregon and was eager to move forward with their plan there. They each made small talk about their lives over the last thirty years before they reached that awkward silence couples often reach on a blind date.

They declined dessert and were sipping coffee, with the faint whirl and chimes of the slots as a welcome distraction.

Ellie broke the stalemate, "He's a good man."

"I expected nothing less," Nolan looked directly into her eyes. "He better be a great man or he'll have me to answer to."

"I tried to find you," Ellie said. "But you know, there was no internet help back then, and every time I got serious about it, my mother somehow found out and reminded me I would break my father's heart. After a while, it seemed too late."

"I didn't realize . . . you were searching for me, and I wasn't easily located. I never kept in contact with anyone here and felt betrayed by about everyone who I thought was my friend."

"Did you ever consider coming back? Before now that is?"

"Oh yeah, lots of times. But then, I got married and was happy and at peace. I was even tempted to return with my wife so I could make amends with my ghosts. However, she was the jealous type." Nolan twirled his cloth napkin into different shapes as he spoke. "I was afraid she would see it in my eyes if I ran into you. She'd a called you a witch like Jake did the other day."

"A witch?" She grinned as her eyes opened wide.

Nolan pumped his open palms down in front of him. "Don't get excited. He told everyone you cast a spell over me."

Ellie muffled her laugh and shook her head.

Nolan told her about his chance encounter with her mother at the cemetery just before Easter Sunday and again the previous morning.

"She's never given up. Her opinion of you is as negative now as it was right after Mary's death. But I don't think she'd shoot you."

"That's comforting."

"I have to ask you a serious question, and I apologize ahead of time for bringing this subject up," Nolan said.

Her expression turned stern as she focused on her coffee. "This isn't about us, is it?"

"No, I'm afraid it's much more grievous than that," he said.

Ellie pivoted her head away, as if she anticipated his direction.

"Did they ever find out about the other driver?"

"No, no. Nothing at all. After you left, speculation increased that you were involved and made it worse at home. There was a time there when I almost believed it myself."

"I should have listened to my instincts the day of your sister's accident. I sensed something might happen," Nolan said. "I never acted on those feelings back then. I had a bad feeling all during the day before my parents died in the train wreck. Yet, I never told my mom or dad. They wouldn't have believed me anyhow. I had a similar sensation when I picked up Mary."

The soft touch of Ellie's fingertips over the back of Nolan's knuckles sent a chill up his back.

"You always had some inner vision," she squeezed his hand, "like sensing when I was in a room. That's a special gift."

"Well, my wife encouraged me to use it. She said I was clairvoyant. I have a heightened sense of awareness. That's all."

A solitary tear escaped Nolan's eye as he stared into the casino.

"I suppose if I was better at what I did, she may be alive today—my wife, that is. She was feeling fine, but I told her it would be a good idea if she had an eye exam. She said she didn't need one. I asked her to do it as a favor to me."

Ellie reached across the table, and her napkin absorbed the tear.

"I'll never forget the look she gave me. She didn't have to ask me. She knew I had an odd feeling again, and they never predicted something good was about to happen. Ten pain-filled months later, she lost the battle."

As they walked through the gaming area, the lights blinked and flashed, but no sounds invaded Nolan's thoughts. His fingertips and Ellie's clung to each other as an attempt at emotional healing. They dared not hold hands, yet they hadn't the courage to separate. Once inside the glass elevator at the center of the casino, patrons could observe a tight embrace that projected the lust of newlyweds. But as the car rose, the couple's tears were concealed from view.

CHAPTER TWENTY-SIX

Lost Love

Throughout the night, Nolan dreamt of his deceased wife and Ellie, with snippets of them alive and together, as friends, or as rivals, or just at peace. He swore he could feel Diane next to him, as he had so often since she left. But in every instance, the dream lacked the warmth of her body. Yet now, his mind felt the connection. This was a total experience, and he could even smell her perfume.

This startled him. The aroma was less sweet than usual but yielded more spice than he recalled. Could she have changed her brand of perfume after death? He was on the brink of awakening but despised the prospect of leaving the comfort of his dream. He then remembered how he would extend his arms to discover nothing but cold linens.

But this time he brushed against delicate strands that tickled the sensory points of his fingertips . . . hair!

"Hair," he spoke aloud while he awoke to a room filling with the grayness of morning light.

Ellie propped herself onto one elbow. Her eyes had lost their sleepiness and were staring at harsh reality.

"Nolan, how dare you sneak into my bed," she challenged. "Get out! Get out now!"

She rolled and her arms thrashed at him, an elbow connecting with the tip of his nose. Blood spurted across his white shirt.

Ellie bolted out of bed to see Nolan gazing in awe at his blood-splattered shirt while he tried to use a sheet to stem the flow.

They were both realizing they had fallen asleep in each other's arms while they discussed the lost opportunities of life, plus the impossibility of any relationship for them beyond friendship.

"I'm sorry," Ellie said. "Oh, dear God, how did this happen?"

"So much for my clairvoyance; I sure didn't see this coming."

Nolan exercised caution as he stood, allowing red droplets to be absorbed by a handful of tissues he snapped up from the bedside table.

"Look at your shirt. It's ruined," Ellie said, giggled, and then expanded to a full chortle as she doubled over and pointed at Nolan.

"What's so funny, Mrs. Ellie Parucci?" Nolan asked. "We have a meeting with a rather stern-faced business leader in just over an hour."

She couldn't stop laughing, trying to express the source of her elation.

"You," she said as she touched his bloody cheek and howled. "Your shirt," she tried again. "Your face," she had a point to make indeed.

"War paint!" She spit out the words and Nolan fell into the contagious chuckling fit that possessed them both.

But the hilarity had to subside as they faced the problem of Nolan's wardrobe, not to mention the swollen nose that oozed a slight stream of red, an improvement from the previous globs. They decided the nose was not broken. Still, the entire center of Nolan's face was becoming a showcase for the color purple.

Over the next hour, Ellie demonstrated her innovativeness under pressure while she purchased items from the gift shop to make the best of the situation. She insisted she bandage Nolan for the visit first, to allow her to better gauge her preparation time for their appointment.

As they entered the casino offices, the same dark-haired assistant displayed a poker face as she led the pair into the private office of Chief Shongo. As he stood to greet them, his expression remained stoic, but Nolan could swear there was a slight wrinkle of a smile at the corner of the leader's mouth.

Shongo introduced the assistant as his granddaughter, and Nolan once again knew her facial features were familiar but could not place her.

"I trust your accommodations were satisfactory?" asked the chief.

Ellie responded, "Yes, the dinner was exquisite, and the rooms were most comfortable, Mr. Shongo."

Her cheeks blushed as she continued, "Please allow me to explain Nolan's appearance is all my fault."

Shongo's left hand extended in front of his chest as he spoke. "I prefer no explanation." Then he lowered his hand. "I consider both of you honorable, and I am certain any spoken details will minimize the tale that is developing among my staff. Your hurried purchases this morning, the bloodstained sheets, and only one bed was slept in. While I know your account will be simple and pure, my staff enjoys weaving their own interpretations."

Ellie and Nolan both relaxed, neither raising any objection.

"Now, I have considered your request and made my decision," the chief said. "However, I have one task I wish you to consider before I give you my answer."

Both Ellie and Nolan agreed to help the chief with whatever he had in mind.

"I ask you delay any further construction of your library so our tribal historians may search the grounds and recover any remains of the ancient tribe."

Ellie and Nolan shared a worrisome look, then Nolan responded.

"Mr. Shongo, we appreciate the respect you have given us, so please accept my words with that in mind. Because of the structure of our government, I cannot assure you we can meet your request. However, you have my word we will pursue legal action to achieve your goal."

Ellie nodded her agreement, and they both peered at Chief Shongo. Nolan could feel the cold drops of perspiration drip down the sides of his chest.

"Very well, your best efforts are all I can expect. Thank you. Now, I have someone who will help me explain my decision." Then he rose, and his open arms enveloped the torso of a female who slipped into the office. As they separated, Nolan recognized Jane, the carpenter who was so impressed with Jake's woodworking skills. She had a striking resemblance to the chief's granddaughter.

"I confess I've had a spy in your midst. Jane is my youngest daughter, and she speaks with high regard of your endeavors."

"I hope you will both forgive me," Jane said, "for I will also be your representative of Native American customs in Hope Landing."

As Ellie drove them back to Erie, they both felt good about their trip's results, despite Nolan's expanding bruise beneath his eyes. Nolan shared his efforts to sell his autographed sports photo to fund the payment of the delinquent taxes on The Bayview and acquire that property. He would also assign Father Andrew to consult with an attorney regarding an injunction to halt the library construction until the court could review the request to search for the burial remains of the Senecas.

Neither broached their evening together until they were about five minutes from the diner.

"I've got to tell my husband, you know."

A full minute passed as Nolan pondered an appropriate response.

"But nothing happened. Are you certain you want to do that?"

"He'll understand, and he'll also believe me when I tell him that nothing happened. If he learns about this later, after the rumors have expanded, it will look like I tried to hide this from him, and the truth would become unbelievable."

"Will you be able to continue with the project?" Nolan asked.

"Don't be stupid. He doesn't tell me what to do."

Before they could conclude their conversation, they noticed Jake leaping up and down in front of the diner, waving his arms in the air. As Ellie parked, and they exited, Jake was sobbing at Nolan's side.

"Jake, Jake, settle down. Please."

The young man was shaking his head from side to side, wringing his hands as he tried to explain.

"Jake, is it your mother?" Ellie asked. "Is Marge all right?"

"I'm so sorry, Mr. David." But his mumbling became unintelligible again, and Clifton strolled out the front door and approached.

"Clifton, what's going on?"

"I hate to be the one to tell you this," said Clifton. Then, while he appeared to reach deep within his soul for the right words, Jake blurted out, "Somebody stole Babe Ruth."

CHAPTER TWENTY-SEVEN

A New Start

"There's nothing under your bed, either," Clifton said. "They must have taken them both."

"Both?" Ellie asked.

"There were two photos of Ted Williams and Babe Ruth in uniform together, but one of them had real signatures," said Jake. "The other was a forgery." Jake spoke with pride and authority.

"Well, what are you planning do now, Nolan?" Ellie asked. "That photo was your seed money for the Bayview."

"First thing is to call the police, although I'm pretty sure I know where that's going to lead," Nolan said.

"I'm afraid I've got to get back and work on this marketing plan. I don't want to be delayed by the police, and then the media will show up," Ellie said.

"Please wait a minute," Nolan said. "Jake, could you let me speak alone with Clifton and Ellie before they leave? I'd like you to talk to the police about this, so get yourself ready, and I'll be right in."

"I can stick around if you need me," Clifton said.

"No, you can't. I want you to take off soon and take my car with you."

Nolan walked toward his SUV and waved for his friends to follow. He lifted the vehicle's rear gate, unhooked a few snaps and raised a carpeted section of the floor. The shrink-wrapped photo lay snuggled in the revealed storage compartment.

"Here's the photo with the authentic signatures. If whoever has the forgery attempts to sell it, they'll be exposed."

"Then you can't call the police and report it stolen if it's not," Clifton said. "And you've got to tell Jake."

"Sorry, can't do that," Nolan said. He explained Jake couldn't fake his concern if the boy knew the genuine photo was safe. He would also report the theft with precise accuracy, detailing that the stolen photo had the signature of Ted Williams. If his car was nearby, it was likely the police would search his vehicle as a matter of routine, so he asked Clifton to drive it somewhere, and Nolan would pick it up later. He next gave Ellie a big hug goodbye before she could object and moaned as she nudged her shoulder into his nose to show her displeasure with his move.

"Wow, that looks painful," Clifton said. "Is it broken?"

"Don't think so." Nolan glanced at the puzzled look on Clifton's face. "I'm not talkin' about it, Clifton. So, don't ask."

"You know, I sort of felt that might be the case. Fine by me." Ellie and he then left while Nolan awaited the police.

Nolan expected his shadow Pete would respond to his report of stolen baseball memorabilia, but an aging team of two officers arrived and conducted a very thorough inquiry. It appeared the pair knew nothing of the photo prior to their arrival.

As expected, Jake was despondent and blamed himself for the missing photograph, even though he was the person who discovered its disappearance.

Of course, the police were more inquisitive about Nolan's colorful appearance, but he remained steadfast with his insistence the injury had no relation to the theft. When pressed, he admitted he had too much to drink the night before and tried to headbutt a slot machine. Neither of the officers believed that, but Jake supported the fact Nolan did not have the injury prior to his trip to Salamanca.

Nolan assured the officers they could call Chief Shongo to get a personal alibi for Nolan's absence during the time in question.

"Besides, there's no insurance," Nolan said. "That sort of takes away any motive for my involvement."

The police agreed but promised nothing. They would broadcast the details of the photo with the state police and local collectors. It was their opinion someone had followed Nolan from Atlanta, then waited for him to leave to allow them the opportunity to steal the photo. Nolan nodded and thanked them for their keen insight. He was also happy when they left. He almost confided in Jake, but the teenager was so sincere in his emotions that Nolan felt he would be unable to conceal the ruse.

As foreseen, a television news crew and Jamal Moore were waiting outside the diner when the police exited. For once, Nolan was pleased to see the media. He downplayed the theft and hinted that the Seneca Native Americans were most willing to become significant investors in Hope Landing. He shared many of the facts of the successful discussion with Chief Shongo and referenced the efforts to obtain a court injunction to stop the library construction. Nolan addressed the successes of their meeting, minus the incident that produced his colorful and swollen appearance.

As the camera crew left, Nolan grabbed Jamal's sleeve and nodded for him to stay. At Ellie's suggestion, Nolan took the reporter into his confidence about his theories behind the theft of the Williams and Ruth photo. Nolan explained that Sly Cermak or one of his associates were his prime suspects, who were out to destroy Nolan's financial ability to pay the delinquent property taxes for The Bayview Restaurant. He wanted Jamal's blog to broadcast the fiscal benefit of the support of the Seneca Nation and minimize the hardship of the stolen photo. They both knew that Jamal's boss monitored the blog and had a direct line to someone connected to Ashley Pershing and Sly Cermak's efforts. Their plan to preach prosperity for Hope Landing might cause some movement by their opposition.

"There's something else you should know," Jamal said. "The horse racetrack has scheduled their grand opening for Memorial Day. One of the other reporters told me my boss is complaining about the Hope Landing project taking away some of the focus from the racetrack because of your plans to open on the same day. That'll make it real tough for Hope Landing to draw any kind of crowd. I heard the track will offer free refreshments and snacks to keep everyone away from your event."

"Well, I'm not worried about that foolish racetrack, my dear Jamal. Our goal is to attract a different demographic customer than the track: families with children, adults interested in our country's heritage, and those who visit for excellent food either before or after their beach time across the bay. We can coexist in peace with the horses. I believe Ashley Pershing's group has something different going on, and she's using the ponies as a distraction."

"What could that be?"

"I hope you tell me when you find out."

"Me? How am I going to find out? I don't know anything about that."

"That's simple. You're the investigative reporter, and I have confidence in you."

Jamal peered at Nolan and squinted.

"I'm serious. Go investigate. Do your blog. The good guys need you."

The reporter plodded toward his car, a rusted compact Chevrolet, with enough dents that it may be a demolition derby reject.

"Hey Jamal, do you have any money?"

"Why do you ask me that? I like your project, but I'm not giving you my savings."

"Of course not. But come by tomorrow with your checkbook. I got a way you can make a great first impression with the ladies."

CHAPTER TWENTY-EIGHT

Lady in Waiting

Nolan continued his activities at a rapid pace the next day. Isabel was meeting in an Oregon prison with the son of the deceased owner of The Bayview Restaurant in an Oregon prison, and he made headway in the movement of funds to step up overall plans for opening Hope Landing's first phase.

He drove Clifton's pickup down to The Landing construction site and discovered the group hard at work. Their progress was amazing, and it appeared they could meet a Memorial Day timetable if they didn't hit any snags. He then noticed the paddle wheeler, which provided tourists with rides around the bay. She was docked and had some movement aboard.

Nolan walked over and stepped aboard, where he located the obvious owner, busy cleaning the bench seats inside the main deck's covered area. The wooden decks were worn but well maintained, and the white gloss finish of the framing showed she was pampered. Nolan was certain the observation deck also glistened and was prepared for the season's first voyage.

"Mr. Hanssen," Nolan called out to not alarm the aging sailor.

The man turned and scowled at his unexpected visitor.

"I see you found the time to come talk with me," the gray-bearded guy said.

"I was waiting for you to show up and get your boat ready for the season," Nolan said. "I didn't know I was expected."

"Li Na warned me two days ago you were going to stop by."

He paused his cleaning and rested his narrow frame on one of the long, varnished benches. "She said you were responsible for all that racket coming from Aaron's place."

"Yes, that would be me."

Nolan introduced himself and got to the point.

"Did Li Na explain what we were trying to do here?"

"Yep, she sure did. I was sorry to hear her father was not doing well. He and I could tip a few in days gone by."

"Mr. Hanssen, I know you've been running this business for many years. I suspect that like everyone else around here, you've seen better times. But I don't understand why you've never transported people to the isle across the bay. Seems like that route would be natural."

"Call me Fergie. I'll be happy to answer any question you toss at me, but you gotta answer me one first."

"I've heard lots about what's goin' on—The Landin', flirtin' with an old high school flame and all the while gettin' some mighty powerful people pissed off at ya for doin' whatever the hell you're doin.' But why here? Why Erie? You're a smart fella, no doubt. But why pick this town where we can't even afford to pick up our own garbage?"

Nolan sat on a bench. "I came here for personal reasons, but something came to me when I was eating breakfast here on my very first day back. There's good people here. Always has been. I remember all the different ethnic festivals my dad would take me to as a kid. We had the Greeks, Italians, Germans, Poles, Brits, Irish, Chinese and so on. Then we have all the churches and clubs that match those nationalities. And you're all getting screwed. There's probably fifty or more cities just like Erie, gasping for their economic breath.

But I'm from here and I want people to be proud of what we have and by God, we just might be able to make this happen."

Fergie nodded and rubbed his bony knee. "Seems like an honest answer so now I'll answer you. I tried that trip across the Bay plenty. I just couldn't get any customers."

"I heard the state park wouldn't give you a permit to land. That true?"

"Hell, that wasn't the problem a'tall. I could've got me a permit any time."

The lanky man rose and gestured for Nolan to follow. Fergie hobbled forward, through a doorway, and then they were on the bridge. The captain bent his frame beneath the instruments, opened a small compartment and displayed a bottle of Canadian Club and two short glasses. His grin revealed more gaps than teeth as he twisted the cap.

"If you want to hear the tale, then you've gotta share some pleasure with an old man."

He poured two fingers of the caramel-colored liquid into each of the glasses without hesitation. The sharing of whiskey was part of the account. Fergie clinked his glass bottom to the tip of Nolan's, then sat on a padded bench and began his story. Nolan sat across from him.

"In good times, I had plenty of customers. Even *Lady* here had a smaller offspring of sorts."

Nolan furrowed his brow.

"Sorry, you were never introduced. This here's *Lady of the Bay*, a fifty-foot diesel paddlewheel that's over seventy-five years old. Back in our glory years, she gave birth to a smaller version, which I called *Babe of the Bay*. I thought plenty of times back then that I may give transportation o'er to the isle, but business was too good right here. There was no need. My wife, Belle, and I even experimented with nighttime dining cruises, but the waters were not agreeable enough, so we gave that up. But the isle rides were always my ace in the hole."

"What do you mean?"

"Belle always told me we would start giving transport if business ever slowed. We both knew the deck was stacked again' us, but we figured the mayor was a sensible enough man that we could work it out."

"What happened?"

"Business turned down in the eighties. Then Belle took sick in the winter of ninety and was gone by spring. So, I retired the *Babe*, and me and the *Lady* here have been a couple ever since."

Fergie took a long sip and set himself on the captain's chair.

"So, I made plans for totin' people across the bay. I found three good spots to dock and had handshake agreements with each of 'em. Next, I got a visit from some hot shot police detective who suggested my plan wouldn't work."

"Sly Cermak?" Nolan asked.

"Yep. He had a piss-poor attitude, he did. Told me he was there to make sure I had considered all the consequences. There would be weather to deal with and the choppy water, the additional cost of insurance and the good chance I'd go broke and perhaps face criminal charges if I lost a passenger or worse during a rough crossing. He was real polite with his words, but it was clear his intentions were not to help me."

"When I told him I appreciated his tips but would take my chances anyhow, he said he would need to report me to the IRS, since he had a suspicion I was not reportin' all my cash income. I made him get the hell off my boat, and then my real trouble began."

"How so?"

"I started my water taxi across the bay, and business got good. I learned some members of the city council and a few of their cronies had considerable investments on the one road with access to the isle. Restaurants, motels, even the amusement park were all owned, at least in part by this group. They didn't want any business in the dock area to do well and considered us a nuisance. Little things happened. First, I never had a mooring fee in all the years I was workin' the bay. Then one day I got a notice that I would have to pay a fifty dollar a day fee to secure my *Lady* to the dock. I had the *Babe* secured right next to her, so had to move her to a slip at the yacht club that a friend of mine donated. The IRS indeed audited me but came out fine other than the weeks of visits from this government character who just drove more customers away."

"Sounds like you were surviving the battle, though."

"I was, at least until they fired the next shot. I came to work one mornin' and found parking meters installed up, down, and everywhere around the dock. Parking meters. They were all installed in one night and with two-hour limits. Now, no one could take a thirty-minute one-way water shuttle to the beach if they could stay a maximum of one hour, then forced to return to feed the meter."

"So, you gave up then."

"Hell no, I didn't give up. I worked it out with my friends 'round here that we would care for each other's meters. We took turns pluggin' quarters whenever we had a chance and promised we'd pay the parking tickets to our customers if we had to. We were winnin' again, by golly."

The old salt tipped his glass again and took a long swig before he continued.

"Then I got the phone call that told me I was finished. The *Babe* exploded in her slip and was a complete loss. Nothing was left of her. That wiped me out 'cause I just didn't lose the boat, but Belle's ashes were aboard. I secured her urn to the wheel, so she'd be real comfortable. When I got to the *Lady* that day, I found that urn right here on the bridge. Belle's ashes were gone, and there was a note inside."

Fergie paused and emptied his glass of the last few drops.

"And?"

"THE LADY IS NEXT. That's what the note said. I stopped the isle taxi that morning. I knew that detective fella was behind it all, but I couldn't call a cop. Anyhow, people knew he had some kid doing stuff for him, 'cause he wouldn't get his fingers dirty himself."

Nolan looked at the sorrowful expression the memories had brought back to this gentle soul.

"I can understand you not wanting to help. And I appreciate you sharing your grief. I'm sorry."

Fergie poured a quick stream of whiskey into each of their glasses, and once again clinked Nolan's glass.

"Hell, that was the worst decision I ever made. I swore if another chance came along, I'd go down fightin' with my *Lady*. So now you're givin' me that. Let's drink to that crazy idea of yours. What do you call it?"

"Hope Landing," Nolan replied.

"Gracious sakes, hope is sure what we all need. Count me and the *Lady* in on your plan."

As they emptied their glasses together, the old man's eyes revealed a slight glimmer that had been in shadows for too many years.

CHAPTER TWENTY-NINE

Busted

While awaiting word from Isabel, Nolan set plans in motion to sell his car and the Ruth-Williams photo, as well as holding another meeting with all the key representatives of Hope Landing. Father Andrew and he filled the last slots on the list of ethnic origins, and Nolan was confident each person had enough strength and stamina to survive a rough start.

Father Andrew closed out Mexico with a family who worked harvesting grapes during the fall but stayed in the area and cooked for an eatery that catered to the factory workers who made food products from the that same fruit. Nolan convinced a fellow restaurateur in Atlanta to allow his son to take over his Indian restaurant there, which enabled his friend to come to Erie and assume the representation of India.

Aaron only worked at the diner on a rare occasion, since he spent most of his time caring for his dainty Irish lass, as he called Marge. She was now on crutches and threatened to use them to crack Aaron's thick skull if he ever thought of cheating on her. She also said if she could figure out how to carry a plate filled with food while maneuvering herself on the cumbersome sticks then she would evict the Turk moocher from her home. Everyone realized they were in love.

Nolan and his growing crew were disappointed with the morning news. After all the attention and television reporters from the previous night, only a snippet about the theft of the baseball photo was broadcast.

The newspaper story was likewise shortened, but Nolan was happy to see Jamal got his byline. Nolan was troubled that Pete was no longer on his tail and did not accept that fact as evidence he was less of a concern for Ashley Pershing and her associates. Also, there was no mention of the efforts to obtain an injunction to stop the library construction, and Nolan had hoped for at least a one-line reference.

Meanwhile, the blog was doing well, and Ellie's advertisements were beginning the following day on some radio stations. Nolan spent over an hour on the phone with her, and he was amazed at the amount of work she already accomplished.

She created several internet banners and ads about Hope Landing, and the park now had its own website. Likewise, the project was creating an identity on Facebook, YouTube, TikTok, Twitter, Pinterest, Instagram, and others. They would broadcast a radio infomercial on Blog Radio. Other sites had streaming media capabilities to post part of the radio spot as additional advertisements.

Clifton offered all good news regarding the construction. All the fittings and connections had passed inspection, and they now waited for the certificate of occupancy. Even the fire marshal had completed his visit and provided verbal approval. But the insurance and licensing needed the CO to issue their credentials, which would allow Hope Landing to open their doors to the public. The project was several days ahead of schedule, with Memorial Day a mere two weeks away.

Nolan also arranged for Father Andrew to deliver the photo to the Pony Express. They decided a priest was perhaps the least probable candidate to come under scrutiny for the shipment of a large package. The collector had a long-standing offer on the table to Nolan, and while he knew he could do better at public auction, time was of the essence. He also placed the memorabilia community on alert to watch for the forgery to become available, and was thrilled to learn Nolan marked the fake so they could easily identify it.

Nolan guessed he could locate his young reporter friend at his customary table in the back of the cigar and sandwich shop. The sign announced, "Sammy's Deli," but Nolan would bet cigars out-sold hoagies by at least two to one. Sammy had a walk-in humidor in a corner at the rear of the store, and their few dine-in tables sat outside that entrance. This posed no problem except when customers would sample the stogies and exit with a trail of accompanying smoke which settled in the snack area.

Jamal was busy tapping keys on his laptop and didn't notice Nolan approach.

"Hey, Jamal, you bring your checkbook?"

"Hi. I was answering some postings on the blog. I'm getting overwhelmed with questions and comments, so had to leave the office and set up shop here for a while."

Nolan shook his head as he noticed the narrow yellow tie, faded and adorned with a pattern of greasy stains. The reporter also wore a dull green blazer over a pale white shirt, which was so thin you could see the T-shirt underneath.

"Don't get up. I don't want to see the color of your slacks."

"They're khaki. I saw some sports guys on TV about a month ago, and they were dressed just like this."

Nolan thought for a moment and put the green jacket combo together. "Oh yeah, The Masters. Kid, I don't want to hurt your feelings, but you couldn't trade your entire outfit for a single golf tee."

"You know, I do my best to be nice to you. So why are you always picking on me?"

"Heck, that's easy," Nolan replied. "I care about you. I'm trying to improve you. Sort of like a father-son thing."

Nolan looked up at the whiteboard with the limited menu options. "Jamal, how about a corned beef on rye with Swiss cheese? Today's special, and I'm buying."

The reporter grinned. "Can you add fries to mine?"

Nolan gave the order, then sat at the tiny table with Jamal.

"You sure have an odd way of showing you care."

"What more do you want? I'm buying lunch. We'll get into my philosophy of parenting some other time, but right now I'm here to help advance your image."

"We're not off to a great start. What'd ya do? Buy me new underwear?"

"Ho, ho, ho. The Comedy Channel awaits you. Listen, let's have a serious conversation."

The sandwiches were up on the countertop already, and Nolan fetched and delivered. "Here you are, my friend."

Jamal slathered his sandwich with mustard, then squeezed an impressive pile of ketchup onto his fries.

Nolan closed his eyes in a long blink. "You keep that up, and your arteries will be clogged before you're fifty." He took a bite of his corned beef. "Not bad for a cigar store lunch, I suppose."

He pointed at Jamal. "Serious question. When was the last time you had a date?"

"Oh no, we're not going there. You can pick on my clothes all you want, but my social life is not fair game."

"All right, let me tell you. It's been longer than you'd like it to be. I don't know your sexual preference, but no matter what, your social activities are not as frequent as you'd prefer. True?"

"Sort of. But I've been busy with the blog and all these news stories. You're somewhat responsible for the slowdown in my social life, so you shouldn't harass me about it."

Nolan nodded. "I agree and am ashamed. That's why I came to help you."

The young man sat back in his chair and folded his arms, then leaned against the wall and balanced it on the rear legs.

"Tell me a little about your last date—a proper date, not an arranged one."

"How did you . . ."

"I have one question about that event. Did you drive?"

"Yeah, I kinda drove. I picked her up at her house."

Nolan relaxed and allowed the silence to dictate the tale.

"Well, we got outta the restaurant, and we couldn't get my car open."

Nolan stared at Jamal, waiting.

"The passenger door never opens, but the girl pressed the button down when she got out, thinking she was doing me a favor. But she didn't know the key didn't open the door. It's been busted for a while."

Nolan remained silent, shaking his head as Jamal continued.

"It wasn't her fault. I tried to open the door, believe me. I even proposed we take rideshare or a taxi, but she'd given up on me by then. She called her mother for a ride home."

Nolan tried not to smile. "Uh, second date go any better?"

"Wasn't any. She wouldn't even let her mother give me a ride. I had to walk home."

Nolan laid his car keys on the laptop keyboard.

"Blue Book's fifteen grand. But I like you and want to help. Plus,

I need the cash for Hope Landing. The tank's full and the tires have plenty of air and tread. $10,000, and she's yours."

"I don't have enough. $7,500. I'm assuming there's no warranty."

"Correct." Nolan chewed his corned beef while he thought. "How about $8,500, and I'll pay for the first oil change?"

"What are you going to drive?"

"Public transportation, hitchhike, you know, all the usual methods of getting around that are used by a successful businessman."

"Seriously. I'm not going to take your ride knowing you'll be out there begging. Besides, your project is now, short term. What are you going to do when you want to go back home?"

Nolan thought briefly. "That's easy, Jamal. I believe in being unselfish and that's one of the reasons I've been successful. Right now, that vehicle is a cash cow, and I want to milk her for the sake of our project. After that my positive outlook will make things happen. Life usually works out that way for me."

"I'll have to transfer some money from my savings," Jamal said.

"Your social activities are about to multiply significantly. You won't be sorry." Nolan was on the bus for only a few seconds before he missed his SUV. Almost every place he visited in Erie was on the bus line, and he could use rideshare as backup.

After he ate dinner at the diner, he got some exercise and walked down to Paddy's. It was about a two-mile coast downhill, and he arrived in time to join Clifton, Jane, and several of the crew. He had a couple of beers and learned most of the hard work was done, so this was a celebration of sorts. The last tidbits were clean up, signage, and administrative items. Jane and Marge were planning to create menu ideas and design interior decorations the next morning. Clifton's wife, Evelyn, would also assist. This pleased Nolan since he felt Marge would handle the practical issues, while Evelyn would add some elegance to the décor.

They were all surprised Nolan sold his SUV but appreciated his efforts to get the injunction. Jane drove him back to the diner and told him the Senecas would have paid for the attorney if Nolan had asked her father.

"We're both proud men, Jane. That wasn't the deal, and I'm not going back on my word," Nolan said.

He bid her a good evening and walked toward the rear entrance to his room. A few patron's cars were still in the parking lot, and he was pleased business held up with all the changes that occurred. Customers in Erie were definitely creatures of habit.

When he approached the corner of the building, the hairs on the back of his neck bristled, and he sensed he was being watched. The few vehicles appeared unoccupied, and he thought of Pete. Perhaps the young police officer was improving his skills.

Then, he noticed a small wisp of smoke, or maybe a release of warm breath into the frosty air. Whichever, he was certain someone was at his entrance. He halted.

"Who's there?" Nolan asked.

His voice was strong and confident, projecting well in the still night.

The figure who stepped from around the corner lay in shadows with an unfamiliar outline. He projected an ignoble appearance, even though he was as tall as Nolan and trim. But the man stood with slumped shoulders and shifted his weight from foot to foot. His gloved hands formed fists, but he held his arms stiff, disabling the fluid movements you would see in an attacker.

"Are you Nolan?" The stranger spoke with a mild stutter, then stopped his advance.

"I'm Nolan David. Who are you?"

"I'm Joe Parucci," the voice said, "Ellie's husband." He emphasized the last phrase with a ring of pride.

"I'm pleased to meet you, Joe. Ellie's told me lots of good things
about you."

The silence continued for at least a full minute before Nolan
spoke again.

"You've been out here quite a while, Joe. If you want to come
into the diner, I'll buy you a cup of coffee."

More silence.

"You slept with my wife," the voice stated this as fact with less
emotion than the words should dictate.

"I sort of slept with Ellie, but you already know the entire story.
Come on in and let me get to know the man who Ellie fell in love
with. I figure if you were going to shoot me, it would've happened
by now, so let's talk this through."

Nolan turned and walked to the front of the diner and heard Joe
maintaining several paces distance between them. Neither Bootsie
nor Aaron were working, but Kade and his wife were inside.

Joe's back remained rigid, with a stiff grip around the ceramic
cup filled with black coffee. He had removed his gloves and was
using the mug to warm his hands.

"Would you care for something to eat?" Nolan asked.

"Please don't be nice to me," Joe said. "I've got some things to
tell you, and I want to be certain you understand."

So far, Nolan thought Joe was speaking like he practiced his
delivery in front of a mirror.

"Alright, Joe. Say what you need to. But you have my sincere
apology and assurances nothing happened that night."

Joe took a sip from his coffee before he continued.

"I wish you never came back, Nolan Kaminski. You've been like a ghost in Ellie's life, and you shouldn't have returned. Not now, after all these years. It's not fair."

"Joe, I . . ."

Joe raised his fist at Nolan. "Let me speak. You have no right to be in my marriage."

Nolan sat back and allowed Joe to explain.

"But you have been. Every few years I heard about the great Nolan Kaminski. Track star, scholar, musician, leader. When I first met Ellie, she told me right up front she didn't expect us to date for long, 'cause you would be coming back. Five years later, I convinced her you weren't."

Joe was now settling in with his emotions and emptied a packet of sugar into his coffee, then proceeded.

"On the night before our wedding, she called every one of your old friends to see if they heard from you. Nothing. You were a ghost. Things got better every year of our marriage. But now and then, one of her friends would bring up your name. A few years ago, I found her searching the internet's obituaries for you. I said, 'Good God, Ellie, it's been over twenty-five years, and you haven't heard from this guy. Why would you be browsing for him on the internet?'"

Nolan lowered his head and did not look at Joe.

"You know what she said?"

Nolan shook his head with compassion.

"Hell no, you don't know. Cause you weren't there. She said she worried about you. Worried about *you*! That was the first time we ever argued in all our years together. I tried to remain calm when she told me you were back in town, and she was going to visit. The right thing to do was support her. I even thought, okay, she would find out you were just a damn human and didn't remember her. Next, she told me she signed you up as one of her clients, *for free!*"

Joe's decibel level rose, and their conversation grabbed the focus of the few patrons, plus Aaron's son and his fiancé.

"Then, she comes back from an unexpected overnight trip with you, and she first warns me to not get upset, but you slept in the same room together. On the same bed, I later learn. But don't worry, honey, nothing happened, and we had our clothes on. Is that supposed to make me feel better? Of course, I believe her, but you slept with my wife."

Joe's voice thundered, and Nolan glanced away to see Kade approaching from the kitchen. Nolan's peripheral vision captured the blur of movement from Joe's arm, as he turned his head to absorb the full force of the punch on his already bruised nose.

Nolan saw Joe's dim figure leave the restaurant as he lay on the floor with another stream of blood spouting from his nose plus a ringing in his ears.

Kade handed him a wad of napkins and asked, "Nolan, are you okay? Should I call the police or an ambulance? We're all witnesses."

Nolan waved his friends off. "Now, it's broken. This just shows you, Kade," Nolan said, "if you try hard enough, you can even hurt a ghost."

CHAPTER THIRTY

Native American Cavalry

Clifton relaxed as he waited for Nolan to be released from the emergency room. The nose indeed was broken this time, and the ER staff bandaged and fit it with a plastic guard to prevent further damage. The once rainbow-like colors that ran in many fine lines across his cheeks were now replaced with deep purple bruises that covered his face from his lips to his hairline. Nolan's pain lessened thanks to the pills, and he was grateful for his decision to get treatment.

"How do I look?" he asked Clifton.

"Like a badger on withdrawal from OxyContin," replied Clifton. "Did you sleep with Ellie? I mean, I wouldn't blame you, but that sure will mess up Hope Landing."

Nolan rose from the required wheelchair as he exited the hospital and noticed the clock on city hall displayed it was almost midnight.

"Clifton, I didn't have sex with her. I promise you."

"For some reason, I believe you a lot more than I did the last guy who used that line."

Nolan turned down Clifton's offer to get the car and insisted on walking to the parking garage.

"Isabel called and gave me a very specific message. She said you just purchased The Bayview for seven thousand dollars' worth of cigarettes and Twinkies. She's on her way to an airport and should be taking off about now."

"That's significant news, Clifton. Even with the forty thousand for property taxes, that's still a great buy on that property. One of those things you can't afford, but you can't afford not too either."

Back in his room, Nolan picked up his active journal for the first time in several nights. He finally had a few moments and began an entry that relaxed him. He summarized the progress of Hope Landing and was finishing his words about Ellie when a tear dropped onto the page.

Nolan slept with unexpected comfort and a trace of excitement. His wife came to him many times this night, encouraging him to pursue Ellie. If he followed her advice, he would tempt Ellie to destroy her marriage. Each time his wife visited, Nolan's desire for Ellie to join him in his room renewed the cycle.

At last, the sequence broke as he awoke to Ellie sitting on his bed and calling his name. He dared not reach out to her—the painful image of his last experience flashed caution to his brain. Then she called his name again, and he mumbled his reply. "Ellie, is that you?"

She touched his hair, and he winced. She was real.

"El, what are you doing here?"

"My tough guy. Joe told me he leveled you, and I wasn't certain he was telling me the truth. You didn't fight back, did you?"

Nolan blinked, fighting an escaping tear.

"I deserved to get slugged." He pushed himself up in the bed, so his shoulders rested on the backboard. "I just didn't believe he had it in him. Joe loves you, El."

"I know he does, and we've now had our second argument, but it's got to stop here."

Nolan nodded, and his head feigned implosion.

"We're having a meeting tonight." He reached out and covered her hand. "Do you think you can make it?"

"I'll be there. Joe knows I'm committed to this project, and what's more important, he knows I love him."

He brushed her fingertips. "Does he know you love me too?"

"I'm sure he told you that last night." She leaned forward and kissed his forehead as he closed his eyes, then drifted back to sleep.

Nolan next awoke to read the digital clock at 10:03 a.m. He remembered his one o'clock appointment with the attorney about the injunction and needed to get an update from Isabel about her trip. Then he recalled Ellie's visit and his dreams. He wasn't sure if her presence was reality or a dream, but figured he would find out as the day went on.

Deep thoughts in the shower helped him plan his to-do list, and he learned a broken nose touched the nerves in his entire face, so shaving became a painful experience. He affixed his plastic guard and thought the mirror reflected an image from a horror movie.

As he strolled downstairs for coffee, he was glad to see Aaron in the kitchen.

"Nolan, my friend, I am here on a mission of mercy from Miss Marge." He approached Nolan with his arms open, prepared to embrace him, but Nolan turned and raised his hand to his face.

"No Turkish greetings this morning, Aaron. I've had more than enough people mashing me over the past few days."

"As you wish, dear friend." He handed him a message slip. "You have many calls from Moe at this number. He pushed me to wake you, but I told him a beautiful woman tried but failed already. How could I do better than that?"

Ellie. Her visit was real.

"Moe's my broker for my baseball collection. He must have received the photo."

Nolan phoned his broker and arranged for the wire transfer of funds into the Hope Landing account. Moe tried to persuade Nolan to wait for the sale until a Sotheby's auction in two months. He promised Nolan he would receive twice as much then, and in all likelihood, much more. But Nolan needed the fifty thousand as soon as possible and couldn't wait.

The broker confirmed the collector community was on alert for the forgery, and that controversy was already driving up the starting price of the authentic photo with anticipation they would sell it at Sotheby's. By the end of the conversation, Nolan was booting himself for his forced decision, but recognized he had no other options.

"Miss Isabel called a short time ago," said Aaron. "She is home and going to sleep. I will be your taxi driver today and take you everywhere. Don't worry about the bus schedule."

"He can also ride with a real Native American chief's daughter." The voice came from Jane, who was leaning against the kitchen doorway, attired in a rich-black business suit and a pleated white blouse. She explained she hoped to accompany Nolan and Father Andrew to their meeting with the attorney.

"Jane, I'm honored to have you join us. Besides, I feel there's much more to you than a pretty face wielding a hammer. Aaron, I hate to break this to you. I have an option to ride with you, or with this attractive young lady. Who do you believe I should choose?"

"I am forbidden from seeing beautiful women from now on. So perhaps it is best I do not drive. I've seen two already, and it's not even lunch."

Jane, Father Andrew, and Nolan organized their presentation prior to their visit with the attorney, who Chief Shongo recommended. They were all aware any legal action would get a powerful reaction from Ashley Pershing.

The attorney's office was modest by comparison to most high-profile attorneys, and Father Andrew heard this lawyer did more pro bono work than was perhaps prudent for his finances. The firm was located on a busy street a few blocks from the courthouse in a large two-and-a-half story port-wine colored brick building. But while the exterior was magnificent, the interior resembled a private residence.

The group entered the front door into a foyer with a simple dome light fixture and polished hardwood floors. A vacant receptionist desk rested a few feet past a rounded archway. The workspace was piled high with thick legal-size file folders, and two beige lateral filing cabinets with drawers askew stood against the rear wall.

A gentleman in a tailored business suit entered the room and introduced himself as Neal Atkinson. As he led them through the rooms, he explained he grew up in this home, and through a long chain of events, he was back again. He decided to practice here, citing its proximity to the courthouse. The group walked into a wide enclosed rear porch, which overlooked a landscaped yard with an array of tulips of assorted colors. They sat on an assortment of auburn-toned soft leather sofas, loveseats and lounge chairs. The group completed their introductions, and Nolan kicked off the meeting.

He outlined the role of each attendee and provided the attorney with a portfolio overview of Hope Landing. While the Native American burial ground was not a part of Hope Landing, Nolan felt it was important to understand all the background associated with their request.

Jane Shongo provided the historical importance of the tribe who once lived in the area, long before the white invaders even considered Erie as a settlement. She was eloquent in her presentation. She stressed the significance of the ancient tribe's sacrifice, by choosing to isolate themselves from others to confine the disease, thought to be smallpox. Legend had passed down a tale that fur traders who crossed the lake from Canada were ill with fever when they arrived. These indigenous were peaceful farmers and cared for the ailing traders who had died in their midst. The disease introduced by the merchants soon infected the entire settlement. Their chief would permit no one to leave to spread the death to other tribes, and it claimed every soul. Jane stressed the modern Seneca Nation owes a significant debt to this clan and would like the opportunity to move their remains to a place of honor. Although it is not believed they were Senecas, they should be rewarded for their actions that saved thousands of lives.

When she concluded her explanation, it was obvious she was so much more than the carpenter who was part of Clifton's construction crew. She spoke with a convincing tone and savvy point of view that explained why her father had chosen her for Hope Landing.

Father Andrew elaborated on the historical data known of this tribe and agreed with the scenario outlined by Jane. He also referenced the more popular historical account that it was the Senecas who eliminated these indigenous for not joining the confederation formed to repel the increasing number of white settlers into the territory.

History identified a very broad area of Erie as the likely home of that tribe, and evidence of their physical existence was never verified. However, it was logical that if a tribe of Native Americans lived in the current Erie area, they would have chosen a site that provided access to waterways, a defensible position, and fertile ground for farming. The early pioneers of Erie recognized the choice parcel of land and constructed a fort where the existing library expansion was underway.

The priest then provided a more recent account of the discovery of bones at that site by a construction crew several months ago, and he produced reprints of newspaper clippings. He indicated he represented the historical society in the area, and no one contacted him regarding the find until concrete was already poured over the archaeological find.

Nolan then linked the activities of Ashley Pershing with the new horse racetrack, the pressures for Hope Landing to stop their project, and the library expansion. These were all political moves to strengthen Ms. Pershing's resume and position her to become the next mayor. He also tossed in the incident of Marge being struck by a police vehicle that was spying on the project, and the confrontation with Sly Cermak at city hall. While those incidents were not connected to the injunction request, they represented the character and integrity of the individuals with whom the attorney would be dealing.

The trio finished their brief and awaited the questions and direction from Atkinson.

"You have all done a good job providing background and your goals," said Atkinson. "However, I see a few obstacles we must address before I will accept your case."

"Please explain," said Jane.

"First, I view the actions of Pershing as civic-minded and beneficial to the citizens of Erie. She was instrumental in obtaining the racetrack and library expansion, so without specific evidence to prove otherwise, I must assume she is pursuing another project in the bay area that would benefit the city. As you yourself admitted, there is no direct link between your Hope Landing concept and the library construction."

"I suppose you want us to keep quiet until you've finished," Nolan said.

"Yes, I would appreciate that. Thank you.

"Now, next is your issue of the actions of the contractors working on the project. I suspect it will be most difficult to trace any order of the construction efforts back to Pershing. We all know she is not there in a direct supervisory capacity with hardhat and steel-toed boots. It will be difficult to prove any professional misconduct on her part if she had no face-to-face involvement. I'm not saying it's impossible, but we have no evidence."

The attorney continued. "Then we have the issue of the building progress itself. I took the liberty of inspecting the area myself, and it appears the parking deck you mentioned is 100 percent complete, and the additional wing of the library is constructed, with only interior work remaining and perhaps some exterior landscaping. If you had come to me several months ago when the skeletal remains were first discovered and construction was just getting underway, I believe we would have had an excellent chance at a delay to allow a search and transfer of any artifacts from the discovery.

"However, you are now talking about razing a completed parking garage and delaying completion of a project with obvious community benefits. While the construction company may have acted with questionable ethics and with no respect for history, I see minimal basis to target for criminal misconduct either. Even if we had other factors to litigate, I believe the best we could hope for would be some financial payback to the descendants of this lost tribe, if they could ever be identified."

"So you won't take our case," Nolan said.

"Please accept my apologies for this next comment, but I try not to make my living by separating a fool from his money. While I could charge a retainer, draw up some briefs and file a motion, I would not be acting in the best interests of my client."

Jane interjected a question, "So, you are saying the primary issues that would prevent us from achieving our goal are the cost of the action and the impact on the community by delaying their access to improved educational facilities."

Atkinson nodded, "Very well stated. Yes."

"What if we could assure you the parking garage would be rebuilt and improved, and I would further expand the current library to house, err, let's say the Erie Historical Society?"

She had Atkinson's complete attention to her remarks. "I have this feeling you have more to share regarding that statement."

"Attorney Atkinson, the Seneca Nation is prepared to pay for the required demolition, and the reconstruction of an enlarged parking garage," said Jane. "In addition, we would fund an annex twice the size of the current enhancement, plus adequate space to house the historical society. I believe the current project's budget is two million dollars. The Senecas will absorb the cost of razing any structures required for the search and excavation, and an additional five million dollars for the next project's completion."

They all stared in awe at Jane's remarks, and Neal Atkinson was agape.

"Please excuse me," Atkinson said, "but on whose authority are you representing the Seneca Nation?"

"My father, Oteliani Shongo." She then reached into her folio and produced a single sheet of notarized paper which documented her claim.

"Whooeeh!" Atkinson's lips puckered and released a soft whistle. "I'd be honored to represent you and your father, Ms. Shongo. My dad and he consulted each other on occasion in the past. I'll work on my cost estimates and create an agreement. I trust this will be but a formality."

He regarded Nolan, "I must admit, I never admired Pershing's style of politics. This is going to be fun."

CHAPTER THIRTY-ONE

Moon Pies, Ho Hos, and a Ticket to Ride

Isabel was still suffering from jet lag but was pleased with the results of her trip.

"I'm telling you, Nolan, I was good. I knew watching all those prison reality shows would pay off someday."

"Prison reality shows?"

The pair sat at Isabel's kitchen table, sipping herbal tea.

"Oh yes, you learn so much. But they're nothing like the real thing," Isabel said. "No wonder the little twit got caught. I swear, he likes it in there. I just got done telling him his father died, and his mother was in long-term care for Alzheimer's. All Harold wanted to do was complain about the rising cost of Twinkies."

"I appreciate you making that lengthy trip. The money from the sale of my memorabilia should be in the Hope Landing account by the end of the day, so you can pay the taxes, then arrange for the property transfer."

"I'll do all that tomorrow. I don't know when the transaction will attract the attention of our friends at city hall, but the clerk's office was up to date on all their recordings when I left. With my absence, I suspect a mild slowdown."

Nolan briefed Isabel on his most successful visit with Attorney Atkinson and was not surprised she knew and praised him. She inquired who Atkinson would target for the motion to halt the current construction, and Nolan said that was not a point of discussion.

"I believe my judge friend would be sympathetic toward your cause," she said.

"Well, please say nothing to him. I don't want him to recuse himself because of information you provided prior to his hearing the case."

Nolan felt Isabel was off her normal enthusiasm for the project. "Isabel, why haven't you commented about my face?"

Isabel's head drooped, and she spoke with a much lower volume. "What you do is none of my business."

"What's wrong? Please be honest with me. Did something happen I don't know about?"

"Frankly, I'm disappointed in you." Isabel bowed her head, then lifted it back up a few inches. "I guess you're like any other man, so I shouldn't be shocked."

"What's going on, Isabel? I have a hunch somebody is telling lies."

"Follow me," she said. She sat at her computer, and in a few seconds hit the print command, then an inkjet printer spit out a brief email.

Have you heard the news? Nolan David, the director of Hope Landing, and his married marketing assistant Eleanor Parucci are an item. The two evidently spent the night together on a recent out-of-town trip to a casino. When they returned, Parucci's husband assaulted Mr. David at a well-known eatery, breaking his opponent's nose while roaring, "You slept with my wife." No charges have been filed, so this makes you wonder. Just what kind of family entertainment will Hope Landing advocate?

Nolan crumpled to a nearby chair and gazed at the email.

"Who sent this?"

"No signature, and I didn't recognize the source name. I tried to respond, but it bounced back as an invalid email address. It's all over social media."

"Right. It was an email address created for this one message and then the account was deleted." Nolan stared at Isabel. "It's not true. This is the work of Sly Cermak. Please, Isabel, you've got to believe me. Ellie and I didn't have sex. We've got a lot of history, but right now, we're good friends and business associates."

As Nolan brushed his fingers through his hair, he realized even his scalp hurt. "I'll bet everyone on the project and others received that message. I'll address it first thing at tonight's meeting."

"Best I call everybody to explain it's rubbish. Oh, my, that poor woman."

"Oh, I'm so sorry this happened. I'll call Ellie right now and hope she hasn't quit," Nolan said.

Several hours later, Nolan paced the front sidewalk of Hope Landing, greeting his participants as they arrived. Isabel was successful in speaking with most, and a few hadn't yet opened their email. Overall, the damage was minimized within the group, and Ellie was working to remove the postings from social media. She told Nolan earlier she shared the responsibility for the situation and intended to bring her husband to the meeting to demonstrate their unity. So far, they were no-shows.

Aaron pulled up to his former restaurant with a huge grin, bursting with pride as he helped Marge out of the car and handed her the crutches. Marge was even wearing a trace of makeup and more than a dab of perfume. Jake opened doors and pulled out a chair for his mom, boasting of his contributions to the rehabilitation of Aaron's former restaurant.

The others arrived and roamed the facility, impressed with the appearance and functionality of the transformation. Jane transformed to her carpenter's wardrobe, with jeans, flannel shirt, and her long raven hair once again tucked under a ball cap.

Jamal arrived and took Nolan aside. He spoke of numerous blog postings he deleted throughout the day that were similar to the email Isabel received. He also said he was grilled late in the afternoon about some effort to stop the library construction, and he was glad he knew nothing about that.

As nine o'clock approached, Nolan was happy to see his restaurant friend from Atlanta stroll from the parking lot, and Fergie Hanssen was making great effort to ignore his arthritic knees as he hobbled from the same direction.

Within a few minutes of the scheduled time of the meeting, Ellie and Joe walked side by side from across the street. Ellie's left hand gripped her suede briefcase, while her right was entwined with Joe's left as they broadcast their bond.

They walked to Nolan, and Joe reached out his right hand.

"Ellie told me I have to apologize, so here it is."

Nolan accepted his firm grip. "I'm sorry too, Joe. I would've done the same if I was you—maybe worse."

The three strode abreast of each other as they entered Hope Landing. Nolan made certain he was on the right, with Joe as a buffer between him and Ellie.

Nolan started the meeting with a sincere and humbling explanation of the email which many of them had received, and the facts of his relationship with Ellie. He categorized the entire situation as a "catastrophic misunderstanding," and assured the attendees all three of them were good friends, and this would not affect the day-to-day working requirements of Hope Landing.

A brief statement by Ellie, who agreed with Nolan's opening commentary, followed.

Coming next was Joe. He spoke with his fingers tucked in the back pocket of his slacks while staring at his shoes. "They didn't do nothin' wrong and I'm sorry I slugged him."

Everyone laughed, and the tone of the meeting changed to the excitement of the opening of the first phase of Hope Landing in just over a week.

Father Andrew introduced each of the ethnic representatives, providing a brief history of their qualifications or an anecdote of their reason for managing that booth.

Clifton next provided a well-thought-out explanation of the operational issues of the kitchen and restaurant. He began speaking with uncertainty, but after a few minutes, he gained confidence that he knew every strength and weakness of the tactical plan. He was most concerned about the certificate of occupancy. Although he had been waiting only a few days, he stressed the importance of receiving this prior to operating their business. The final license approval and liability coverage would also have to wait for that CO. The building had a new hazard insurance policy, and he explained he built everything to code and well beyond the minimum specifications.

Ellie spoke the longest, explaining the progress of her marketing plan and her need to meet one-on-one with each of the owners over the next few days. She would create website profiles and was working with Evelyn and Marge on the menu designs. Each of them needed to finalize their menus and be certain they could produce all food items with the limited amount of kitchen space and equipment. She handed out coupons for distribution at each of their current facilities. Many were trying to direct an existing customer base to Hope Landing, and the discounts would entice first-time visitors.

Clifton popped up and encouraged everyone to test their machinery as soon as possible, so he could repair or replace as needed.

Ellie created a smooth introduction to Jamal, who spoke of his blog and asked their cooperation in spreading the URL address with family and friends.

Nolan addressed logistical issues of management and teamwork. Their initial supplies would arrive the next morning. He announced the acquisition of The Bayview Restaurant building and asked Jake and Clifton for some recommendations on the utilization of that structure and land. Jake seemed thrilled to have his name mentioned and penciled some notes.

Their plan for free parking and the water taxi to the isle was now in place with the addition of Fergie and *The Lady of the Bay*. By offering free parking and transportation, the expectation was that customers would be more likely to eat at Hope Landing.

The meeting then opened to questions to any of the speakers. Several people raised thoughtful and pertinent questions. Most were tactical items that would be addressed as they all worked together in the next week prior to opening.

The Russian gentleman had a menu question which caught Nolan off guard.

"I know the rules require all the food be as authentic as possible from our native countries. I also believe there should be no duplication. My opening menu features pickled pigs feet, and I've heard that Africa will have pig knuckles. What should we do?"

Nolan wanted to question why anyone would eat either of these delicacies, but was formulating a response when Mrs. Bennett, the representative of England, raised her hand.

"Yes, Mrs. Bennett, so you have a suggestion?"

"Well, no, not a 'tall. I was going to say I was planning to serve pig wings and wanted to be certain they wouldn't be a problem either."

"Pig wings?" Nolan asked.

Mrs. Bennett nodded.

"I'd like each of you to provide me with a broad description of your creations, and I will review for similarities. To start, let's agree to rotate your menus so only one of you has these pork specialties each week. How's that sound?"

The trio nodded in agreement, and the group sensed they had run out of important topics.

He concluded the meeting and reminded everyone they now had access to the building at any time so they could familiarize themselves with all its operational aspects. Almost every attendee asked him if he needed a ride back to the diner, but he turned them all down. He wanted to walk to clear his mind, and the night air was cool but no longer frigid. The two-mile hike would be beneficial. He missed his wife during these times of success, for he most had the desire to call her and tell her all about the progress of Hope Landing, plus how proud he was of all the participants. But he knew in his soul his spouse was with him tonight.

By the time the parking lot of the diner was within sight, he was exhausted and felt his entire face might implode. He skipped his pain medication so he could be sharper in the meeting, but he needed to pop some pills and get a pillow under his head.

As he inserted his key into his exterior lock, a shiver rolled through his spine. He looked about and noticed a dark, late model four-door sedan parked at the back of the lot. Someone was lurking in his immediate surroundings. He continued forward, alert and ready.

He opened the door and stepped to the side, but no one rushed outward. He slipped into the foyer and locked up behind him as if everything was normal. He focused on picking out the slightest sound and detected the odor of fading cigarette smoke.

A flick of a switch lit the empty stairway. He took the stairs at a cautious pace. If someone was waiting for him, they already knew he was here. As he reached the top, the fresh smell of smoke was stronger.

He slid his key in the door and pushed it open, again standing to the side. The stairway light slivered into the room onto his bed, where Sly Cermak lay atop the covers, exhaling smoke rings.

"We're having some trouble issuing your CO," he said.

"No smoking in my room, Cermak." Nolan flicked the switch, and his room flooded with light. Cermak appeared to be alone.

"I should have gotten rid of you thirty years ago," the former detective said, "but you left town before I had a chance to finish you."

"Sorry I disappointed you. If I had known, I'd have stuck around."

"You were just another punk kid, Kaminski." Cermak shifted to sit on the bed and stamped his cigarette butt with the heel of his boot.

"Why are you here?"

"You're not as bright as I thought you were. We had a similar discussion thirty years ago. You made the right decision then and skipped town. I even felt sorry for you, with your girlfriend's family turning on you like that. And that poor girl—Mary, wasn't it?"

Nolan moved further into the room and stood at the foot of the bed to Cermak's left, as the detective's thumb crossed two fingers and twirled his ruby ring. It reminded Nolan of the detective's same habit from so long ago. "I'm not leaving this time. It's you who needs to leave."

Cermak snickered, "Me? You have guts, Kaminski. I'm on the verge of the payday I've been shooting at for all these years. I'm not going anywhere."

"You need to back off and leave Hope Landing and the people in that project alone. It's good for the city. Why should you care?"

"Care? I don't give a damn about your project. But you're in the way. I could give you your CO, since you're confined there with no room to expand. It's a shame your picture was stolen. I thought you would try to get that restaurant across the way to get caught up on their back taxes and make this more interesting. Such a pity."

"I haven't seen Pete, your young gopher, around the past few days. I'm guessing he's sitting on the photo. Haven't you figured that whole photo, movie, digital image scenario out yet?"

"You're bluffing, but you got guts."

"So what are you still doing here? You told me to leave, I'm staying. End of story."

"Oh, you're leaving all right. You just need to make your decision on how you want to exit. I may let you have your fun for a few months. I'll enjoy watching all those weak people, and how they crumble when they see their hero in prison. Our mayoral candidate has the strength that none of the other administrations had. When she gets elected, we'll stop dealing with all this penny ante bullshit. The ponies. The library. Those are merely a warm-up."

"You're talking too much, Sly. Aren't you afraid I'll expose your scam?"

"You know something, Kaminski? Police departments are solving cases all the time now with cold evidence. DNA. Forensic advancements. There's no statute of limitations on murder. So, if you want to play, I'm ready."

"I don't care what happens to me anymore. You should have figured that out. I have nothing to live for since I lost my wife. Bring it on, Sly."

Sly chuckled as he got up and sauntered toward the door.

"This time I'll take you out, but the genuine pleasure will be to ruin your girlfriend Eleanor too."

Cermak handed an envelope to Nolan. "Here's a bus ticket back home, kid. Use it, or you and Ellie will share different cells together."

CHAPTER THIRTY-TWO

Ship Storm

Fifteen minutes after Cermak left the diner's apartment, Neal Atkinson received a phone call. Nolan took the chance the attorney would answer late at night since his office was within his home.

Atkinson picked up with some alarm in his voice, as most people would with any unexpected call after midnight. Nolan provided a broad overview of the conversation that was fresh in his mind and was told to write down his entire recollection of the visit. They agreed to a 9:00 a.m. appointment.

The threat to Ellie tore through Nolan's gut, and his head never hit the pillow. After he listed as many quotations from the meeting he could recall, he started his second pot of coffee. He decided Cermak was either baiting him with his clues, or the former detective was so confident he didn't care what he said. Nolan parsed his notes to highlight the keywords and how Cermak used them.

One of the most obvious points was the longtime history of Cermak's corruption. He had been angling for a big payoff from his political relationships for many years. Nolan recalled his conversation with Fergie Hanssen, and this seemed to corroborate that point.

It was also evident the recent construction projects of the racetrack, and the library were somehow connected to Ashley Pershing. Kickbacks for contracts were as old as politics itself, but the proof was always the challenge. Nolan penciled Jamal's name next to this topic and placed a visit with the reporter high on his priority list.

The threat to deny the certificate of occupancy showed Cermak's ability to manipulate current government actions, even though he was no longer an official city employee. That connected him by his own words to Pershing. Still, by the time that complaint came before a judge, Hope Landing would be a memory of a whacky idea doomed to failure. No, he had to find a way to get the documentation without criminal allegations. That was why he needed Atkinson.

Then there was the risk to Ellie. He didn't care about his own well-being, but the involvement of Ellie made this personal. This represented a definite pattern by Cermak. He threatened to mar her reputation when she was first introduced into the project, then the email smear, and now this direct approach. Cermak wasn't using physical harm, but rather incarceration on trumped-up charges. Nolan underlined this thought and sensed there was something he couldn't connect from a previous conversation.

That damn ruby ring. Cermak must have twirled it a hundred times in his five-minute visit. Nolan wanted to rip it off his finger and toss it in the bay.

As he greeted Kade and Cat as they opened the diner, he was silent about his late-night visitor. He shuffled off as if it was just another day and rode the bus. Clifton would be available to make certain the facilities were functional and identify any concerns from the individual booth owners. Nolan would try to join him later.

This time, there was a receptionist at the attorney's office, who turned out to be Mrs. Atkinson, who was stowing a diaper bag under her desk when Nolan entered.

The detective's open remarks alarmed Atkinson, who advised Nolan to consider some sort of security until the issue was resolved.

But Nolan's focus was on Ellie's safety and the CO. The attorney wanted to contact Pershing and file an official complaint of harassment and misconduct by one of her staff, but Nolan felt that would only provoke Cermak to take harsher action.

They agreed the best plan was to research the track of the certificate to determine why someone had not issued it yet. Atkinson would focus on that. He was confident they would issue the document or at least identify the problem if there was a flaw in the construction or safety of the building. He stressed verbal clearance from an inspector was not adequate to confirm the restaurant had passed all the requirements to open for business.

Atkinson insisted he personally contact Eleanor and believed this would strengthen the message that she be concerned for her personal safety. Despite strong objections, Nolan at last agreed to a joint call from the attorney's speakerphone so he could be a part of that conversation.

Ellie was glad Joe wasn't home to hear this. She explained he would leap at any opportunity to have her stop working on the project and saw no reason to incite their third marital disagreement. Like Nolan, she downplayed the likelihood of a physical attack and was not concerned about any charges being brought against her. She was not as confident Nolan would stay in the clear and dreaded that issue may return. She was also very worried that another investigation into her sister's death would prove fatal to her mother.

As Nolan left the attorney's offices, he felt guilty about the strain in Ellie's voice. He remembered how shame drove him away thirty years ago, but this time he wasn't about to give up. There were too many people counting on him.

The city buses were old, noisy, and uncomfortable, but provided the necessary transportation within certain parameters. As he rode, he again micro-analyzed the visit from Cermak. Just then, he realized he was passing the library expansion site and pulled the cord for the next stop. He didn't know what he could gain from an impromptu stop but felt the urge.

As he approached, he jotted down the names on the sides of the various trucks parked alongside the building. Swensen General Contractors, Tyler Heating & Air Conditioning, Erie Plumbing—they all seemed hard at work, and he didn't even know why he stopped. He saw no activity that would lead him to believe the project was anything more than what it appeared to be—an expansion of the library resources for the residents of Erie. Then he thought of Clifton's union association, and that he worked on the construction of the racetrack. He wondered if he also worked on the library project.

Nolan wanted to get to Jamal but detoured his route to visit Clifton first.

As the bus pulled up to the pier, Nolan was excited to see Hope Landing's red, white, and blue sign being erected. Several of the booth owners lined the street and observed the crane twist the sign toward the workers prepared to secure it in place. Clifton was among the crowd, with his back turned to the bus.

"Pretty cool, huh?" Nolan said, as he had walked up to Clifton without being noticed.

"Oh, I'm so glad you're here to see this," Clifton said. He patted Nolan on his shoulder, and they all watched with pride at the crowning of their accomplishments.

Then Nolan tugged on his larger friend's shirt and motioned him away from the bulk of the crowd. Clifton followed Nolan to the

Lady of the Bay, where they stepped aboard and sat on the benches in the enclosed main deck.

"I don't think Fergie will mind us using the *Lady* for this purpose."

"What's up, guy?"

Nolan swore Clifton to secrecy, then briefed him on the events since the conclusion of the meeting last night. Nolan learned Clifton was assigned electrical construction work at the racetrack, then again in the parking garage for the library. It surprised him when Clifton admitted he declined working in the library because of his commitment to Hope Landing.

"Okay, help me here," Nolan said. "I saw three different company trucks at the library site, Swensen, Tyler HVAC, and Erie Plumbing. Do you know those guys?"

"Oh sure, they're genuine people all right."

"Why'd you say that?"

"Well, I figured you were leaning toward the fake contractor angle, but these guys are not only real, they wouldn't play any games either."

Nolan thought for a moment, then pushed on.

"Tell me more. How would something like that work?"

Clifton scratched his chin and shook his head. "It doesn't work very well in recent times. Years ago, the GC would sometimes create a shill company, generate invoices, and get extra payment for the same amount of work. But that won't function anymore, since everything is audited."

"What if the auditor was involved?"

Clifton shook his head again. "You're stretchin' too far there. Auditors are subjected to spot audits by the state and workers' comp companies too. The entire process is wrapped up pretty tight."

"Do me a favor and make a list of all the companies you remember working at the track and the library," Nolan said. "Will you do that?"

"Sure, that's easy."

The first testing of the neon sign of Hope Landing sent a chill up Nolan's spine. The group had come together with a supreme effort so far, and he could almost taste the success.

"Say, one more thing, Clifton. You said you turned down work at the library project. Anyone else in your crew here may have walked away from that chance?"

Clifton stood up and looked over at the building, creating the list of laborers in his mind.

"Yeah, at least a few. We don't have too many union guys in there, and believe me, I've heard about it. But the union would have called our first workers to work the library deal. Sean, Jerry, and Jane."

Nolan nodded and grimaced. "They still working here?"

"Nah, Jane is, of course, but not on construction. We're all done with that phase, but I paid them this morning and told them I may need them for the expansion."

"One more favor, Clifton. Call Sean and Jerry tomorrow and ask them if they can start work in The Bayview next week."

"What? C'mon, Nolan. I can't be ready to start so soon. I don't even know what bugs we have here yet."

"Calm down. I'm just setting a notion in play. I'd like to find out how long after you ask them that Pershing and Cermak blow up about The Bayview purchase."

Clifton grinned and shook Nolan's hand.

"I sure am glad you're on our side. I'll let you know the moment I talk with 'em."

Nolan saw a bus coming down the hill and jogged past Fergie and waved, then climbed aboard and was on his way to see Jamal at the cigar store.

Even from a distance, Jamal Moore's appearance projected confidence. He had a bit of lift in his step and was wearing a simple blue long-sleeve shirt with a button-down collar. He had shed his coat of many colors, and his tie was stylish with calm dark blue and bold red stripes.

"Jamal, what happened to you?"

"What? Nothing happened. Not yet anyhow, but I am in one hell of a shipstorm over my blog."

Nolan gripped the reporter's upper arms. "I mean the clothes."

"Oh, these were my girl's idea. I've got to hand it to you, Nolan, you were right about that car. I've become a chick magnet."

"So, you had a successful first date?"

"Boy, did I. Second date tonight, but I almost blew it again."

"How so?"

"We came out of the restaurant and I found out I locked my keys in the SUV. Man, I had this déjà vu thing going through my mind. Then I remembered I could use the code on the door to open her up, and she thought that was so cool. I plan to repeat it if this doesn't work out with her."

"I wouldn't press your luck, kid. The next girl may find locking your keys in the car in the first place wasn't all that brilliant."

"You got a point," the reporter said. "Say, I'm hungry, how about if I buy you lunch?"

Nolan glanced inside at the combo cigar store and deli counter and looked around the nearby buildings.

"I suppose this will do," he said.

While they ate, Nolan asked the reporter to see if he could get as much information about the contracts and the company names associated with any new construction. Jamal agreed with Clifton that the system had pretty much a stranglehold on that type of scam. Nolan skipped the coverage of Cermak's surprise visit and inquired of the latest concern over the blog.

"Oh man, the chief is pissed. Clifton told me last night he was worried about the CO, so I posted some questions on the blog about how long something like that should take. My responses were coming back with it's a mere stamp of approval after all the inspections were complete, so I called and spoke with the person who issues the certificates. I found out it was approved days ago and should be issued. So I slid that tidbit on the site."

The reporter continued to empty mustard and relish packets onto his hot dog while Nolan looked on in amazement. "That's a total of ten packets, five each of mustard and relish, which you've slathered on that hot dog. You can't even taste the meat."

"That's the point. I don't like hot dogs." He smiled at the messy mixture in front of him and grinned. "I think that ought to do it," and he took a huge bite, squirting the mustard concoction onto his new blue shirt. "Damn."

Nolan pushed a handful of napkins across the table. "Now I know what happens to your shirts."

Jamal made a quick run to the restroom for cleanup, then returned and started talking like he hadn't missed a beat. "I next contacted the city manager's office and within five minutes, my head was back on the chopping block. Fitz told me to disable my blog right then, or I was off the payroll."

"Well?"

"Well, that's when you called my cell phone, smack dab in the middle of the shipstorm."

"Shipstorm? That's the second time you've said that. What the hell does that mean?"

"My mother used to say that all the time. I figured it was a nautical term that meant lots of stormy seas."

Nolan chuckled and patted the young reporter's upper arm.

"It's shitstorm, not shipstorm. Get it?"

"Oh, gee, shipstorm makes more sense to me, and my mother would never cuss."

The reporter's cell phone had been ringing every few minutes, but he sent the calls to voicemail. The phone rang behind the deli counter, and a gruff voice called out, "Mr. Jamal? Do you want to be found?"

He had a look of concern as he hopped toward the counter.

"Tell your friend we don't take calls for customers. That's our to-go line," said the proprietor.

"Yes, sir, I will."

Jamal listened for a few minutes, with an occasional "yes, sir," or "no, sir." Then he said, "I'm sorry you feel that way, sir. Thank you for the opportunity."

He ended the call and returned to nibble at his sandwich. Nolan waited, knowing the reporter couldn't keep a secret.

"Well, the shipstorm is over."

"Boss settled down?"

"Sort of. He is a lot calmer now. He just fired me."

CHAPTER THIRTY-THREE

Shimmering Light

"Fitz told me the folks at city hall were receiving too many calls about my blog and the certificate of occupancy. He said he could no longer ignore the conflict of interest, and I should use my investigative talents to support the paper and not my internet rag."

"You'll land somewhere. Don't worry. That blog's a great boost to your resume. I need to get down to our project. Now that you're unemployed, do you want to drive me?"

Jamal jumped at the chance to be more involved in Hope Landing and wanted to introduce Nolan to his new girlfriend. On the way, Nolan received a call from Mayor DeLuca himself, who promised he would personally review the status of the project's inspection and make certain the proper action was taken. He wouldn't approve the opening if the inspector had discovered any safety issues, but implied he already knew such was not the case.

He was curious when they pulled into the parking garage at city hall as Jamal almost dragged Nolan to introduce his female companion. As soon as the pair approached the receptionist's desk, Nolan's intuition leapt into overdrive. The young lady who Nolan had called Buffy was introduced to him as Shyann. Her personality seemed anything but representative of her name. From the few moments Nolan observed her, she was spirited and witty. Plus, she was a terrific contact. She may have information that could help them about the recent whereabouts of Pete, who was no longer Nolan's shadow.

Once out of the building, Nolan quizzed Jamal on how well his new girlfriend knew Pete. Jamal boasted he stole the heart of the officer's fair maiden while her unsuspecting boyfriend was out of town on a business trip. Patrol officers rarely travel outside their jurisdiction for days at a time, and Pete's vague explanations strained his romance.

Jamal's official position on the matter of the stolen heart was one of opportunity, and he claimed Pete's relationship with Cermak already displeased Shyann. Her lover had become more secretive about his assignments and whereabouts, so much so she warned him she would stop dating him if Pete did not become more forthcoming. When he refused and disappeared again, Jamal stepped up to offer his shoulder of comfort.

If Pete was involved in the theft of the autographed baseball photo, then a logical deduction was he transported it to a secure site. Jamal explained Pete was absent for at least three days and perhaps four. His travel started the night the memorabilia disappeared. That meant Pete had adequate time to take that photo to almost any place in the world.

"Jamal, I'd like you treat you and your new friend to dinner—tonight, if possible."

The reporter didn't jump at the opportunity for free food and fell a few steps behind Nolan as they approached Hope Landing.

"I don't want to appear ungrateful, but I can't have you scare Shyann away."

"I won't scare her, I promise. She won't even know I'm gathering information." Nolan gripped Jamal's shoulder, "But she may hold the key that could at last bring the activities of Ashley Pershing and her group out into the open. I won't do anything to jeopardize her safety, and you can stop me at any time during our conversation."

Jamal agreed, but insisted the location be confidential and secure. Nolan said he had just the place and put the arrangements in motion as soon as they arrived at the pier.

The aroma of foods from around the world welcomed them upon entry into Hope Landing. About two-thirds of the booths were active with test cooking, sign installation, or simple primping to make the space more inviting. Nolan roamed the stalls, broadcasted the forthcoming news, and felt the growing excitement among the members.

As he spoke, Nolan gave his young friend all the credit when he announced the expected issuance of the occupancy document. Spirits were high and almost all the equipment performed without a flaw. Clifton said he only had a few tweaks, and no appliances needed replacements.

Mrs. Bennett approached with two other interested chefs trailing behind.

"Young man," Mrs. Bennett began, "we were wondering if you've made your decision about the similar recipes."

"I'll allow each of you to sell your particular items, but you must stick to the recipes you've provided to me. Pig knuckles and pickled pigs' feet use the same part of the hog, but you vary your preparations enough to be considered native to your ethnic origins. But Mrs. Bennett, your barbecued pig wings sound unique. I'm looking forward to having one of those myself."

The cooks were all pleased.

"Mrs. Bennett, please hold on a moment," Nolan said. He peered into her gray eyes as he spoke. "Thank you for all you did for me in the orphanage, and I am happy you're a part of Hope Landing. I wasn't the easiest kid to handle growing up, but you managed me just fine."

"Well, I appreciate you saying so. Your words mean a lot to me. My life hasn't had many rewards, and I'm glad you feel I did some good with you."

"I'm sure I didn't show it when I was a boy, but I appreciate you now. If there's ever anything I can do to help you, please ask. I promise to do my best."

Mrs. Bennett opened her arms and hugged Nolan tightly.

Nolan then made his way toward Ellie. She was interviewing Cai Li Na for her internet profile, and Nolan shared his optimism about the CO. Their conversation was brief and professional. Nolan's facial bruises were still severe, but his discoloration showed some graduated purple, an improvement from the blackened blotches of the day before. Li Na had her menus prepared and her equipment tested, so Nolan asked if she could accommodate his need for a dinner delivery later that evening. She was glad to oblige, and they worked out the details.

Nolan concluded his status check with all the other owners, then coaxed Clifton away from his tasks and across the street to The Bayview. They were walking the odd question-mark-shaped property when Jake caught up with them, toting a fistful of lined paper.

"I have all the parking spots figured out and brought my sketches to show you."

He plopped down on the ground and sorted his papers, placing pebbles atop each to secure them against the wind. Nolan and Clifton had no choice but to pay attention.

"Now, as you may already know, standard parking spaces are 160 to 180 square feet, which is eight and a half to ten feet wide and eighteen feet in length. Handicap spaces are twelve feet wide and the same length. Since we will park the cars ourselves, we won't need handicap spots, but I thought it would be safe for calculation purposes."

Jake was businesslike as he pointed at his sketches.

"I balanced the lack of need for the handicap spots by creating spaces for compact cars. They can be seven and a half by fifteen, and that saves valuable room. Because of the peculiar shape of the land, I assigned the compact spaces for the rounded corners, and that was another big savings of space."

"What's the bottom line?" Clifton asked.

"One hundred and twelve spaces in all."

"Wow," Nolan said, "that seems incredible, but I've learned to not question your abilities."

Both he and Clifton looked at the sketches and the land, still impressed with the calculations.

"But Jake, this will remain gravel, you know. At least for a while," Nolan said. "How will anyone who's parking the cars know where the spaces are?"

"Oh, that was a problem for a while," Jake said. "But the guy at the hardware store told me we could use orange luminous spray paint to mark the spots. Getting them aligned will be a challenge, but I believe I can do it. The lines will fade with the weather, but repainting will be easy."

"Jake, you're amazing. If your mom could see you working down here, she'd be so proud."

Jake ignored the compliment.

"We'll face some problems with erosion, topographical soil movement, and rain, but if you let me manage this parking lot, I will be the best parking space manager ever." Jake grinned like he slugged a walk-off home run at the World Series.

"Clifton," Nolan said, "looks as though we have a new member of management in Hope Landing."

Jake looked down and took off his ball cap, stammering a bit.

"Mr. David, does management get paid?"

"Yes, management gets paid." Nolan looked at Clifton. "We'll work on the budget and come up with an official job offer for you in a day or two."

Jake just stood there with his cap in his hands, as he seemed deep in thought.

"That's very good, Mr. David. I'd appreciate it if you told me how much I'd get paid as soon as you can."

"Jake, you've done a magnificent job for us, and we're all very proud. I apologize for not recognizing before your need for money. Has something happened that sort of brings your desire to a higher level of importance?"

Jake snatched at his sketches, careful to keep them in order. "I kinda heard my mom talking with Mr. Erdogan. I think they want to get married, but my mom said she didn't want to burden him with me."

Jake swallowed hard and kept his head lowered, so no one could see the tears in his eyes.

"I think if I moved out and got paid for working, then my mom would be happier and could get married."

Both men glanced at each other, then Nolan spoke.

"Jake, I think your mom was making sure Aaron cared for you besides loving her. Anyone who marries your mom will understand you're a big part of her life. Every mother is afraid of losing her son when he moves out and becomes a man. I guarantee when you tell her you've got this job, she's going to cry because she'll be so proud of you. And when you discuss what you overheard, I'll bet her explanation will make you feel a lot better."

Jake bolted across the field and toward Hope Landing, wiping his face with his sleeve.

Nolan noticed that Clifton too rubbed his cheeks by rolling his shoulders inward and could see the slightest glisten of a tear.

"Jake got to you, huh, tough guy?"

"Oh, hell no. I was only feeling sorry for Aaron."

Nolan slapped Clifton's back, and they walked to the rear entrance of The Bayview.

The establishment was similar to Aaron's Landing restaurant, prior to the recent renovation. The Bayview's décor was a bit more nautical, but the layout was a mirror image of its sister eatery across the street. The structure had more windows with views of the bay, and beyond a light layer of dust, the business appeared it could open in the morning.

"I almost hate to clear it all out," Clifton said.

"I understand. But she's a major part of our plan. Besides," Nolan said, "I have a feeling this building will be mighty important to us a lot sooner than we intended."

"What do you mean?" Clifton asked.

Nolan shrugged, "Don't know for sure. But my hunches are right more often than wrong."

Nolan noticed the framed business license and occupancy certificate near the front entrance.

"Clifton, do me a favor and have this place checked out as soon as possible. Fire extinguishers, insurance—the whole works. Our plan was to clear everything out and renovate, but let's do the checkup first."

"Seems like a waste of time to me," Clifton said. "Why make sure it's all operational like it's opening day, then start ripping the place apart?"

"Just humor me, my friend. Let's pretend we have The Bayview warming up in the bullpen."

Clifton thought a moment and then nodded. "Okay. When you say it like that, it makes sense. I'll work on it right away."

Nolan made his way to the *Lady of the Bay* and reviewed the plan for the dinner cruise with Fergie Hanssen. Li Na delivered her Chinese hot pot dinners, complete with an excellent bottle of white wine.

Jamal and Shyann were waiting for the paddle wheel boat as she pulled into the marina. Nolan remained below while Fergie was docked, so it appeared Jamal and his date were merely taking an evening cruise. But to Nolan, this meeting had the promise of providing possibly real insider information about the workings of Pershing and Cermak.

Jamal beamed with pride as he helped his date aboard, then slipped and grabbed the rail to avoid falling into a very frigid spring lake. Li Na acted as the server, and Fergie grinned with pleasure. He guided the boat into the still waters of deep lagoons, where even the glasses of wine didn't ripple.

After their introductory greetings, Shyann mentioned she was impressed with Jamal's ability to arrange this special dinner. Hope Landing was creating quite a stir in Erie, and Nolan's presence as their host had Shyann glowing with adoration of her new beau.

Jamal and Nolan learned Pete and Shyann dated for about a year, and his personality and availability deteriorated as his relationship grew with Sly Cermak. Pete had been a patrolman for over a year when he was selected for special assignments. At first, Pete's rapid promotion thrilled Shyann, but she never appreciated his total secrecy. The job transposed her boyfriend from the man who told her amusing stories about his day to a stern-faced police officer with no comments at all.

Shyann became concerned for Pete's safety, since she knew he had no special training, and worried his plainclothes work for the department would place him in situations where he may face harm. One day, she found a list of addresses that had fallen out of his pocket and called the station to leave him a message. She couldn't call his cell phone when he was on duty, and she thought he might get in trouble if he lost the list.

He returned in a matter of minutes after she made that call and cursed at her, instead of thanking her. This was the last straw for the young girl. Shyann explained she was never afraid of Pete, but after that day, she was fearful for Pete, because she thought he may be involved in something illegal.

Li Na served the hot pot special as if they were on a private yacht with a complete galley, and Jamal's date was in awe of her treatment. Shyann even voiced how pleased she was with the change of pace the reporter provided. She didn't even know one could rent a boat like the *Lady* for a private dinner, and here she was as a privileged guest.

"Jamal sure knows how to treat a woman," she said.

The group raved at Li Na's egg tarts and were sipping coffee when Nolan led Shyann one more time back into her experiences at city hall.

"So Shyann, do you have much exposure to Pete's bosses while you're at your post?"

Her nose scrunched, and her eyes squinted.

"Him. That man's eaten too many sourballs in his life to ever change his disposition. He's going to get Pete killed one of these days. And Miz Pershing already acts like she's the mayor."

Jamal picked up the lead, while Nolan looked disinterested. Shyann was going exactly where he wished she would, and he didn't want to appear as anxious as his heart was pacing.

"So, Detective Cermak is giving Pete dangerous assignments?" Jamal asked.

"I suspect so." Shyann peered to her left and right like she expected a crowd of people to overhear, then whispered.

"I just think wherever Pete disappeared to for those few days, he was up to no good for that man. I heard he got thrown off the police force, and now he walks around city hall like he's the police chief."

"Do you see the detective a lot?" the reporter asked.

"I see him, but we don't talk ever since Pete and me broke up. He used to come up to Pete, put his grubby hand on his shoulder and say, 'Young lady,' like he didn't think I had a name, 'you've got yourself a fine man here to take care of—reminds me of my own son.'"

Nolan choked on a sip of coffee, then wheezed as his mind raced with all the possibilities. A son . . . Fergie had commented that Cermak had a boy doing his dirty work for him. Nolan's mind concentrated. There seemed to be another reference to a young man he was missing.

"Anyhow," Shyann continued, "he would then slap Pete on his back and send him off like a pit bull on one of his trained errands."

Nolan asked Li Na to give Jamal and Shyann a tour of the *Lady* while he climbed to the observation deck and leaned against the rail, searching his mind for the other suggestion of Cermak having a son. He didn't arrive at the answer, but sensed he was close. First thing in the morning, he would ask Isabel to begin another research project. But something else was gnawing at Nolan, and he had that feeling of imminent danger once again. The paddle wheeler seemed to run fine, but Nolan checked for the locations of the life preservers just the same. He also confirmed with Fergie that all gauges were normal and was glad to learn they were on their way back to the marina.

By the time the *Lady* tied in, it was almost midnight. Fergie decided to spend the night aboard and invited Nolan to join him in a nightcap. The offer was tempting, but Nolan wanted a clear mind to focus on pushing his memory about Cermak's mysterious son. Shyann placed her hand in Jamal's as they strode off with the hormones of youth guiding them. Nolan shook his head with fond memories and bid Fergie a good evening.

Nolan was grateful to spot a taxi parked by the main gate of the marina, saving him from having to walk back all the way back to the diner. But as they rode in that direction, the dark sentiment returned, and Nolan asked the driver to make a detour.

Nolan wanted to check on Hope Landing one last time before he turned in. The day had seen a flurry of activity at the facility, with equipment being tested, people coming and going, and he wasn't even certain someone owned the responsibility of locking up the building for the night.

As the taxi approached the docks, two figures came into view from around the corner of the building, then were gone.

When the cab pulled to the curb at the front of Hope Landing, a light flickering inside the building came into view. Then a slender shadow came from deep inside and rushed toward the front door.

A faint howl increased as the silhouette crashed through the plate glass window.

The shadow now had substance, and stumbled wailing in agony, projecting two flaming posts that reached out to Nolan. His reaction was to avoid the extended pillars of flames until he recognized them as the arms of a pleading torso.

"Fire! Fire!" Nolan yelled as he lowered his shoulder and tackled the person onto the sandy soil. He rolled and scooped the earth onto the smoldering arms of the body beneath him, noticing this was indeed someone he knew. The pebbles and sand had suffocated the fire, but the victim had slipped into unconsciousness.

Nolan didn't notice the spreading blaze behind him, and the approaching sirens couldn't penetrate his awareness. He feared the phone call he had to make to inform the leader of the Seneca Nation that his daughter Jane was suffering from severe burns.

CHAPTER THIRTY-FOUR

Call the Cavalry

Nolan refused immediate treatment for his burns until he could reach Oteliani Shongo and set that shipstorm in motion. *Perhaps Jamal had the most correct spelling of the slang term after all,* he thought.

Jamal put the phone on speaker and held it so Nolan's hands would avoid any contact. At this early hour, the Golden Deer Casino would be at the height of operations. Still, it took Nolan nearly thirty minutes to identify himself as a serious caller, then finally heard Shongo's sleepy voice. He awakened with a jolt once he learned the purpose of the call, and assured Nolan he and his son were already on their way.

Jamal and Clifton flanked Nolan's sides and directed him back into the ER. His burns were minor, but the doctor was more concerned with the sand and pebbles mixed with the scraped and blistering skin. It was Jane's condition that was foremost on everyone's minds.

The doctor explained he couldn't release any information about Jane because of the privacy regulations, but he would ask for Jane's permission after Nolan's treatment.

A nurse injected a local anesthetic into each of Nolan's arms and handed him a tiny paper cup of pills to ease the pain. "Once those hands are numb, the doctor will be back."

Nolan looked up at his two friends who hung their heads, their torsos half-turned away. They were there for visible support, but their body language projected they rather be ice fishing in a blizzard.

"How bad?" asked Nolan.

The question lingered in silence. Jamal reached out his left foot and circled imaginary designs on the tile floor. Clifton jammed his fingers so deep into the front pockets of his jeans that the stitching stretched. The room was so quiet one could hear the whir and click of Clifton's prosthesis.

Nolan was about to rephrase the question when Clifton replied in a voice spoken as if he didn't want to wake a sleeping baby.

"We can rebuild it, I guess. But not in less than a week."

"What about the equipment?" Nolan asked.

"Don't know yet. The firefighter in charge would only allow me to peek through the openings, but it looked like most of the damage was to the counters and frames. We sure are lucky you were driving by."

Clifton's voice inflected in his last phrase like he was expecting a more detailed explanation from Nolan, who peered at Jamal.

"Sorry for taking you away from Shyann. You two seemed real cozy when you left the marina."

He grinned, and his face flushed. "She, uh, is out there waiting with everyone else."

"Who else is up at this time of night?"

Clifton and Jamal raised their heads in unison, and Jamal nodded to his elder.

"About everyone you know is out there, including friends and foe. And there's more coming all the time."

"Friends and foe?"

"Well, yeah," said Clifton. Then Jamal picked up the explanation.

"Ellie's here, and so's Joe, so I guess that covers both sides. Of course, almost all the managers are here, some of the crew too. Heck, even my boss Fitz is here."

"You mean your former employer. Perhaps you can get your old job back."

"Jamal already turned that down," Clifton said. "I heard the whole thing. Fitz offered him the feature story, and this kid here was so cool, telling the old man he was working freelance now, so he could bid on it."

"Man, you should have seen the look on Fitz's face."

"Now listen," Nolan said. "I saw two figures leaving the building as I arrived, but they were just shadows from afar. I'll bet Jane knows who they are. Don't let anyone talk to her until her father gets here—very important."

"We're on it. That lieutenant goon is hanging around, waiting for Jane to wake up so he can question her," Clifton said. "He's even got another cop with him, to make it all official like."

The doctor informed Nolan he would release him after he finished treating his wounds and if he didn't show any symptoms of shock. In the meantime, Clifton and Nolan strategized about the next moves for Hope Landing. Clifton would call the crew in to work on preparing The Bayview for business as soon as possible. They knew they would miss their scheduled grand opening but would do the best they could. Quitting was not an option.

The pair left, but their replacement surprised Nolan.

"I didn't think Joe would let you alone with me in a room with a bed again."

Ellie leaned forward and touched her lips to Nolan's forehead, then stood back. "I promised him I would leave my clothes on."

"Well, I recall that's how this entire rash of injuries started."

They chuckled a bit more and then got into the business of how to spin the fire story, and persuade people to stay away for a while, then come back. The delay of the grand opening was a kiss of death they knew would be difficult to avoid.

"On the bright side, TV, radio, and social media will pick this story up. We might be able to spin this so people will cheer for a comeback."

Jamal trotted into the room, catching glares of warnings from two nearby nurses. "Jane's father and brother just got here, and based on their expressions . . ." He stopped midsentence when he realized he interrupted a conversation.

"Shipstorm?" asked Nolan.

"Big time—an entire fleet I'd say."

The nurses asked Ellie and Jamal to leave so the doctor could continue with Nolan's hands. Within thirty minutes, a pair of oversized white mittens accompanied Nolan's bruised face and nose guard. He wouldn't be cooking in the immediate future.

A nurse entered and whispered into the doctor's ear, and that ended Nolan's treatment for the moment. They both exited and before the door closed, Oteliani Shongo slipped inside the room.

Nolan lowered his feet to step down from his perch atop the bed, but Shongo pushed down on his shoulders.

"Don't get up." The chief's clear voice commanded attention. "I judged you correctly when I first met you," he said. "I know your type doesn't need my gratitude for saving my daughter, but you also realize I must express my appreciation."

Nolan nodded.

"But on my travel here, my anger grew at you without cause. I blamed you for getting us involved in all of this and believed some-how your impatience with having this project finished so soon caused a mistake that started the fire. I was wrong, and I ask your forgiveness for my thinking you capable of such action."

Nolan reacted in the next breath.

"Mr. Shongo, I accept your unnecessary apology. The love you have for your daughter just brought out the instincts of a father."

Shongo nodded. "You need to call me by my first name, Otel, like hotel without the H. I visited Jane and got her account of what happened. She was trying a new hot pot recipe and slid on her oven mitts. A flaming bottle whizzed past her and exploded on the countertop of the booth next to hers. She glanced back at the flight-path of the bottle, and she remembers the two men turning away. Instinctively, she reacted by trying to smother the fire with her insulated gloves. Not a good idea. The gloves absorbed the gasoline or whatever it was and caught fire, which spread to her shirtsleeves. She was running to dive into the bay when you grabbed her."

"What's her condition?"

"Could have been much worse. Second and third-degree burns to her arms, some lacerations from cut glass. Remarkably, her hands were burned, but not badly. The gloves did a fair job."

"The two men?" asked Nolan.

"Yes, they worked on your construction crew. Sean and Jerry. I'll find them."

Sean and Jerry were the strapping lumbermen lookalikes who complained of the lack of union wages and no overtime. Nolan damned himself for not reading them better.

"I figured out they were on Ashley Pershing's payroll, but didn't see this attack coming. I had a bad feeling tonight, and that led me to check on the project."

273

"What will you do with Hope Landing now?"

Nolan explained their plans to evaluate and build at The Bay-view as soon as conceivable, hoping a surge of interest could allow them to have a limited grand opening in three to four weeks.

"What if you had a hundred carpenters and construction crew to help?"

"I'd put them to work and open sooner. We'd spend some time to redesign our site but could start construction almost immediately."

"You have my complete support, and I'll assign an engineering firm and my architects to arrive here at lightspeed. I might get a few of them here today to work on the plans. The Senecas will supply the building materials and the labor force. We will work with your friends to rebuild what my daughter loves so much."

Nolan was speechless, his mouth open with awe of the offer—no, the plans of Otel Shongo. They scheduled a meeting at The Bay-view in less than twelve hours, and Shongo was positive he would deliver on his promise.

"This will push our opposition against the wall. I don't know their scheme yet, but with the arsonists ID'd, Pershing or Cermak will make an obvious move."

Chief Shongo strode into the emergency room waiting area, and the media greeted him with microphones and cameras. Lieutenant Hutchinson approached and introduced himself to the sternest expression the Seneca leader could offer.

"Mr. Shongo, I must speak with your daughter. I understand she's awake and may have information about the fire."

Shongo searched the crowd, waved at someone in the rear, motioning him to come forward. Neal Atkinson advanced and stood next to the ombudsman.

"Lieutenant, this is my daughter's counsel, and he has advised her to not talk to anyone at this time. And before you object or begin your own legal maneuvers, I feel obligated to inform you that a representative of your state police will be here soon."

Shongo paused, and his steel eyes locked on the deep-set stare of the sizable officer.

"Based upon the information Jane has provided to me, and I have discussed with Attorney Atkinson, the state police will take my daughter into protective custody."

"Protective custody?" asked the lieutenant. "Protection from who? We wish to apprehend whoever started that fire as much as you do, Mr. Shongo."

"Well, perhaps. But you don't know what my daughter said now, do you? And you've made a sudden judgment the fire was arson. You must have privileged information. Has an anonymous tip led you to jump to this conclusion? Normally the police would postpone an announcement of that nature until the investigation was complete."

Shongo didn't wait for a reply and stepped forward to within inches of the much taller officer. The chief put his hands on his hips and spoke in a tone of syrupy sarcasm.

"Lieutenant, please tell me. Are you a man of faith?"

With the news crew recording images and video, Hutchinson replied in a calm manner.

"Yes, indeed, I am. And I will pray for a full recovery for your daughter, Mr. Shongo." He snickered and grinned, appearing proud of his sound bite.

Shongo increased his volume and turned to the media and increased his volume.

"Well, if you're such a man of conviction, Lieutenant, then you better pray real hard you find those two men responsible for my daughter's injuries before I do and learn who paid them to light that fire."

CHAPTER THIRTY-FIVE

Family Tree

The first light of dawn provided a faint grayness to the bay area. The hospital rested atop a hill that overlooked the pier that was striving to become the site for Hope Landing. The library expansion was two blocks further east, and from this perch, Nolan understood why this setting would develop into a focal point of a new encampment. Native Americans, trappers, or colonists—it didn't matter. A level vantage point with a strategic view of a natural harbor would have tempted settlement and growth.

Morning also bestowed good news to Otel Shongo and his son, with the gift of Jane making excellent progress in her recovery. They had transferred her to the burn intensive care unit, and she did well with the painful cleansing and initial treatment. Now she needed several more days of satisfactory healing, with infection remaining as the most serious concern.

Much to Nolan's surprise, many of the franchise owners from Hope Landing stayed the entire night, including Father Andrew, Marge, Aaron, and even Jake. Perhaps the most pleasant thrill was the presence of Ellie, who sent Joe home and demanded he trust her. She ended up doting over Nolan like he was her long-lost brother, and he grinned through every second of her attentiveness.

"I just told Joe he was my husband and I loved him. You're my long-lost best friend, and I love you too. He had to live with it," Ellie said.

The night culminated with Ellie giving coffee to Nolan in a sippy cup with a straw, while he conversed with his new friend, Otel Shongo. Nolan was twenty-five years his junior, but the pair formed a close bond.

Isabel had visited for a short time, then left to get some rest before she began her new assignment in a few hours. Her job was to search for a birth certificate which identified Sylvester Cermak as the father of record.

Meanwhile, the chief and Nolan hatched an elaborate strategy for the next several days to corner the corruption in Erie, plus open Hope Landing on time, or very close to it. They were both confident the political savvy and contacts of Chief Shongo, coupled with the ingenuity of Nolan, formed a winning combination.

The plan had an official kick off at 8 a.m., with a brief meeting at The Bayview. Nolan preferred they did not involve Ellie in the action at all, but she pointed out he wouldn't even be able to grip a cup of coffee for a few days. Therefore, she became his designated chauffeur.

One nurse befriended Nolan and secreted him into an unoccupied room where he could get about two hours of sleep before Ellie would pick him up. When he asked Ellie if she wanted to share the bed with him, with her clothes on again, she threatened to slap his hands with a ruler, for old times' sake.

So, the group embarked on their plan to return the city of Erie back to the people.

At 8:45, Fergie Hansson pulled his 1983 Chevy pickup in front of the exit of the employee parking lot of city hall, turned off the ignition, and pumped the gas pedal to the floor. The flooded engine wouldn't turn over, and Fergie's bent frame slid from the vehicle, then lifted the hood to ventilate the carburetor.

His efforts were legitimate, and passersby commented as they inhaled the fumes of gasoline. A few marked police vehicles ignored the sailor as they departed for work. Another few nodded and referenced his tough luck. One motorcycle cop even stepped up and offered to help, then they both agreed a little time and air drying would solve the problem. Fergie had lifted the filter assembly to reveal the believed-to-be faulty automotive part.

That persuaded the motorcycle police officer to return to his appointed duty, as Pete pulled his unmarked white Toyota Camry out of the lot. Fergie next made his inaugural cell phone call, and it worked just like in practice.

Jamal picked up the first trail of the Camry, followed for a few blocks, then phoned Cai Li Na. Thus, the rotating tail continued, with a team of Hope Landing members posted throughout the city. No matter the direction or distance, the next tag of the team was a few blocks from the interception of Pete's path. If the police officer stayed on surface roads and within the city, he should be unaware of anyone following him for more than a half mile.

It was Father Andrew who followed at a safe distance when Pete pulled into a subdivision on the city's northwest side. The priest slowed and proceeded past the Camry while Pete was walking up the steps to a well-maintained bungalow. Andrew jotted down the address, then called Marge, who acted as dispatch. She sat next to Shongo's son, who used an interactive online map with many color-coded pins to identify the locations of the drivers.

The street then became a thoroughfare for one of the team members to drive past the Camry every sixty seconds. While they prepared for this to continue for quite a while, it was Rose who giggled into her phone that Pete had returned to his car, carrying a number 10 white business envelope.

Marge relayed the address to Isabel, who waited at the clerk of court's office where she chatted with old friends. Once she identified the owner's name of the property visited by Pete, she called Nolan and shared her findings. He sat with a laptop with a wireless internet connection outside The Bayview and watched Ellie search for any information about the owner.

Meanwhile, the tag team resumed their pursuit of Pete, and Nolan was confident he would uncover the link between Pete's visits. Clifton was elated the invasion of the promised help from the Senecas was already arriving and peered over Nolan's shoulder at the list being created.

Pete continued his stops, all to residential homes, and drove away from at least two of the three with envelopes.

"Hey, I know that guy," Clifton pointed at the top name Adam Larkin. "He was a pipefitter at the forge where I worked, but I haven't seen him since the plant closed."

Ellie and Nolan froze, then Ellie pushed the list with all three names at Clifton.

"What about the other two?" Ellie asked. "Do you know them?"

Clifton turned, lifting the legal pad to better light.

"Nah, not well enough to say," and handed the pad back.

"Not well enough?" Ellie became impatient. "You saw them at bars but didn't buy them drinks? They were in your bowling league, but you didn't date? What's the deal?"

"Hey, watch it," Clifton said. "I don't date guys, or dames for that matter. You know what I mean."

"Well?" Nolan asked.

"The last guy, Dudenhester, he couldn'ta bowled anyhow. And I didn't know him and never met him. He was a classic demo guy for the union safety talks. His hand got mangled by a riveter, and they judged him at fault. Still, the union stood up for him, and he came back and retrained in a new position. Few months later, a band saw sliced off three fingers at the knuckle and whammo, his career was over."

Nolan's and Ellie's eyes met, and their thoughts melded. Nolan even forgot about the pain in his mittened hands and wrapped his arms around his friend and planted a kiss on his forehead.

"Clifton, I love you," Nolan said.

"Hey, you cut that out," Clifton said. "There's people watchin' us."

"Otel," Nolan called out, "it's time to roll."

Within seconds, Ellie, Otel, and Nolan were on their way to visit Pete's first stop of the day, Adam Larkin. The news that the team may have a lead filled them with excitement, and their focus increased as their teamwork became flawless. They recorded the addresses and names of the police officer's stops, while an odd-appearing trio approached that initial bungalow.

A timid female voice and some strands of silver hair were visible as the Larkins' door opened a crack. The woman sounded fearful as she told them all to go away, then shut the door. The click of a sliding chain lock further discouraged their entrance. As the three were about to leave, the sound of the chain jingled again, and the door opened wide.

"You're the man whose daughter was burned in that fire last night," she said. "How is she?"

"She's in intensive care, ma'am, and I appreciate you asking. The doctors are confident, and Jane's a determined young woman."

Within a minute, Millie Larkin was introducing the three visitors to her husband, planted in a vinyl recliner and gripping an

Iron City longneck. After Millie's introductions, her spouse took a long pull on the bottle and returned his focus to the Sons of the Pioneers, harmonizing one of their all-time classics, Tumbling Tumbleweeds. No surround sound, no high definition, just pure Roy Rogers and his cowpoke friends entertaining in rustic black-and-white on a forty-five-inch Smart TV.

Nolan explained the purpose of their visit as a follow-up to Pete's earlier stop. Adam didn't even flinch as he took another long swig of the beer, swirled the longneck to determine how much beer remained, then glanced at his wife.

She returned with a full bottle and thumped it on the cardboard coaster on the end table. He handed her the empty bottle, but instead of leaving, she slid it into the side pocket of her apron.

Ellie tried next, exuding sweetness in her voice and shifting her body with the charms that attracted the admiration of many a man. But Adam Larkin's face turned to stone, or so it seemed.

Shongo's powerful speech had to compete with the clip-clop and gunshots of Roy's posse, with thundering hooves across the dusty plains. He too was ineffectual and for a moment, he slid to the front of the sofa, and it appeared he was going to leap across at the man who ignored him so well.

After all three failed, Adam Larkin looked again at his wife and said, "See what you've done now, Millie?"

Millie reached out and swiped the longneck from her husband's grip and shot out of the room before Adam could even react. He raised himself in haste and trailed after her.

Shongo rose to follow, but Nolan lifted his gauzed hands and shook his head. The tiny house offered little hope for complete privacy, and Adam didn't seem the violent type. Loud whispers with harsh tones could be overheard but not deciphered. After a few minutes, Adam and Millie came out together. Millie was guiding her husband with sadness and support in her eyes.

Adam settled on the edge of his recliner, and Millie returned his bottle of beer. He inspected the label as if he was reading it for the first time.

"My husband wants to talk with you, but we're both concerned for our safety and that of our children." She paused, filled her chest with a deep breath, then continued. "We'll discuss this with you if we have some sort of protection—more for our kids than ourselves."

Nolan explained they would not record the Larkin's interview, but Ellie would take notes and deliver them to the state police. The pair would then need to cut an official deal with those authorities. This information gathering was unofficial, and a tiny part of the overall evidence being collected.

Mrs. Larkin confirmed to Adam she already heard the state police were protecting the chief's daughter at the hospital, and this one fact authenticated the tale of the three visitors.

Adam Larkin passed his almost untouched beer to Millie and jerked his head toward the back of the home. After all the years they shared, this wordless communication made sense to her, and Millie left with the beer and returned empty-handed.

"Okay," said Adam. "But no notes—they make me nervous. And I won't repeat this again until I'm facing a statie."

All three agreed, and Millie shuffled up to her husband and rested her clasped hands on his right shoulder.

"Not long after the forge shut down, I got into a conversation with a guy at the bar down the street. He agreed it wasn't fair the owners closed the plant and told me about a way that would help out a little until I got myself another job."

"Who was the man?" asked Ellie.

"I'm getting to that—just let me tell it my way."

"I sort of thought this guy was a schemer, and it was the beer talkin'. He said he was with the police and could recommend I'd become a beneficiary of their special funds for the underprivileged. He made it sound legit, and it would be temporary until I got on my feet."

Millie ran her fingers through Adam's sparse hair, and he twisted his head and pecked the back of her hand on his shoulder.

"Well, as soon as the process started, I knew there was something wrong. This big guy I met, Hutchinson, would come to the house once a week and deliver a payroll check made out to me. I would cash it, then give him back half of the net amount when he came back the next week. I tried to hide this from Millie for a few weeks, but she ain't stupid and sure as hell isn't blind. She insisted I stop—told me to tell the police. What good was that gonna do? It was the cops who began this whole thing. So, we kept it up."

"Was it Lieutenant Hutchinson who always made the deliveries?" asked Nolan.

"Most of the time, yeah. Now and then another guy would show up, and he looked like the devil stole his heart a long time ago, that's what Millie used to say about him. And the new kid is this fella who just left a bit ago. Pete's his name."

"Do you recall the other man's name?" asked Ellie.

"It was Cermak," answered Millie. "He used to be the head detective for the city. That man's parents can't be proud of how he turned out."

"I got to know Hutchinson pretty good over time," Adam said. "One day, we were sharing a beer while Millie was out, and he told me I was about to get a raise. With the horse track comin' in, I was being designated as a supervisor and would get a real nice increase for my loyalty. It was like I was doin' somethin' to earn this money. Hell, I was stealin' it."

He looked up at Millie, then moved his tongue around to build some saliva in his dry mouth.

"You want your beer, honey?"

"Nah, I think I'm through with that stuff. I need to be sober to see this through from here on out."

Adam returned to his story.

"That's when I figured out how they were payin' me. You know, with special projects. They would list me as an employee, pad the budget, draw me a check, and keep half for themselves. And they trapped me. If I quit, I'd lose my health care, and I couldn't do that. And that isn't even considering what they might do to my family if I stopped. So as much as we need the money right now, it's time we fess up and deal with it."

Millie didn't even bother wiping her tears as she leaned forward and wrapped her arms around her husband's neck. He slid back in his recliner and slipped his arms around her waist to prevent her from falling. It seemed like a maneuver they had orchestrated before but were a bit out of practice.

Prior to the group's departure, they discussed the secrecy that must continue for a brief time until they gathered more evidence. Of course, the Larkins vowed to remain silent until they received a visit from the state patrol with a promise of safety for their family.

When the trio returned to their car, they learned Pete had already completed fourteen deliveries, then stopped for lunch. Marge relayed a frantic message from Clifton that over fifty workers had already shown up, and all were eager to build something. Otel Shongo grinned with satisfaction that his people were following through as promised.

They agreed to stay together for two more visits, then the head of the Seneca Nation needed to meet with the current mayor and Attorney Atkinson about "formulating an agreement of spiritual cooperation," as he phrased it. Isabel had provided a list of all fourteen homeowners who Pete visited and could identify the others later. Now that the group understood the workings of the illegal machinery, Nolan requested Isabel start her next quest at the Bureau of Vital Statistics. Even though the Larkins hadn't mentioned a young man other than Pete who was involved in the deliveries, that possibility was still a thread that was foremost on Nolan's mind.

The following two visits on the list were not as melodramatic as their first but yielded similar results. It relieved each of the victims to have the scam come out in the open, although Dudenhester shook with fear. He said his disability would prevent him from working at all, and he couldn't afford the medications for his wife's various ailments without some sort of financial supplement. Ellie mentioned the option of litigation against the perpetrators of the crime, meaning Ashley Pershing and Sly Cermak, and the couple perked up and became gracious hosts. After scarfing down an assortment of cookies and a slice of chocolate cake, the three left and once again called in for a status report from Marge.

Clifton was meeting with the architect and engineer as promised by the chief, and Pete was back on the trail of contributing his part to the graft at city hall. Ellie was driving Clyde Shongo to check on Jane, but the chief's son reported her spirits were up, although she was in significant pain. Marge next insisted the most urgent message was from Isabel, who stood where she'd been pacing in circles for the past forty-five minutes.

Isabel's voice projected loud and clear.

"Nolan, you were right. Holy Mary, you were right." Isabel was almost shouting over the phone with excitement. "I found a birth record with Sylvester Cermak listed as the father, just as you suspected. But I also found a corresponding death certificate."

At last, Nolan thought, *the first day he saw Cermak at the cemetery. He was there to grieve for his son, who Nolan sensed was the key to an aging mystery.*

CHAPTER THIRTY-SIX

The Fugitive

The pier was brimming with activity as Ellie pulled up to Hope Landing. She couldn't even locate a parking spot, then spotted Jake fervently waving a red flag toward an area behind The Bayview. Surveyors, construction workers, law enforcement and news media were all moving about like a school of fish at feeding time.

Ellie noticed two police cruisers with their blue lights flashing parked in front of The Bayview. Nolan saw a makeshift stage set up on the back of a pickup, with a bank of microphones atop the roof, and an American flag covering the windshield. This impromptu press conference would face The Bayview, and the television audience would never suspect the speaker was standing in the bed of a truck.

Ellie turned the car around and headed back up the hill when her phone rang with Marge as the identified caller. She listened for a few minutes more than Nolan could bear, then Ellie asked about the whereabouts of Fergie Hansson and his *Lady*.

"Nolan wants you to raise Fergie, Marge. He may still have his cell on from earlier today. Have him meet us at the old marina. He's got a slip there."

Ellie hung up and filled Nolan in on Marge's call. "The police are searching The Bayview and surroundings, looking for you," Ellie said. "Marge doesn't know what's going on, but Ashley Pershing is holding a press conference soon."

Ellie drove within the traffic flow, careful to remain part of the curious crowd.

"I'm not running," Nolan said.

"I'm not suggesting you run. If we find Fergie, he can anchor right off the pier, and we'll have prime seats for the press conference where no one will see you."

Nolan used Ellie's phone to call Shongo and get his take on the activities. He had just left a visit with Jane and was pleased with her progress. He also relayed that his meeting with Mayor DeLuca was most productive. DeLuca was cooperating in every way possible, even if it meant issuing building permits and certificates of occupancy under his own signature. The mayor also promised the injunction to halt construction at the library would be unnecessary, since he would issue a cease order until they could conduct a hearing about the burial ground.

"Nolan, I hope you won't feel I've left you out on this decision, but it was one of those judgment calls," Otel said. "I discussed the fraud we uncovered this afternoon, and he'll involve the state police. He knows of a few officers within the Erie PD who he can trust and will include them when he is confident it is safe for them and their families. He portrays himself as being powerless to the activities of Cermak and the councilwoman, but he may loosen his balls just in time."

As Ellie drove down the narrow lane to the marina, Fergie was waving from the bridge of his *Lady*. Fifteen minutes later, he anchored the paddle wheeler within thirty yards of Pershing as she stepped to the bank of microphones.

"I speak to you as a candidate for mayor of Erie, as a current representative of the city council, and today, as a concerned citizen. The pier area here is a prime location for the city redevelopment that will become part of my administration. However, the city and our citizens are victims of a recent scam focused right here."

"The building behind me was the scene of an arson last night, which hospitalized a female worker with burns suffered in that fire. Her father has requested the state police to investigate, and we applaud and support those efforts. In fact, I have asked my chief of security to conduct his own investigation. It is unfortunate our citizens cannot trust their own law enforcement to make the proper decisions, but thanks to Sylvester Cermak, we have worked with key police department officials and are here to announce our initial conclusions. It will shock many of our citizens who have been supportive of this pier-side endeavor labeled Hope Landing. But our investigation has concluded that Nolan Kaminski, known to most of the city as Nolan David, committed arson at his own project for the substantial proceeds from an insurance claim he intended to file."

The crowd gasped and mumbled among themselves as the council member continued.

"Therefore, we have issued a warrant for the arrest of Nolan David Kaminski for arson and conspiracy to commit insurance fraud. Additional charges are pending the outcome of the burn victim who remains hospitalized. We recognize this announcement will deflate the spirit of many and we are prepared to counsel those who may be affected. I will now take a few questions."

Nolan's empty gaze targeted the polished texture of the varnished wall in front of him. Ellie shook his elbow, concerned the announcement somehow shocked him.

"Nolan, it'll be all right. She doesn't know we've got enough evidence to bring her down."

"No, that's not what's on my mind. I think I've figured it all out, after all these years."

"What are you talking about?"

He reached and touched her cheek, then whispered. "Mary. Your sister. That night."

Nolan leapt to his feet, and Ellie yanked him down.

"They'll see you, Nolan."

"Get me to Jamal, and to Shongo. I should have figured this out years ago."

Within an hour, the *Lady of the Bay* was the site of a strategy meeting with some of the key players of Hope Landing. Clifton admitted the plans designed by the architect overwhelmed him, but the construction engineer was ordering lumber and equipment to begin work in the morning. Besides the several crews supplied by the Senecas, most of the country representatives of the Hope Landing project also showed up with talent of some type to pitch in.

They would work in continuous shifts, and while it seemed improbable, both Hope Landing and The Bayview might be finished in a few days. Clifton said crews were busy at that moment ripping out the damaged sections and preparing The Bayview for the remodeling phase. Since the building inspector was on scene, he would review and issue all the necessary permits.

Ellie planned to use the media hype to ramp up the announcements and advertising since Clifton was serious about opening on the original schedule.

No one had seen or heard from Sean or Jerry, but rumor said they fled to Canada. Nolan felt they would return if offered a plea bargain for their testimony.

Shongo assured the group the state police were already investigating the fraud discovered earlier in the day. He also told Nolan even if he was arrested, he would personally post his bail as soon as they announced the amount.

That didn't sit well with Nolan, who had plans to make a quick trip to North Carolina. They greeted his announcement with gazes of curiosity.

Ellie asked the question on the minds of every attendee.

"I'm afraid to ask, but first, you're in no condition to travel, and second, why would you leave now when everything is coming together?"

"That's simple. I picked up on something our young reporter mentioned a short time after we met."

Jamal formed that look of dazed confusion on his face, one which he had perfected without effort.

"I asked Isabel to do further research of public records. I figured since she was checking births and deaths, why not go for the middle? Marriage records. And she hit pay dirt."

Nolan spoke with excitement, waving his white-mittened hands in emphasis.

"Sly Cermak had a son who would have been forty-four now. But he died a few years ago. Well, the detective lived apart from his wife for many years, but didn't get divorced until after their son passed. Isabel learned the one person who knows Sly Cermak better than anyone—his ex-wife, who married Duane Zuccola, the reporter who preceded Jamal on his job. If I'm right, both have enough information to put Sly in prison for life, and most important to me, solve a mystery that's haunted me for thirty years."

"So Otel, you think your son would use that fancy plane of yours to transport a fugitive of justice across state lines?"

CHAPTER THIRTY-SEVEN

Old News, Good News

Nags Head, North Carolina was approaching peak tourist season, and it was a congested drive from Dare County Airport across one of the two access roads to the island. While he waited for the rental car, Nolan picked up a copy of the *Isle Rag* and was not surprised to see the editor and publisher identified as Duane Zuccola. He supposed even someone who retired to this area needed, or perhaps wanted, to make some extra money and newspapers were in his blood.

The address Jamal provided was on the main road, with the Atlantic Ocean to the east, and a combination of inlets and sounds to the west. The cottage appeared to be a small hotel or bed-and-breakfast. A fine spray of salt water could dampen one's skin, but not enough to moisten clothing. An odd paradox indeed. Perhaps the ocean's breeze dried the fabric before the skin, Nolan thought.

The turquoise shutters were appealing as they hung open and contrasted with the worn brown-shingle siding. The long flight of stairs to the main entrance appeared stately, and Nolan assumed the area behind the lower-level trellis was designed for the high water that would wash over the isle in any significant storm. Hope Landing was being built just a few feet from the breaking waters of the bay of Lake Erie, but none of the storms of the Great Lakes could ever bring the devastation of a hurricane surging across the barrier isles of North Carolina.

The squeaky screen door reminded him of his childhood, and

he recalled a similar sound when he opened the back entrance to his porch in Erie. He thought it odd how a forty-year-old memory could jostle him in a place he'd never been. He could still hear his mother's voice telling him to take off his muddy shoes before he came inside. In Erie, the season didn't matter, for he always possessed footwear caked in mud, snow, or grime.

The connection with Erie was here, with the people behind the screen door. The silver-haired woman at the check-in desk would have been radiant in her youth, and she reminded Nolan of the hairstyle and posture of Sophia Loren.

"Checking in, sir?" she asked.

"No, not this time. I'm looking for Duane Zuccola."

"Perhaps I can help you. I'm his wife, Sally."

"Uh, probably not. You see," Nolan held up the *Isle Rag*, "I wanted to speak with him about the paper. I think I have something that will interest his readers."

Sally gazed at her visitor for more than a glance, noticed he had no luggage and nodded to a wicker sofa near the window.

"I'll go get Duane. You have a seat, and he'll be out in a few minutes."

The man who came around the corner explained where Jamal formed his fashion sense. He was a head shorter than Sally and wore a sleeveless yellow sweater vest that was last stylish in the 1960s. The dark plastic frames of his glasses looked like they came with the sweater.

"Hello, sir. My wife said you were interested in the paper?"

"Well, I'm afraid that's not the truth. I'm here to talk to you and your wife about your old hometown."

"Oh, I knew it, Duane," said Sally from behind the counter. "No one comes to see you about that rag."

Duane peered out the window above the wicker sofa and noticed the imposing figure of Shongo's son standing beside the rental car. He squinted his eyes and raised his brow in concern.

"You know we never talk with anyone up there anymore," he said.

"Mr. Zuccola, I'm Nolan David, or you may know me as Nolan Kaminski."

"Oh my," said Sally, as she covered her mouth with her hand and came around to the side of her husband.

"We've been followin' the blog by that reporter who replaced me," said Duane. "Jamal—that's his name. He's doing a mighty fine job, in my opinion."

"He got fired from the newspaper for working on that website."

"We could see the wheels were comin' off the entire town, and we're mighty glad we got out," said Duane.

"I think you both know why I'm here. The citizens of Erie and I need your help."

"Well, we've been talking about what we'd do if the police came asking," said Sally. "You ain't the law, but from what we hear, you've stuck your neck out more 'an once to help our friends there. So yes, Duane and I already decided to help."

With that said, the group moved to the living quarters. They explained they were mere managers of the cottage-type hotel and received in return the two-room suite. This kept their expenses down, and Duane made a bit of profit from running the small newspaper.

"I know folks here don't like the name, *Isle Rag*, but it targets the tourists and newcomers, and they seem to pick it up because of the name. So, the moniker stays," said Duane.

While admitting that financial assistance from her ex-husband was an option, Sally made it clear she wanted nothing more to do with him. She hated she still heard from him now and then.

Nolan told them he uncovered the payroll scheme Sly Cermak was operating, and that the state police were investigating.

That Nolan had gotten that far in his investigation, and was still alive, shocked Sally.

"The state police will have questions about the payroll fraud, or whatever name they give it. Was your son involved in that as well?" Nolan asked Sally.

"I knew Sly had many schemes he worked on, but he never shared details with me, that's for sure. Now, Wayne would leave me the occasional tidbit of information. He said that linked me to having knowledge of the crime, and I'd be charged the same as them if I ever went to the staties or the feds. I swear, that boy was as evil as his dad, if not worse." Sally looked defeated but relieved at the same time.

Nolan used this lead-in to push into the distant past. He told them that while their testimony about the payroll scheme could be useful, that wasn't the focus of his visit. He came there to discuss Sally's son.

"Wasn't ever my son, no sir," Sally said. "I may have given birth, but as soon as that child was old enough to walk, my husband's evil took him over. It wasn't long before Wayne figured out how to manipulate his father. He would get into trouble, and his father would get him out. I think sometimes that boy got himself caught just so he could see how his father could get him outta the mess he was in."

"Sly and me separated about the time Wayne John was ten.

Wayne John, you can figure out where Sly picked that name from. Well, I couldn't take it anymore. It was bad enough when that boy would beat up on his friends, but one day he threatened me, and Sly told me I musta done something awful bad to provoke the kid like that. Do you hear what I'm saying? My ten-year-old son threatened to hurt me, and my worthless husband took his side. Why, the next morning I packed and left."

"Did you see them often after that?" Nolan asked.

"Oh my, rarely. But once in a great while was too much. That's how I first met Duane, so I guess some good came of it."

"I was the crime reporter for the paper back then and pretty fired up about my job. I kept on getting these leads that this cop's son was getting arrested, but charges dropped for no reason," Duane said. "You can imagine my attempt at questioning Sly Cermak got me nowhere. So, I followed the trail to Sally."

"So Sly got his son out of some pretty tight jams, fixed some tickets, had some charges dropped, is that all there was to it?" asked Nolan.

"At first, yeah. But then, the two of them teamed up. I mean, they worked together while on different sides of the law," said Duane.

"I don't get it," said Nolan.

"As Wayne got older, he was big for his age, and hung around even older kids. He would steal a car, and while everyone knew he was the one who took it, Sly would arrest someone else, an innocent person," said Sally.

"Sly would frame them. I don't know how that all started, but before you knew it, they assigned Sly to the detective squad, since he was making so many arrests. Hell, his own kid was a one-person crime wave, and Sly was setting people up with false evidence.

His son was having a good ole time—muggings, B&Es, stolen cars, selling pot, and his old man was moving up the police department ladder because of it," Duane said.

The conversation lagged for a moment, and Sally and Duane looked at each other with a mixture of dread and fear. Duane spoke next.

"And then you came along, and it all got worse from there on."

"What? Me?" asked Nolan.

"Yep. You stumped Sly. Kids wouldn't testify against you. He couldn't figure it out and never had that problem before. He would go out, tell the kids what to say, and he made his case. With you, every time he got an angle on some kid, it wouldn't work. And you didn't even know it was happenin', which Sly couldn't believe either. So, he turned the girl's family against you. He planned to ruin your life one way or another," said Duane.

"And he would have gotten you if you'd stayed," said Sally.

"I'm sorry, I still don't get it. Why did he want to throw me in jail? I didn't know him or his son."

Duane continued, "There was a set-up that night for a drug bust. The kid who was driving the car with the girl in it sold pot and LSD to the high school kids, and Sly was going to bust him."

"But my no-good son wanted to prove he was in charge," said Sally. "So instead of going up and buying pills from this other boy, he taunted him into a drag race. And Wayne put something in that boy's gas tank that made the engine catch fire. Wayne killed that boy and girl just for fun, and my husband knew it."

"You mean . . ." said Nolan.

"Oh yes, I'm very sorry to admit this," said Sally. "I should have come forward thirty years ago, but I was afraid and have been ever since. Then when Wayne overdosed on pills a few years ago, I told Sly that Duane and me were getting married, and if he had any plans of stopping us, I would tell the FBI what I knew."

"So . . ." Nolan said.

"Yeah, you got it now," said Duane. "Sly Cermak was there the night your girlfriend's sister died. He was there and didn't do nothin' to stop Wayne from sabotaging that car, then let the race go on. And pinning it on you was Wayne's idea. He said you were an orphan, and no one would care about you doin' time. That was their routine—pick someone who didn't have enough money for a good defense."

"That would mean Sly was sending innocent people to prison."

"Hell, yeah," Duane said. "Bunches of them. It was one of those cases that got Hutchinson thrown off the force, and then Sly went into retirement. But when Pershing rose to power, Hutchinson came back, and Sly became her security chief. But yeah, Sly ruined dozens of lives, and some are still in prison."

Nolan sat down on the sofa and clasped his hands in front of him, thinking about this devastating news.

The detective was there when Mary died. Cermak's son was responsible. He was the other driver, the kid who helped Cermak do his dirty work, and who vandalized the car in which Mary was killed. The entire plot had come together, and Nolan needed to return to Erie as soon as possible. He had more than enough to put Cermak away and wouldn't miss the look on his rival's face. Then he would tell Ellie and her mother he was now absolved without a doubt of any wrongdoing in connection with Mary's death.

As the three looked at the urgency of the matter in Erie, Sally agreed she would be the most appropriate person to give a statement to the state police. She therefore agreed to fly back and leave Duane in Nags Head to manage the cottage inn, so she prepared to leave.

As Nolan was about to walk out for a breath of air, Duane entered the lobby and carried a wide package wrapped in brown paper.

"I forgot to tell you," he said, "I haven't opened this, but Sally and I are pretty sure this belongs to you."

At one glance, Nolan was confident of his judgment of the contents and snickered at Duane's presentation.

"A young man named Pete brought this down here a few weeks ago," Duane said, "and told us not to open it under any circumstances. But from reading the blog, this has to be your baseball picture."

"I love it when evidence is gift-wrapped."

CHAPTER THIRTY-EIGHT

Hippety–Hoppity

By the time Nolan's flight landed in Erie, it was too late to set up an interview with the state police. Evelyn would help Sally relax to prepare for her testimony, while Nolan and Clifton brought each other up to date.

A full day of work at Hope Landing exhausted Clifton, who spoke with amazement at the progress made in such a short time. The crews had ripped out every piece of damage from Aaron's former restaurant and gutted The Bayview, all by five o'clock. They were working through the night with real architectural blueprints and construction engineers who were creating a Hope Landing that Clifton and Nolan envisioned as their third phase. The cheap plywood that Clifton's group had crafted to make things presentable was being replaced with solid oak stalls and granite countertops.

Every food station would have its own mini-kitchen, and they expected new tables and chairs tomorrow. Behind Hope Landing, outside dining would be available in a newly designed covered pavilion. The Bayview would house a few food stations plus a booking area for transportation to the beaches aboard the *Lady of the Bay*, which would soon offer dinner cruises with Li Na's guidance.

"We won't have everything up and running on day one, but the visitors will see what's scheduled, and they'll want to come back," Clifton said.

"When do you think we'll open?" Nolan asked, then added, "Please be honest."

"Hell, we're running three shifts right now. They've got enough generators and floods down there to light up the whole county. And these guys are good. I'm proud to be on their team, and they treat me like I know a helluva lot more than I really do."

"When?"

"They're telling me Saturday, and I believe 'em. Ellie's had spots on the local TV station and all the affiliates up to five hundred miles away. Rumor came swirling through about seven tonight that we may have live coverage on one of the national morning shows on Sunday."

Nolan made a few calls and learned Jane continued to make modest improvement, although she was still in intensive care. Even though it was late, Nolan called Ellie to tell her he was back in town. Joe didn't appreciate the call at all and grumbled just enough in the background to be heard. Nolan couldn't bring himself to tell Ellie over the phone about the depths of involvement of Sly Cermak's son, but said he needed Ellie to come to Clifton's in the morning for the entire disclosure.

Nolan didn't sleep well, as his anxiety over the upcoming events overwhelmed him. He was in a restful twilight on a lawn chair in Clifton's yard when Clifton jolted him back to consciousness with a whisper of his name.

"Gee, you're jumpy."

"Yeah, with good reason," Nolan said as he displayed his bandages. "My hands are on fire again, or so it seems. I don't think the saltwater mist was proper therapy."

"Evelyn told me your burns looked pretty raw when she put on the fresh dressing."

"Seems like a minor problem when I think about what Jane is

going through. I wouldn't want to be Sean or Jerry if any of the Senecas find them."

They both sat in silence for several minutes, and the night air frosted their breaths.

"What are you thinking about back here all by yourself?" asked Clifton.

Nolan took more than a minute to respond. "I was speculating about what my life would have been like if I'd stayed here and never left. I wouldn't have met and married a damn near perfect woman, so I don't have any regrets."

"But don't you think you and Ellie would've, you know, made it work somehow?"

"It would have been rough, for sure. That detective may have used one of his tricks to put me in jail for a long time."

Clifton went back inside and returned with two beers, his metallic hand pushing one toward Nolan, then chuckled at his gesture.

"I don't guess you can't hold that longneck very well, can you?" Clifton asked.

"I'll manage as a two-fisted drinker. Perhaps it'll help the pain, since I'm not taking those pills. The alcohol wouldn't mix anyhow."

The pair continued to talk about the expected events for the day and the grand opening of Hope Landing. Another round of silence slid between their conversation. They both watched a rabbit spring across the lawn until he halted from full throttle as he noticed the humans.

"I've got to tell you something," said Nolan. "I owe it to you since you've become my friend up here."

Clifton tugged at his beer and waited.

"As soon as Hope Landing becomes successful, I'll be moving on."

"I was wonderin' about that. You know you've made a home here. Folks here in Erie owe you big time. You could be mayor."

"I'm honored. But I've already become an imposition in Ellie's life. Because I love her, I've got to honor her marriage and let that take its course."

"Have you told her?"

Nolan shook his head, and the rabbit scooted away. "Nah, can't tell her I'm leaving until I give her the complete story on Sly and see that through to the end. If he's not arrested, then she and her family would remain at risk."

Morning light crept into the sky, and they went inside.

Evelyn was already brewing coffee, and Sally was in the shower. The entire household had the expectations Erie would be a different place to live in the future, and they were a proud part of the reason. Within minutes, the doorbell rang and everyone paused their motion, wondering who would stop and see them before six in the morning.

"Let's be careful, but I don't think Cermak would ring the bell," said Nolan.

Clifton came out of the bedroom with a shotgun lowered to his side, stood five feet to the right of the entrance and called out for the person to announce themselves.

It was an irritated and commanding voice that responded, and Clifton opened the door for Chief Shongo.

"I've been sitting in that patrol car for over an hour waiting for you to show some signs of movement in here, then you greet me with a shotgun." He grinned.

They all shared news over mugs of fresh coffee. Shongo told them the lead investigator of the state police and a representative of the state bureau of investigations would arrive at the house at eight to interview Sally.

Jane was complaining more and expected to be moved from ICU later that day. She was indeed fortunate and told her father God had spared her shooting hand so she could take revenge on Sean and Jerry. No one laughed at this statement, including her dad.

Ellie arrived a few minutes after seven, and she and Nolan perched themselves on Clifton's rear patio. Nolan provided comprehensive details of his discussion with Sally, and the relationship of Sly Cermak and his son. He eased into the account of the evening when Ellie's sister passed away in the auto mishap. He dropped a few hints of the father-son team framing unfortunates, why they picked him as the fall guy, and had no choice but to home in on the devastating news that Mary's death was not an accident, but a homicide.

Ellie felt responsible, as she had all these years, at not being more aware of her sister's level of involvement with the boy who sold pot to the high school teens.

"You know, I knew Mary took a toke every now and then, but back in those days, we all did. How could I say anything? And if I told Mother, wow, the gap between us would have widened even further. After all, I was the egghead sister."

The investigators arrived while Nolan and Ellie were still conversing outside, and Clifton left to check on the progress of Hope Landing.

"That crew's been at it for eight hours; I doubt I'll even recognize the place anymore," he said as he hopped into his pickup and drove off.

Nolan finished sharing all the details of the depths of the plot as concocted by Sly Cermak and Ashley Pershing, including the good news that he once again possessed his fraudulent baseball memorabilia photo. By then, Ellie was adrift in her mind, eager to tell her mother about the circumstances of Mary's death and that Nolan was cleared beyond a doubt.

"I only wish my father knew. He was so angry at you—at me."

"He knows."

Ellie's tearful gaze melted Nolan's heart again, bringing his own release of drops rolling down his cheek.

"Yes, I suppose he does."

The investigators insisted Ellie not leave alone, and they assigned an officer to follow her home and stay with her until the principal parties were all in custody. Nolan was glad to see this precaution.

He paced while he waited for his turn to be interviewed. He tried to imagine Ellie's mother's reaction to learning of his innocence. While he was still uncomfortable with Ellie springing the news until Cermak's arrest, he felt better knowing her home was being guarded.

Sally concluded her statement and Nolan rolled through his, recognizing the investigators were making phone calls and plans even while they took his testimony. As soon as he finished, the investigator from the state bureau of investigations tapped the stop icon on the notebook and leaned back in his chair.

"Mr. Kaminski," he said, "we rarely involve private citizens in our arrest procedures, but I've requested and received an exception. Besides, I think you deserve the chance to see the rewards of your efforts."

The investigator went on to explain the two state agencies, along with a few loyal local police officers and the support of the mayor, were about to embark on arresting the key people implicated in the current fraud, and the long history of false arrests and imprisonments.

"I'm most fearful of the number of innocent citizens with convictions because of the efforts of this detective and his son. This town is about to be ripped apart by class divisions, racist implications, and a loss of confidence in their government and law enforcement. The townsfolk will need your positive influence and your leadership."

He reached his hand out and placed it atop Nolan's shoulder, "I hope this all goes down without violence. You should also know my wife and I are looking forward to the grand opening of your project."

In an instant, they guided Nolan out of Clifton's home and led him to the back seat of an unmarked vehicle. He watched as a stream of vehicles encircled city hall, and Nolan was secured in an alcove overlooking the main entrance. He could see Shyann's amazement at the invasion of flashing badges that whirled past, including one attached to a guy who stopped her from any announcement of their presence.

Within ten minutes, Ashley Pershing, head hung low and arms behind her back, was led from the building and escorted to the rear seat of another unmarked car. A defiant Lieutenant Hutchinson was next, and the mayor strode abreast of him with a satisfied grin.

At this same time, they apprehended Pete with a folder full of paychecks he was delivering on his regular rounds. But all were disappointed the big fish, Sly Cermak, had eluded capture, and his whereabouts were unknown.

While the police were all confident the former detective would be located soon, Nolan was filled with that familiar, dreaded feeling.

CHAPTER THIRTY-NINE

Pistols and Prayer

Sly Cermak remained free as Saturday dawned on Hope Landing. The police now believed he fled the area, but they would remain on alert throughout the grand opening weekend.

The appearance of the rebuilt Hope Landing impressed Nolan and his project managers. In place of the meager booths designed by Clifton with plywood and low-end appliances were sleek kitchens fitted with stainless steel equipment behind each sizable stall. Slate floors, granite countertops, and enhanced lighting would greet the first customers.

They set the official opening time for ten, but almost every participant was in their booth three hours before the doors would open. They constructed a small grandstand for the ceremonies that area television stations would broadcast, and live feeds would stream across the internet.

About everyone was thrilled except Nolan. He couldn't ignore the sense of dread that pulsed through him. His senses were overpowered by an emotion that told him something big was about to happen. Ellie and Clifton tried to convince him he sensed the grand opening ceremonies, and too many representatives of law enforcement were nearby for Sly Cermak to be considered a threat.

Nolan addressed the crowd gathered between Aaron's former restaurant, The Landing, and its sister, The Bayview, across the street. Nolan expressed his appreciation to all the visitors and citizens of Erie who believed in and supported the project during the struggles the group overcame.

He next thanked the key players and called each of them up to the podium to accept kudos from the crowd. Marge had progressed from crutches to a cane, but of course, her doting boyfriend, Aaron, carried her almost the entire way. Jake followed, and his coworkers increased the level of applause as he took the stage.

Aaron fumbled with the microphone, then bellowed to the audience.

"My friends, Marge and I are happy you are here. I wish to say to you who have been loyal to Marge and her diner, and my customers at The Landing, you are all invited to the cemetery on Tuesday, where Marge tells me we will get married."

The crowd cheered with enthusiasm, but a buzz of soft conversation filled the air.

"Did you mean to say cemetery?" one man bellowed, the question bouncing among the audience.

Then Aaron spoke up again, "Yes, the cemetery is correct. That way, Marge's first husband will bless us, and we have other business there that day. Please. Come. All of you."

The ceremony continued as Nolan informed the crowd of the future phases of Hope Landing, which would include a historic walkway from the library to the pier. This was the path once used by the Native Americans who first inhabited this settlement by the bay. The street where the gathering now stood would become a park, so visitors could traverse in an eco-friendly environment without traffic concerns. By mid-summer, the second phase of Hope Landing would add a cluster of buildings surrounding Li Na's tiny snack bar, and this would be the focal point of the history of each nation represented at Hope Landing.

Construction would use today's safety standards to build replicas of the living quarters the immigrants faced when first settling in America. The park would focus on a theme of education, with the celebration of prosperity expressed in the sale of foods from each country.

As Nolan spoke, he remained cautious of any odd movements in the area. The appearance of an ambulance troubled him. He then noticed Otel and his son, along with several other gentlemen helping Jane into a wheelchair and toward the podium. Nolan stood back to allow the Shongos to address the increasing crowd.

Chief Shongo was accustomed to speaking before significant numbers of people and was very much at ease. Even though it was early in the morning, he wore a deep ebony tuxedo, enhanced with a lariat tie that appeared to be crafted of black onyx.

"We all want you to enjoy Hope Landing and all it represents. A strange man and an intelligent woman came to me about a month ago and told me of a dream they had to celebrate the ancestry of the townspeople of this city."

He nodded and pointed at his daughter, who sat nearby. "They were unaware my daughter, Jane, who will speak to you next, was already very much involved in their project and was active in her campaign for the Seneca Nation to become an integral part of Hope Landing.

"What they also did not know is I have been looking at a very special parcel of land here at the Bayfront for many years. I purchased the former grain elevators and shipyard several years ago and was seeking proper commercial usage. When I learned of your project, I asked the council of the Seneca Nation to consider my idea. They have agreed with my suggestion, and I am pleased to announce construction will begin soon on the Golden Deer Resort

Hotel, a year-round facility with each floor representing a different nation."

The unexpected announcement was another boost to Hope Landing and added many options for additional revenues. The chief introduced his daughter, who could stand on her own once they helped her to her feet. She gripped the microphone with her right hand and spoke to the gathering.

"While I've been recovering in the hospital, I've had a lot of time to think. I thought of the mess our economy is here in Erie, of all the illegal activities that have occurred, the money stolen from you, and of all the people who no longer have confidence in our local government. I thought of Hope Landing and the efforts that you, our citizens made with only a slight chance of success. There is an approaching election, and while I have never held public office, I have a vision for Erie. Like the project that surrounds you, my vision has hope too. And so, it is today, that I, Jane Shongo, announce my candidacy for mayor of Erie—where we make hope a reality."

The crowd's excitement rose to a frenzy as Jane waved her right hand, with a grimace of pain on her face.

Nolan was standing off the podium next to Ellie, who told him her mother wanted to apologize for holding a grudge against him for so many years.

"I'd like to see her too. Is she nearby? I'm going to thank the crowd and let them enjoy the day."

"She doesn't care for crowds," Ellie said. "I think she stopped at the cemetery and should arrive soon. I'll meet her at Li Na's old snack bar. She knows where that is."

Nolan's eyes widened as he realized the connection from Ellie's words.

The cemetery. Of course, Marge and Aaron were getting married there, Ellie's sister was there, Cermak's son was there.

Nolan reached out to Ellie's arms and twirled her around.

"Ellie, I know where Cermak is. I need you to take the stage and handle the crowd. I've gotta run."

"But Nolan . . ."

He ran ten paces, then darted back. "Keys, car keys. Please give me your keys."

Then Nolan dashed away and through the crowd.

As he drove, he gained confidence in his theory that he would locate Sly Cermak somewhere in the cemetery. His first guess was the caretaker's office, or perhaps the mausoleum. He expected to find a nearby building which housed the maintenance equipment.

The structure with the crypts was closest to the entrance, so he stopped there first. There were no living occupants. Next, he discovered the cemetery office was locked. Nolan thought this odd, but if the persnickety buzzard who managed it was on the grounds, then that made sense.

Nolan couldn't see any outbuildings which may have housed equipment, so he drove to the plots where he encountered Cermak on his first day in town. He drove by Mary's grave and was pleased Ellie's mother was not there. He realized he had no weapon, beyond a mini-promotional pocketknife, with a slender one-inch blade. They considered this a weapon only if one tried to carry it aboard an aircraft. His bandaged hands couldn't even fit into his pockets to retrieve it.

He parked Ellie's car near Mary's gravesite then headed toward the area where he thought Cermak's son might be buried. As he walked closer, he noticed a canopy erected nearby for an upcoming funeral. The open side faced away from the street, so he needed to alter his path. He still saw no movement but was overcome by a powerful feeling he was not alone.

His wife always told him, "Do that thing you do," which meant to concentrate so he could sense who was nearby. She had joked he was like a dog more than a man.

These senses now told him Cermak was the who, and he was near. Nolan viewed the inside of the canopied area, listened to the wind flapping the canvas, but no one was inside. The rigging for the burial was in place, and the hole prepared.

"How nice of you to visit," the bitter voice said from behind.

"Sylvester, you're missing the party. It's not the same without you."

Nolan pivoted slowly, but the old detective's words boomed.

"Hands up and out, Kaminski, then pivot on your right foot, nice and slow."

Nolan complied with caution and found himself face-to-face with the man he had despised since he was a teenager. Cermak pointed a large gray revolver at his prey, and Nolan was unarmed with nowhere to run. Less than five yards separated them.

"You know the good thing about your visit, Kaminski?"

"You've got fresh coffee?"

"Always the smart ass," said Sly. "But you couldn't have picked a better place and time. After I kill you, I can roll you under that casket holder, and no one will ever know. They'll lower a coffin and fill that grave before anyone even knows you're missing."

"The police are still hunting all the roads for you, Sylvester. You won't get away."

Cermak chuckled and never moved his two-handed grip on

his gun. "You forget I know procedures. After this weekend, they'll assume I have slipped their dragnet, and everything will go back to normal. I can leave without a care."

Nolan spotted motion in the corner of his peripheral vision, but it was slow and unstable. Then he focused and identified Ellie's mother, hobbling across the lawn with the aid of her cane. Nolan couldn't think of one good thing about this development.

Nolan hoped for a chance drive-by of a security patrol or even the maintenance staff who may come to check on the gravesite preparedness. But he also knew his time was running out.

"What did you do to the caretaker? Did you kill him too?"

"Tsk, tsk, Kaminski. You're spreading lies about me again. I'm not a killer. I've never killed anyone, at least face-to-face. No, he's in safekeeping you might say, until Tuesday."

Cermak took one stride forward. "Now I will make an exception in your case, Kaminski. You'll be the first I've killed personally. You should be honored."

Cermak took another step, and this one aligned him, so the slow-moving rescuer was now behind him and out of his vision. Naomi Thompson wobbled and almost fell but grasped a monument to steady herself. She reached into her coat pocket and withdrew that same tiny pistol, shifting the cane to her left hand.

Nolan was not a weapons expert but knew the accuracy of a handgun that small made him as much of a target as the detective. Add in the distance factor and the unsteady hand of the shooter, and the element of surprise may be his only salvation.

Nolan lowered his hands, and Cermak barked a command.

"Hands back up. I don't expect you're smart enough to bring a weapon, and I ain't never seen a man draw for a weapon wearing white mittens, but let's keep 'em up just the same."

"Give me some peace of mind before you shoot me, Sylvester. That's the least you can do. Tell me what was going through that brain of yours the night your son rigged the car to blow up. Were you a proud father?"

"Shut up, orphan boy. Wayne was just havin' some fun but used too much of that juice in the carburetor. The car would have never blown if that kid hadn't pushed the engine so hard."

Nolan laughed aloud, "That's your logic, is it? It was the kid's own fault for driving too fast. If he had only ignored Wayne's taunts and walked away, he'd be alive today."

"That's right. He was a dope peddler anyhow."

Mrs. Thompson had limped to within twenty feet of the aging detective, who had lost a trace amount of hearing. A slight breeze disturbed the canopy just enough to camouflage the noise of her motion. She set down her cane and wobbled again, then found a bit of stamina, then wrapped both arms around the pistol and leaned against a tombstone. Nolan was no longer in the line of fire but had little confidence in the woman's ability to hit her mark, or her courage to pull the trigger.

"Well, you go ahead and pull that trigger, Sylvester. But don't miss. 'Cause I'll figure out a way to send you to hell, either now or soon thereafter."

Cermak smiled and leveled his arm with his target when a meek voice interrupted him.

"You put down that weapon, Detective. Or I'll blow you away."

"Why, that must be Mrs. Thompson. I'm losing my touch to let you sneak up on me."

Cermak snickered at her threat.

"And don't you think I won't shoot," she said. "I've had plenty of practice with this here gun, and my Elmer used it to kill sick dogs and wounded coons. I put you right in the same category with the sickest animal."

"Now Mrs. Thompson, you wouldn't shoot a man in the back, would you?"

Cermak exuded an air of confidence and developed a sneer as he listened to the old woman.

"I promised my Elmer I'd avenge my daughter's death if they ever proved who was responsible."

The crack of the weapon echoed through the cemetery, and for a split second, Nolan wondered if he was hit. Then, he noticed a burst of red and pink globs in the air and Cermak fell to the ground.

The shot provided enough recoil to the unsteady woman to cause her to fall on her back. Sly Cermak propelled himself up off his knees and back on his feet, charging the fallen shooter.

At that instant, Nolan launched himself full speed at the converging couple. Cermak stood above the prone woman and pointed his weapon. He then noticed Nolan was almost upon him and swiveled to fire. The 22-caliber pistol cracked another round, which punctured the detective's cheek and exited the other side. He turned with surprise at the source of the shot, and the frantic lady fired a third shot, this one exploding through the left pupil of Sly Cermak, who collapsed to the ground next to the now-sobbing woman.

The detective lay motionless while Nolan tried to soothe Ellie's mother. She was unharmed but shaken, and Nolan feared the woman would have a heart attack from the stress and shock. Blood spattered her face and clothing, and Cermak was sprawled face down, still with a firm grip on his revolver.

Nolan wished someone heard the shots, but the echoes had receded and not a soul was in sight. He had a difficult time prying the pistol from Mrs. Thompson's hands, then lifted the frail lady and carried her to Ellie's car. Nolan had misplaced his cell phone, and Mrs. Thompson did not own one. Their only choice was to drive for help. Mrs. Thompson stayed in the car while Nolan kicked in the door to the cemetery office and called the police. A stainless-steel entry was visible in the back, which Nolan learned was cold storage for special temporary guests. He pulled on a horizontal handle similar in style to an old refrigerator and revealed the caretaker, cuffed and gagged.

Nolan gripped a letter opener between his two hands and cut through the rag.

"It's about time," the victim complained. "Now get me out of these handcuffs before they slice my arteries, and I bleed to death."

Nolan stood up and stared at the whining man. "Your gratitude is touching. Let me guess. You got this job because you failed undertaker school."

"You call the police this instant, or I'll sue you for any permanent damage to my hands."

"Chill out, man. They're on their way. I suggest you use this time to reconsider your policy on floral arrangements in the cemetery."

When he returned to the car, his passenger maintained a steady gaze through the windshield and into blank space.

The welcomed sirens and flashing blue lights entered the grounds from three directions. Nolan stood next to Ellie's car, waved his arms and pointed a white-gauzed mitten at the canopy. He stayed to comfort Mrs. Thompson and wait for the police to return to the car which he was certain they would do in short order.

It relieved him the ordeal was over at last but was uneasy about Mrs. Thompson's condition.

Nolan recognized the lead state investigator who approached.

"Mr. Kaminski, you phoned in a shooting and that Cermak was dead?"

"Yes, officer, but I think this woman is in shock and needs medical attention."

"An ambulance should be here any second," he said. He turned and pointed toward the scene. "Are you sure that's where Cermak was shot?"

"Well, of course it is." Nolan then noticed the confusion on the investigator's face. "Oh no, what's wrong?"

"We see some blood, and maybe some pieces of flesh. But no, there's no body—dead or alive."

CHAPTER FORTY

Love, Marriage and an Edsel

A crowd which approached one hundred encircled the three-foot-high stage the caretaker permitted with reluctance. Initially, he refused Aaron's request to allow the cemetery to be used for a wedding, but gave in after numerous phone calls encouraged him to change his mind.

Father Andrew prepared for the event, and Nolan approached. "You do many of these weddings at cemeteries?"

"I must admit, this is a first," Andrew said. "And I won't be boasting of this to the bishop either. I doubt he'd view this as a proper location for the sacrament of matrimony."

"Got it. I'll pass the word."

The ceremony proceeded without incident, and Nolan was honored to be Aaron's best man. He and Marge made an odd couple indeed, but it was their diversity that would create many pleasant years of pursuing the depths of each other's personality. Nolan was also pleased he no longer required his nose guard and had free use of several fingers. His palms suffered more serious damage, but they too showed improvement.

As the bride and groom kissed to a raucous applause, Rose tugged at Nolan's sleeve and whispered in his ear. The maid of honor delivered a message that Chief Shongo needed to speak with Nolan as soon as he could slip away from the stage.

Nolan wasn't concerned, since he hadn't any feeling of impending doom. But his friend grasped his arm and led him to his limousine.

"Please," he motioned Nolan inside, "accompany me for but a few minutes."

As they drove off, Nolan felt like he was abandoning his duties to Aaron, but realized his importance to Erie was more diminished each moment. Shongo's expression was stern.

"You have news?" asked Nolan.

"I do. I've learned Sean and Jerry fled to Canada under different names. Their Canadian citizenship papers were flawless, and they have new identities. I assume this was a courtesy provided by Mr. Cermak and his crew."

"So that's it? We can't touch them?"

"Well, they ran short of funds when they were unfortunate victims of a mugging. However, when the police arrived, the constables connected their description to some unsolved drug thefts. During their processing, substantial quantities of cocaine were found inside pockets of their jackets. They are now awaiting trial."

"They were framed."

"I am just the messenger."

"Anything on Cermak?"

Shongo reached into his left pocket and slid an object into his fist. "I've been trying to find a proper time to tell you about your former acquaintance." Otel held out his clenched hand. Nolan cupped his hands to receive a familiar ruby ring and a piece of folded notepaper.

"How did you . . . ?"

"I saw you rush off, and after a brief conversation with Ellie, I guessed your destination. But by the time I arrived, I saw Ellie's car driving away from that canopy near the office. I thought it was you who plugged the detective and had no idea it was Eleanor's mother."

"So you stole the body."

"I prefer to think of it as recycling. Any change to that man would have been an improvement. I'm not even certain the carp will find him an acceptable food source."

"I need to tell Ellie and her mother," said Nolan.

"I suggest otherwise, my friend. Right now, the old woman is relieved she didn't take the life of another human, no matter how strong her hatred. And she is more self-confident, knowing she defeated him. I think that family is assured the former detective will not return to challenge them."

The limousine returned to the cemetery, and it disappointed Nolan that the crowd left Marge's deceased husband's gravesite, and the stage was being dismantled. But less than a hundred yards away, it appeared they gathered again. Otel stopped his car, and Clifton opened the door for Nolan, who now recognized the group collected around the graves of his parents.

The gathering parted, and he forced himself to walk, flanked by Clyde Shongo and Clifton. As he entered the open circle, Father Andrew, who pointed at a new headstone, greeted Nolan.

"Your friends all contributed to fulfill the reason you came to Erie—to honor your parents. Your friends have also completed another task on your list. We got the information from the stone mason about your relatives who are buried here, and the gravesites have been trimmed and are most presentable. I'm here for a very special reason. When you were eight, I couldn't convince you to attend your parents' funeral, so I am honored to preside over the service you missed as a child."

And Nolan cried. All the tears he kept for forty years flowed out, as he knelt and sobbed as if the deaths were a new slash in his heart. Ellie lowered herself to the ground and hugged her friend with the unique love they shared for each other. Nolan wept for his parents and yearned to hold his father's hand one more time. He wanted another chance to tell his wife he loved her, even though she left him with that full awareness. He wanted to tell Ellie he was sorry he left her but would leave her again. After a while, Father Andrew abandoned his efforts to get Nolan into the chair which was designated for him, so held the ceremony and dedication of the headstone while Nolan knelt.

Nolan composed himself enough by the end of the service that they helped him up the few steps and he sat and overlooked the crowd. The priest had vanished, and Nolan glanced about, searching to express his appreciation to his friend.

He noticed a car entering through the gates of the cemetery and rubbed his eyes to clear his tears. The car was still about one hundred yards away, but the color reminded him of the shimmering turquoise Edsel that carried his parents to their death. He couldn't stop studying the slow-moving vehicle and confirmed the horse collar grille that was the first sign of an approaching Edsel.

His mind calculated the odds of this coincidence, then glanced around to his friends, wondering if they too were seeing this vision from his past. But they were watching him, and this was the telltale sign the vehicle was not imaginary.

He stood and could now see the driver was Father Andrew, and this was indeed a 1958 Edsel Citation convertible. No, this was his dad's convertible. Somehow, it survived, with whitewall tires, the wrap-around windshield, and the ivory ragtop that folded into its housing behind the rear seats.

As Father Andrew parked, the throng again parted and revealed a priest who had a hop in his step and a broad grin on his face. He jangled a set of car keys accompanied by a tan rabbit's foot, identical to the set Nolan now recalled his father owned.

Nolan almost stumbled down the stairs as the emotions were too many and too sudden.

"Andrew, how? Is this really . . ."

The priest slipped the key chain around one of Nolan's unbandaged fingers and embraced his younger friend.

"You were so angry as a child, I couldn't tell you. But the car was struck in the rear, and the train's impact threw everyone out of the vehicle. Over the years, I worked on her as my therapy. I intended to present it to you when you graduated from college, but you disappeared. I couldn't find you, but I kept your prize in prime condition. It runs great, and since Jamal refused to return your SUV, I thought this was an appropriate day to turn over the keys. Here."

Another embrace, followed by more tears, but Nolan was more composed and lifted the keys in triumph to the cheering crowd. As he pivoted away, Marge stepped into his path.

"You don't think I'm going to let you slink away without giving the bride a kiss, do you?"

She wrapped her arms around him and their lips met with tears streaming down Marge's cheeks. She then held him close and whispered in his ear. "Thank you for saving my life—for giving me a new start." She pushed back and grinned while she used the sleeve of her beige wedding dress to wipe her tears.

"I'll visit. I promise. Oh, and please don't let Rose cook anything or the entire park could shut down."

She slipped an advertising flyer into his shirt pocket. "This has the list of countries and their top menu item listed. You can read it when you settle." She glanced at her side and waved as she walked away.

He felt Ellie's presence at his side and hugged her as they both mixed some tears of joy and sorrow.

"You're leaving again, aren't you?" asked Ellie.

Nolan nodded and his lips touched her hand, then ran his tender fingers through her hair.

"This time, I'll keep in touch. But I love you too much to stay."

"I understand—me too," she said, and they let go of each other's fingertips as Nolan plopped himself down on the leather turquoise seats with white trim. He lifted his bandaged hand to the crowd as he pulled away.

As he left Erie, he sensed new and long-time friends who appreciated him and would welcome him back. Their resilience gave him inspiration that would empower him to proceed with the rest of his life. He had arrived in his hometown burdened with despair, and was leaving with the air of hope, whipping around the inside of his dad's Edsel.

His newfound courage inspired him as he drove the Edsel toward his childhood home. As fate presented, bells clanged, and the signal arm lowered as Nolan approached the railroad tracks where his parents had died. As he waited for the passing freight train to pass, Nolan wondered what direction he should take.

He then remembered a scrap of paper that Otel had found in Cermak's pocket. Someone penciled a street address and city, and Cermak felt it was important enough for him to keep. Nolan sensed a connection to evil.

As the caboose clanked past and the signal arms rose, Nolan glanced at the modest bungalow where he spent the first eight years of his life. There was nothing there any longer, so he set his destination to the address on that scrap of paper.

ACKNOWLEDGEMENTS

My writing journey would have never resulted in this publication if it were not for my friends at the Atlanta Writers Club. George Weinstein and the critique group in Roswell, Georgia encouraged and prodded me to bring *Hope Landing* from my shelf and into a format where readers can become a part of the lives of the characters within.

In addition, my good friend Jackie always believed my written words deserved to be shared with others.

Thanks to my editor Janie Mills of Alliance Book Editing who gave me the chance to reconnect with Ellie, Nolan, Marge, Clifton and whole Erie gang.

ABOUT THE AUTHOR

 Marty Aftewicz spent the first 21 years of his life in Erie, PA. He came to love his hometown except for the overwhelming winter snow. He is an Officer Emeritus of the Atlanta Writers Club and a board member of the Cherokee Senior Softball Association, where he remains an active softball enthusiast. His friends enjoy his culinary delights which he creates from his home in a suburb of Atlanta, GA.